THE ADVENTURES OF ELSABETH SOESTEN

GONNES
OF
NAVARRE

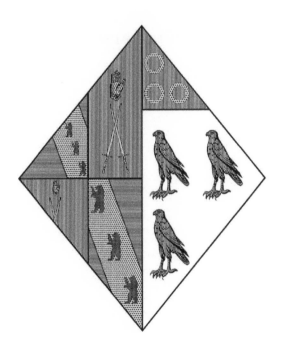

THE ADVENTURES OF ELSABETH SOESTEN

NO GOOD DEED...

BAIT AND SWITCH

PRIZE PLAY

GONNES OF NAVARRE

FORTHCOMING

THE CONFESSION AT GODRA

THE ADVENTURES OF ELSABETH SOESTEN

GONNES
OF
NAVARRE

D. E. WYATT

Wyrmfyr Press
St. Louis, Missouri
2023

The Adventures of Elsabeth Soesten: Gonnes Of Navarre

Copyediting by Debbie Manber Kupfer
Cover Art by Rebecca Frank, Bewitching Book Covers, LLC
(bewitchingbookcovers.com)
Heraldry image resources sourced from HeraldicArt.org

ISBN-13: 979-8-9853905-5-1

Thanks to Lori and Corey Cole, for sparking my interest in fantasy through five adventures in Gloriana.

A NOTE FROM THE AUTHOR

A number of terms contained within this work may be unfamiliar to you, the reader. As such, I have provided a glossary at the end of the book for your convenience, along with a quick guide on how to read the blazons for the coats of arms described herein.

THE ADVENTURES OF ELSABETH SOESTEN

GONNES
OF
NAVARRE

"BUGGER!"

Elsabeth raised her head above the seat of her wain and gazed at the black-shafted bolt stuck quivering in the back of the bench. Had she not thrown herself over and into the bed when she did, it would assuredly have passed neatly through her belly. She twisted her lip in irritation, snatched her hat from beside her, and returned it to her head. Then she turned her attention to the six men barring the road in front of her.

They were a ramshackle lot, dressed all in homespun doublets and hose that had seen better days. Once, perhaps, their cloth might have been diverse and brightly colored, but sun and weather left them all now the same dingy shade of brown beneath their ragged coats. Their features matched their dress; tanned and cracked by the elements, assuming they had ever been lovely at all. Shaggy hair hung round their shoulders, and unkempt growths of beard warmed their faces against the chill of winter. They gripped spears and cudgels in rough hands, and their leader casually slipped his foot into the stirrup of his crossbow and spanned the bow. The sharp *click* of the nut locking into place echoed ominously across the road.

"'Twas a warning shot, my lovely," he called across the space between them. His Boehman was rough and uncultured, and touched by a hint of Navarrese as was common among the local dialects along the border regions.

His voice broke the peaceful stillness of the flat, snow-swept fields stretching for miles in all directions. Only here, where the road dipped into a small wooded grove, was there a place where an enterprising sort might set such an ambush, and Elsabeth chided herself for having driven right into it unprepared. Had she been alone upon Felis she might have spurred her forward and ridden them down before they could bring arms to bear. Unfortunately, the old draft horse hitched to her wagon was not up to the task, nor did she trust the wheels not to come apart when they struck the roadblock spanning the way ahead.

"Some bloody warning!" she called back. Elsabeth stayed low, peering over the seat from the back of the wagon, scarcely showing more than the low crown of her hat for him to shoot at. "Had you been a little faster on the draw we likely would not be having this conversation now."

"Well, would that not have been a pity," he said with a laugh. "But 'tis what you get for not slowing down as you were asked, to pay our toll."

"'Twas a bit high for my liking, I don't think you can fault me that."

The leader of the group casually fitted another bolt onto his crossbow and leveled it towards her wagon. Elsabeth hunkered down and peered between the slats of her bench.

"Well, it has not changed in the last few minutes. Toss down that lovely bit of steel you have at your side, raise your hands, and step down. We'll be having that cart and your goodies. You can go your way after that if you play nicely."

"Ordinarily, love, I might find it hard to refuse such a polite request, but I am afraid the cart and its wares are not mine to hand over, and hardly anything you might find of value leastwise. Just a few meager odds and ends for the poor souls in Pruck's monastery up the road for the holiday, as a good turn for the Lord."

"Oh I doubt that. I wager there is food and blankets, and a few baubles worth a bit of coin. Along with whatever you might be carrying on your own person." His voice took on a harder edge. "And I am beginning to lose my patience. Lads!"

Four of the men started forward, and Elsabeth muttered a curse under her breath. They advanced in a disorderly fashion, neither supporting the other, and under normal circumstances Elsabeth had no doubts she could put the wagon between her and one pair while dispatching the other two.

That crossbow makes all the difference; I can't risk exposing myself, as I doubt my doublet can stop a bolt even at this range. And this fellow is a good enough shot I would rather not take my chances on him missing. He likely poaches fowl on the wing in fairer months.

She considered her cargo for a moment. There were barrels of flour and barley, a good-sized goose huddling quietly in a cage covered by a blanket, and baskets of dried fruits and vegetables left over from harvest and laid aside for the winter months. Bundles of spare clothes — none by any means large enough to fit her assailants — and blankets were piled among a few other packages and parcels sealed against the weather. All lay under a heavy canvas tarp, which she tore free during her mad scramble into the box when the leader of the brigands first raised his crossbow. Unfortunately, there was nothing at hand she might use as a suitable shield.

"Come now, love," she said. Elsabeth pressed her back against the bench and thumped her head against it at the plan taking shape.

3

'Twill be a desperate gamble, but I don't have much choice. "Surely you and I could come to some sort of arrangement."

"You have heard my terms."

"But you have not heard my counter-offer!"

"Well, let us have it, then," he said.

Elsabeth craned her neck enough to peer around the bench behind her. The men advancing on the wagon paused, but their leader kept his crossbow aimed squarely at it. The last of the group, a rather big and brutish man who likely stood at least a head taller than her, flanked him with arms the size of tree trunks folded across his chest. He alone showed any sort of weapon more complex than a spear or cudgel; a heavy iron mace hanging from his belt.

"For a start, I don't think you have considered just how useful I could be to your outfit. You won't find a finer sword-arm in this part of Boehm."

He laughed sharply, little more than a dismissive bark that echoed across the glade. The others all broke out into laughter along with him, and Elsabeth's face heated indignantly.

"A woman? I think you have been out in the cold too long!"

Elsabeth screwed her lip into a scowl. "Set aside your toy, love, and you can see it for yourself."

"I think not. Besides, even if I might consider it despite your sex, 'twould still be an extra share to divvy up, and pickings are slim as it is."

"Well, I assure you that you shan't find pickings like me. Use a bit of imagination, love! I am sure you can think of more pleasant things to stick me with than a quarrel in the belly."

Contemplative silence hung over the little grove, disturbed only by the soft hiss of the wind, and the faint creaking of naked branches swaying. A few small flurries drifted aimlessly down from the slate sky overhead.

"Well?" she prompted, when no answer was forthcoming.

"Don't you know anything about husbandry? You don't take on a brood-mare without a chance to inspect the goods first." he said.

Well, now I have him thinking with the wrong head. That ought to have him off his guard.

Elsabeth unbuttoned her coat and unfastened her doublet. The winter chill blasted right through her, and raised her finer hairs on end. She turned round in the wagon to face her assailants, and in one smooth motion she popped up above the bench that was her only cover and pulled down on her blouse. The men howled their approval when she flashed her breasts for just a moment, then dropped back out of sight into the box. Elsabeth shivered — from disgust as much as the cold — and covered herself once more.

"You make a compelling offer," he said. The rest of his men all voiced their agreement, and Elsabeth curled her lip into a twisted smile.

Oh, this just got too easy.

"There is, of course, one small thing," she said. "I am still a woman of some respectability, you know, and not a common bawd to be passed round."

"Of course you are, and I can't imagine a man wanting to share you, either. So, I take it we let you pass, and you come with me."

"That is the offer on the table, as it were."

"And how do I know 'tis not just some scam to save your own neck, and you intend to make good on it?"

Elsabeth shrugged, though the other could not see the gesture. "The roads are dangerous this time of year, you know. A stout man doing a good deed by escorting this delivery would not be unwelcome."

Another moment of thoughtful silence passed, and that started grumbling among the others when the prospect of a windfall from the wagon seemed to evaporate before them.

"And what about us?" one said. "We don't get a single trinket, and you walk away with the real prize?"

"I sure did not sign up for the benefit of another man's cock," said another.

"I can't believe you would even consider it!" came a third voice. "There are six of us and one of her; 'twould be a small matter to have a share of all the goods, if you mark my meaning."

"Oh, there are six of you," Elsabeth said, and quietly slipped her sword from it scabbard. The cold air frosted on the four and a half spans of naked Boehman steel. "I have no doubt should you all come at me I would be overwhelmed. But! How many of you will die before that should happen? And what if in the chaos some unfortunate stroke should fall and stove my head in? Then you would not have me at all?" She chuckled. "Well, at least you would have yourselves for company."

"Quiet, all of you!" the leader snapped, "I am the leader of this outfit, and I'll not tolerate any such arguments!"

But the others were now pensive.

"Of course," Elsabeth said, in her most off-handed manner, "I am flexible and agreeable to other terms, and an enterprising sort might find an opportunity to negotiate for himself."

The leader of the band let out a laugh. "So that is your game, is it? Well, my lovely, it won't work. Enough of this: Take her!"

But contrary to his assertions, the grumbling amongst his band only grew louder. *Prospects round these parts must be slim indeed if all it takes to stir up this sort of mutiny is the brief glimpse of an admittedly exceptional pair of tits.*

"And if we do, how do we know that you intend to make good on your part to us?" one of the men growled at his master.

Elsabeth leaned around the bench. In spite of his orders, the men who were advancing on the wagon now started back towards their leader. He shrunk behind his big guard, but they were not cowed by the mountain of muscle standing between them and the subject of their ire.

"For that matter, how do you know he has not been holding out on you all along?" Elsabeth said. "I suppose he does all the counting for you."

"That is quite enough out of you!" he spat, and raised his crossbow at the wagon once more. But he could not get a clean shot at her hunkered down in the bed, and not even the crown of her hat peeped above the bench to offer him a suitable mark.

"I think she brings up a fair point," one of the four said, his voice thick with accusation. "Remember that job two weeks ago? I thought my share looked scant, but I said nothing! I wonder now if you have been holding back on us after all."

"He certainly laid claim to the finest things from the loot," said another, and he tightened his grip on his cudgel.

"Because I am the only one with a bloody brain between us!" the leader snapped.

Elsabeth tsked. "Well, that is hardly a show of respect for you all. I wager you lot do all the fighting for him, too."

"And he stands back with his bow safe, while we do all the wet-work!"

7

"I warn you all, get back and get to it, or 'twill be Cunlin knocking your heads together!"

The big fellow at the leader's side uncrossed his arms and made a show of rubbing one meaty fist. But if the others had been cowed by the big man in the past, now the threat only riled them further, and they snatched up their spears and cudgels against him.

"'Tis always how it is with you, Wendel: Do this, do that, I'll have that, don't make me set Cunlin on you! Well, I for one have had my fill of i—"

One of the men started forward with leveled spear as he spoke. The twang of the crossbow cut his protestation short, and he fell to the snow clutching at the black shaft of the quarrel buried so deeply through his throat the squared head jutted out the back of his neck. Blood sprayed in a brilliant crimson arc as he spun into the ground, and spurted between his fingers. He writhed and thrashed in the snow, choking and gagging around the bolt.

"Endres!" Another cried, crouching momentarily at his fallen comrade's side.

Wendel backpedaled in a mad scramble with Cunlin between him and the others, desperate to gain enough ground to reload his bow. An angry cry went up, and chaos erupted. Cunlin whipped his mace from his belt in a futile bid to fend them off, and went down after being set upon from all angles. His size availed him little against the spear that slipped past his arms and pierced his belly, while the other two fell on him with their cudgels.

Elsabeth spared no time watching how the battle would unfold. She seized hold of the rail and vaulted from the cover of the wagon bed. The snow covering the road was well-packed, and she easily maintained her footing on her rush across the ground.

She flew past Endres, who now lay still in a pool of red slush with his mouth gaping. She leapt the prostrate form of Cunlin, writhing in agony with the broken haft of a spear buried in his belly, and bleeding profusely from many wounds in his head and face. Another of the outlaws lay sprawled beside him and clutched the other half of the spear in a death grip. His head had been crushed by Cunlin's mace; his reward for the fatal blow he had struck against the big enforcer.

Steel rang, and Elsabeth fixed her eyes on the end of the fight between Wendel and his two remaining companions. He discarded his crossbow and went to work against them with a longsword he had concealed beneath his coat. He dispatched his first opponent in deft fashion, then turned to face the last of his erstwhile comrades. But Elsabeth was upon them both before they could conclude their argument.

She ducked low, put her shoulder into the back of the latter, and upended and hurled him behind her. He cried out and landed with a muffled *whump* in the snow. Then she took her sword in both hands, vaulted to the side, and met Wendel with the *zornhau* when he leveled a wild and desperate blow at her shoulder. Her sword rang as her blade caught his, and at the moment their blades crossed she thrust stiffly towards his face from below. The awl-like point pierced his throat where it met the underside of his jaw, and he gurgled sickeningly. His sword fell from his hands, and his legs collapsed beneath him. Elsabeth continued past, turning her sword in her hands and allowing him to fall off her point.

Her lungs burned from the exertion and the frigid air. She checked her advance and turned, sliding a bit in the snow as her momentum carried her forward a few paces more. By now the last of the outlaws was scrambling to his feet again, and his eyes flicked between the reddened blade of her sword, and Wendel choking on his blood at her feet. More hot blood pooled in the snow and painted its white surface with angry red splotches.

Elsabeth raised her hilts to her shoulder in *vom tag* and prepared for another exchange, but her adversary blanched and threw down his spear. He slipped and fell in the snow in his mad scramble away from her.

"Mercy!" he cried, and cowered.

Elsabeth did not let down her guard, but she did not level her sword for the fatal strike he expected. "Well now, our situations seem to have reversed, have they not?"

The fellow looked up at her from between his arms. "'Twas Wendel, Gnädige Frau! He put us up to it all."

"Of course he did, love. Well, Wendel is not in a position to put you up to anything else, now, is he?"

"No, Gnädige Frau." His features turned pensive as he looked up at her standing over him. "You...ah...would not still be amenable to making an offer, would you?"

Elsabeth rolled her eyes. "Oh, just get the fuck out of here."

He slipped and fell face-first into the snow in his effort to scramble away, while fine powder flew into the air in a white mist. He eventually got his feet beneath him again, and flew like a frightened hare across the drifts, falling at times as his speed got the better of his footing.

Elsabeth watched him go, her lips curled slightly in amusement, until he was safely away and unlikely to return to harass her again. Then she wiped her sword clean on Wendel's coat, and went about gathering up anything of value her erstwhile assailants left behind.

2

ELSABETH LOOKED OUT AT THE SEA OF FACES GAZING up at her from the floor. Her audience sat enraptured by the tale, and hung on her every word. All were boys of diverse ages, the youngest having seen no more than three or so winters, the eldest no more than thirteen. They dressed plainly. Not in rags, but in well-worn garments donated by those who no longer needed them, and sought a more charitable end for their use than to simply toss them out into the rubbish or use them for cleaning.

For the boys of Pruck it was a small consolation for many who had been viewed as no less disposable. But here, at least, their bellies were full and their eyes were bright, which was more than they could ask when the alternative was the cold and hard life of the streets.

She paused in her story and leaned back in her chair with a tankard of ale cupped in her hands. A fire crackled in the hearth beside her, rolling back the cold chill of winter from the common room, but offering little in the way of light. Ordinarily, lamps and candles would fill the space beneath the heavy timber beams supporting the ceiling, but when it came time for the telling of tales they were extinguished; her audience preferred the warm intimacy of the darkness, the better to let their imaginations run wild over wide green fields and deep tangled forests they had never themselves seen.

Elsabeth tossed her head back for a long drink and let them hang. An expectant silence filled the darkened common room, and the only sound was the sharp *pop* of the fire. The slightest intake of breath was deafening.

"What did you do?" came a high, anxious voice, breaking the stillness.

She did not answer right away, and instead brushed a few drops of ale from her lips with exaggerated slowness. A mischievous smile tugged at her mouth when she swept her gaze across the expectant faces leaning towards her. Their eyes widened, and firelight danced and cast wavering shadows on their features. Some wrung their hands around their shirttails.

"What did I do?" Elsabeth finally said, savoring every moment. "Well, I was trapped, of course, in the middle of that bridge. A dozen men on either end — some as big as giants! — and all of whom wanted to see my pretty head mounted on a pike. Even at my best I could not fight so many at once, and I did not even have my sword. It all looked very black for me, and maybe that would have been my last adventure.

"But 'tis a remarkable thing the feats one can accomplish in desperation. As my enemies charged towards me, I took the path they had not considered, and leapt over the rail and into the river! 'Twas quite the sight, I am sure; a hundred feet or more into the ravine." She threw her hands up in the air. "Splash!"

The boys all jumped when she suddenly raised her voice, and they laughed, caught up as they were in the tale.

"Oh, 'twas quite the harrowing journey," she continued, more softly now. "No one had ever swum the Rot above Goslar. 'Tis swift and choked with rocks, and perhaps 'twas the most foolish decision I ever made. And yet I rode the rapids with not even a tree trunk to hold onto, in naught but my chemise! 'Twas quite a cold dip, I'll tell you."

Elsabeth offered them all a wink. "Fortunately, by the end of my swim I found a wandering minstrel to warm myself with, and I wager he still sings of the mysterious wood-nymph he plucked all but naked from the river to this day!"

The boys laughed again, and the eldest blushed furiously at her innuendo. The youngest did not comprehend but laughed anyway. Elsabeth laughed with them and drained the last of her drink.

A door at one end of the common hall swung open, and lamplight spilled in from the hallway outside. A solitary figure bearing a candle stepped within and glided across the floor with carefully measured steps. His graying hair was cut in a tonsure, and he wore a simple habit of brown wool knotted about his waist with a belt of cord. Elsabeth playfully hid her tankard behind her and pressed a finger to her lips. The boys all stifled giggles.

"Good evening, Father!" Elsabeth said. "Why you are just in time; the tale was about to get truly interesting."

Father Ottin smiled patiently as he approached, and he regarded her with a twinkle in his kindly grey eyes. He was perhaps twice her age and not quite her height, but had been a man of formidable girth in his youth. There were still signs of his old muscle beneath his plumping frame, and every time Elsabeth laid eyes on him she was reminded that despite his appearance he was not a man to be trifled with.

"Then it seems I have arrived just in time," he said. "'Tis long-past time for my dear boys to be off to their evening prayers and to bed."

A chorus of disappointed groans filled the common room, silenced with a stern glare from the Prior.

"There will be none of that, now," he said. "I allow you all a bit of leeway on your curfew when Frau Soesten comes to visit, but you are still to go to bed when I call you off."

Elsabeth pouted. "Must they? Why, they have not even had a chance to see the presents I brought them!"

The boys leapt to their feet as one, and excited chattering broke out as they all began talking over one another. Father Ottin rolled his eyes, and she favored him with a playful smirk.

"All right! All right!" he said, holding up his hands in defeat. "But then 'tis right to prayers and bed!"

Father Ottin had the common room lit. The sparsely appointed chamber brightened, and the eyes of the children gaped when they discovered packages of all sorts piled upon a trestle table running the length of the wall opposite the fireplace. They scrambled towards it in a mob, and could not contain their excitement as, one by one, Elsabeth handed out each carefully selected parcel. For the youngest were wooden toys, often of simple craftsmanship, but for the unfortunates in the care of Pruck's monastery they were a prize beyond value. For the eldest were new clothes to replace their threadbare garments. Everyone received something sweet to nibble on (the goose she turned over to the care of the kitchens, to cook for tomorrow's supper).

The children departed in ones and twos once they had received their presents, and Elsabeth laughed and returned their embraces and their thank yous. She gave them a peck on the cheek or brow, and sent them scurrying off to their cells with a playful pat on the bottom. Father Ottin observed the routine in silence, maintaining an aura of solemn dignity, but a slight curl of his lips broke his austere countenance at the joy lighting the children's faces.

One tall boy — one of the eldest, at about twelve years — approached her with a slight bow.

"Thank you for coming, as always, Elsabeth," he said.

"You are most welcome, Nestler," she said. "How have you been?"

"I have been very well. In fact, I have some news for you! I will be taking my vows soon, and will be joining the Order here in Pruck."

Elsabeth smiled broadly. "Why that is wonderful! I am sure you will make Father Ottin proud!"

Nestler beamed. "Thank you, I will do my best!"

She tossed him a wink. "'Twill be many a maid in Pruck sad to hear it, but the Lord of All will be gaining an able servant."

He blushed and ducked his head shyly. "I hope you will be back again when I take my vows."

Elsabeth laid a hand on his shoulder. "Well, you know how the Church is. 'Tis a rarity that I am even allowed in here, after all, but even if I cannot attend, at the very least I will do my best to be in town."

Nestler then excused himself, and the rest of the presents were passed out, until only one boy remained. He was a lovely child just past six years of age, and when Elsabeth laid eyes upon him her throat tightened. Chestnut eyes peeped out at her from a rounded heart-shaped face, and his strawberry blond hair neatly framed his cheeks. His expression was solemn, and when he looked at the now empty table he rolled out his lip.

"Well, hello, Paulus!" she said. Elsabeth swallowed hard against the lump in her throat and forced a smile to her lips. "And how are you tonight?"

"Frau Soesten, there is nothing left for me?" he said.

"There is not?" she replied, and made a show of looking over the table. "That cannot be right!"

She retrieved a long packaged wrapped in a cloth that had been tucked out of sight on the bench on the far side of the table, and slowly knelt in front of him. She undid the twine knotting the bundle closed, and Paulus's eyes went wide as saucers when she laid bare the sword she claimed from Wendel after the brawl that afternoon. She slowly drew it from a battered scabbard covered in blue leather and laid it across her palm.

The sword was competently made, if not up to the craftsmanship of her own, and of far more worth than she suspected a common brigand could afford. It was of similar construction to hers; a long and slender blade tapering to a fine, awl-like point, and hollow-ground with a prominent central rib. The guard was slightly S-shaped, and its waisted grip was covered in blue leather from the guard to its middle, and then wrapped in copper wire for the rest of its length. A heavy wheel pommel counterbalanced the blade.

Paulus tentatively reached out to take hold of it in both hands, but the blade dropped, for the sword was taller than he was, and he had not the strength to lift it. Elsabeth smiled and laid a hand on his shoulder.

"If you intend to be a great swordsman, you will need a fine sword," she said. "Now, you are not quite old enough to manage it yet, so Father Ottin will keep it safe for you, for now. Is that right?" Elsabeth looked askance in his direction.

Father Ottin's expression was strange, but otherwise unreadable. He gave a short nod. "Of course. I will see to it that 'tis kept properly."

She returned her attention to Paulus, who gazed upon the polished steel blade with no small amount of wonder.

"Now, you must promise me that you shan't shirk your studies — all of them! Not just your fencing lessons, but your history, and your geography, and your reading and writing. Are we agreed?"

Paulus's face beamed when he looked at her, and tears welled up in his eyes. Elsabeth fought down the bile rising in her throat, and it took a great effort to maintain her composure.

"I promise!" he said.

"Good! Now, I also ask that you remember what I and Father Ottin have taught you about humility. This gift should be between us; 'twould not do to go bragging of it to your friends."

Paulus regarded her as if she had suddenly sprouted three heads. "But 'tis such a wonderful present, and I bet none of the others have something like it!"

She offered him a smile. "And that is precisely why; 'Tis a special gift, and you would not want to make them sad, or jealous, would you?"

He considered that for a moment, and it was evident he did not truly comprehend. But he shook his head anyway. "No, I would not."

"Good lad," she said, and gently reclaimed the sword from him. She slid it back home in its scabbard. "Now go on to bed. 'Tis late, and even the mightiest of knights need their rest!"

Paulus threw his arms around her and squeezed her in a powerful hug belying his size. Elsabeth hugged him back.

"Do you think we can have a lesson before you leave Pruck?" he asked in her ear.

"Of course!" she said, and her voice broke in spite of herself. "I am eager to see just how well you are progressing. Now, go on to bed! The Father and I have business to discuss."

HE OFFICE OF THE PRIOR OF PRUCK MONASTERY WAS AS austere as the face of the Prior himself. Elsabeth slumped in her chair, cradling a generous cup of wine in one hand. Father Ottin sat at his desk across from her. A crystal decanter filled with a strong red vintage out of Arras sat on one corner and was the most decorous thing in the office. Even the sign of the Wheel hanging on the walls of cream-colored plaster was little more than a roughly hewn and shaped spoked wooden circle. The simple but heavy desk, the hard-backed and seated wooden chairs facing one another across it, and a tall shelf laden with a few manuscripts and record books of the Monastery's operations were the only furniture. Lamps filled the chamber with golden light and allowed the Prior to work into the late hours. Elsabeth's saddle bags sat on the floor beside her.

Father Ottin leaned over a large and heavy strongbox bound with iron sitting upon the desk. A loop of iron welded to the box's framework allowed for the passing of a chain, permitting it to be locked securely wherever he placed it. Elsabeth's eye drifted to a back corner of the office, and a matching loop embedded so securely into one of the wooden pillars framing the interior of the office one would need to cut out the entire timber to remove it again. The door to the Prior's office was no less reinforced, with heavy timber joists embedded deeply in the floor and ceiling, and she mused that even a company of men with a ram could hammer at the door all the day long and not breach it.

"The children were delighted to see you again," Father Ottin said. He turned from the strongbox to a sheaf of parchment and scratched a few notes with a quill pen. "I don't know if you realize just how much they appreciate your visits."

Elsabeth lightly swirled the wine in her glass. "'Tis always a pleasure to help as I can. And Nestler becoming a novice?" She chuckled softly. "Oh, you'll have your hands full with that one."

Father Ottin answered her with a chuckle of his own. "Yes, I don't think he entirely thought through just what it meant, but he has always been good with the youngest. And who are we to judge when the Lord of All calls someone to his service?"

"And how is Paulus doing?" she asked. Her mouth went suddenly dry, and she took a hasty drink of wine.

"Quite well. He is proving to be a bright boy, and an eager student. He is excelling in all his studies when I can keep his attention on his lessons and away from chasing after imaginary dragons. And he is picking up Brother Simon's lessons faster and more readily than Brother Simon can keep pace with him."

Elsabeth's face heated. "I should hope so!"

"Brother Simon suggests that his enthusiasm might be better served studying with the Schwertbrüder."

Her cheek twitched, and she took a long drink to stifle the sharp retort forming on her tongue. "As if the Brotherhood would take him. You speak of dragons? Well, the Grand Master guards their rolls of enlistment as if 'twere his own hoard."

"They might, perhaps, with his pedigree."

Elsabeth speared him with a glare, but Father Ottin focused on his work, and paid her no mind. "Absolutely not. With all the trouble and bad blood I have with the Brotherhood, especially after that business in Ain this past autumn, for his sake least of all I rather they never know about him."

Father Ottin sighed. "He is quite enamored of you, Elsabeth. He deserves better."

"Yes, he does," she said sharply, more so than she intended.

"Then why not be honest with him?"

"I already have one meddlesome priest in my life judging my every thought and action, Father. I don't need another."

Father Ottin chuckled softly. "Meddling in the thought and actions of others is the purview of the clergy, my dear. As is giving counsel. Sometimes that counsel may be cold, but I am a servant of truth, as the Lord sees it." He set his quill aside and raised his head to look at her with his fingers steepled in front of him. Elsabeth shrunk from his gaze and took a drink.

"Why do you torture yourself like this? Every day you visit I see the pain it causes you."

Elsabeth leaned forward in her chair and cupped her glass in both hands. Tears formed in her eyes, which she fought back and stomped down with a mighty effort. But it was some moments longer before she could speak again.

"I have a responsibility to him," she said, and her voice wavered against the old pain threatening to rise up and drown her. "I won't abandon that. I do the best I can, Father, little as it might seem."

"I don't mean for you to think I say otherwise. That sword was certainly a princely gift." He narrowed his eyes in suspicion. "It cost no meager sum, I warrant."

"Some trouble on the road to Pruck with my cargo," she said, in an offhanded manner that drew a raised eyebrow from the other. "'Twas certainly dearly bought, though I did not pay for it in the end. But 'tis also why Paulus is better here. The road is too dangerous and uncertain a place for him."

"'Tis not the only way. He deserves to know."

"There are a lot of things he deserves. There are even more that I deserved, but that is not how the Lord saw fit for my life to unfold. I regret that his was caught up in it, as well, but 'tis what is and I can't change that!"

Elsabeth swallowed hard and mopped her face. The old argument threatened to dredge up bitter memories, and grief seized her heart in icy fingers. "'Tis the world we live in 'tis better he be thought an orphan than known a bastard."

She fell silent, and keenly felt Father Ottin's eyes on her. Elsabeth did not need to look up to picture the Prior's expression of solemn compassion. He sighed audibly, and his chair creaked as he sat back in it. His fingers knocked thoughtfully on the top of the desk.

"The account is good for the next year," he said. "'Tis enough to cover all the expenses of his education, with some to set aside, as we agreed."

Elsabeth nodded. She drained her wine with one last swallow and set the glass on the desk. Then she turned in her chair and threw open the flap of one of her bags. Within a well-hidden pouch was a modest bag of some weight, which she removed and hefted in her hands for a moment. She tossed it on the desk, and it landed heavily and with the clinking of coin.

"I lost count of how much, precisely, but it ought to come to maybe three or four *pfunde*. 'Tis everything I have made since my last visit, minus my own living expenses."

Father Ottin pulled the bag towards him and undid the thongs holding it closed. He gave it a cursory look.

"I'll be sure to do an accurate counting and have a receipt for you before you set out again," he said.

"There seemed to be a draft in the common room tonight. You can take a few *skillings* to hire a good man to patch it up, and maybe buy the boys an extra treat at supper for me."

"And invest the rest as we discussed?"

She nodded again. "At least I can offer him that."

Father Ottin heaved another sigh, and Elsabeth's belly churned when she realized it meant there was something more on

21

his mind he was loath to bring up. For a long moment he sat in silence, and Elsabeth sat and stared at him. Finally, when it was clear he would not broach whatever thought was on his lips uninvited, she spoke.

"Out with it."

"There was another matter, though I hesitate to bring it up now."

"I doubt there is much you can say that would make me feel worse than I do already." She offered a half-hearted smile she did not particularly feel. "Best get it over with."

Father Ottin leaned forward with his hands clasped in front of him, but did not look her in the eye. He hesitated again, and when he spoke it was slowly and carefully.

"Herr Peter von Aigel and his wife visited the monastery not long ago. Their son is about Paulus's age, and Frau Nes Aigelen was struck with an illness last year that left her barren. They have a daughter of about two, but they have desired a companion for their son."

Elsabeth's throat tightened. She reached for the decanter of wine to refill her glass. However, she paused just as a red drop rolled to its mouth, and instead tossed her head back and took a long draught straight from the bottle.

"I can't say that I have met them, though word round Pruck is that they are a family of good account."

Father Ottin nodded. "'Tis a lesser house, and Herr von Aigel is a *ritter* only, but they are respectable and make a good living. Frau Aigelen was quite taken with Paulus on their visit, and he got on quite well with Young Peter. Herr von Aigel expressed an interest in adopting him to serve as a companion for his son. I stalled him, but I suspect they shall want an a—"

"I won't stand in the way," Elsabeth said, and she wished now that Wendel had proven a faster touch on the lever of his crossbow.

3

THE INN AT PRUCK WAS LIKE ANY OTHER; TRESTLE tables dominated the large common room where locals and travelers alike gathered to drink, gamble, and share the news of the day. It was a place of raucous cheer, with a good hot fire blazing in the hearth to drive out the chill of winter, and serving girls dodging through crowds of groping hands bearing trays of food and drink. Lamps filled the room with golden light and cast flickering shadows on the walls, and large glass windows in iron frames let in moonlight from outside. The aroma of freshly baked bread and roasting meat flavored with herbs and spices concealed the fouler odors of the sweat of many bodies in close quarters. There was no music, but laughter shook the rafters, punctuated by the rhythmic clatter of tankards and platters, and the occasional roll of the dice.

Elsabeth's table in the far corner, however, was a lone island of gloom in a sea of merriment. She slumped in her chair with her back against the wall, her head bowed by the immense weight settling over her heart after her visit to the monastery. Her head swam in a dense fog, and the room around her was a blur of light and motion. Her foul mood shrouded the table, like a rampart raised against the jollity of the inn, and she took long, slow pulls of the inn's strongest drink. Her supper was left mostly untouched as she descended deeper and deeper into her cups, seeking the blissful warm oblivion that she would eventually find at the bottom.

Dried tears stained her cheeks, and for much of the evening her somber mood was enough to deter any intrusions upon her despondent reverie, as ghosts of things that might have been haunted her thoughts. She took another drink, draining her tankard dry in an effort to drown them and wash them away, but they clung tenaciously, like the icy talons of some beast of minstrels' fancy sunk deeply into her heart.

A serving girl appeared at some unspoken arrangement between them with a fresh pint the moment she thumped the empty tankard in her hand onto the table in front of her, before disappearing back into the crowd to attend to other guests.

Elsabeth soon lost all sense of time, and floated in a queer detached state in which she was scarcely aware of her surroundings, yet utter forgetfulness remained frustratingly beyond her grasp. She idly fingered a golden ring hanging from a chain round her neck, marked by the crossed swords of the Brotherhood; her costly prize from the venture in Ain that autumn, and a reminder of the fleeting hope for normalcy snatched from her grasp.

A shadow fell over her, and when she looked up, she laid eyes upon one of the inn's patrons — or was it him and his twin brother? And why were they spinning round one another? — standing over her.

"'Tis a lovely night," he said. "A pretty lady ought not to be drinking alone."

Elsabeth muttered something unintelligible to her own ears, but she wagered it was not particularly courteous judging from the indignant scowl upon the intruder's features.

"That is hardly language one ought to use in polite company, and I have certainly only been so!" the interloper protested, and made to sit. Elsabeth's eyes flashed dangerously, and she gripped the table to rise.

"Here now!" a stern voice interjected. "Go on back to your own table, Marquart. I'll have no trouble out of you."

"What are you on about, Wernhart? I came over polite as can be and the bitch can't even give me a 'How do you do!'"

"I don't care if you were taking donations for the monastery up the hill! Go back to your own folk. Now get!"

The intruder grumbled something under his breath, but departed nonetheless. Another face replaced him in Elsabeth's vision.

Wernhart casually tossed a cloth over his shoulder and slid into the chair opposite her. Elsabeth glowered at him, though out of annoyance rather than unwelcome.

"I could have handled that lout," she slurred, and it took a great effort to keep her words intelligible.

"Oh, I don't doubt it, Elsie. But I would rather not have to call a leech to put him back together, nor pay to replace the crocks and tables you would break in handling him."

Elsabeth twisted her lip. "Bah. 'Twould be a pittance, and I have a mind to crack a skull or two."

He heaved a sigh and leaned his arms on the table. "So, you have been up to the monastery already, I see."

She speared him with a glare, but with her eyes finding it difficult to focus the look was lost on him. "I already have the good Prior stabbing me in the conscience," she said. "I don't need it from you, too."

"'Tis not my intent, just an observation."

"Well, you keep your observations. I am just here to have a drink after a long road, and then to bed. 'Tis all. A drink after a long road, and then to bed."

But tears welled up in her eyes and her breath came in ragged heaves, putting the lie to her words. She hastily swiped at her eyes to bat the tears away, and drew a choking breath as guilt twisted like a dagger in her bowels.

"I don't know. Tell me what you really think of me; Am I just selfish?"

Wernhart frowned at her. In better light, and if the room were not spinning madly around her, she would have found him handsome, though he was ten years her elder. He had deep hazel eyes, and neatly groomed brown hair beginning to thin up top. And his troubled expression was out of place on features she was more accustomed to seeing laughing at some ribald tale — many she herself told.

"How do you mean?" he asked, unsure how to respond.

Elsabeth considered her tankard of ale and took a long drink. "How do I mean? I would think 'tis plain. Yes, 'twould be plain. Am I just selfish? In leaving, I mean?"

Wernhart sighed. "Don't think like that, Elsie. You did what you had to, and no one would fault you for that."

She shook her head and slammed her tankard down. The other patrons all craned their necks at the sound, curious over the sudden outburst. But when no punches were thrown, they soon turned back to their own business.

"The good Prior does, though he daren't say so openly. I could have stayed. I could have stayed," she said, and again her voice broke. "I could have kept on serving ale and food for you in the common room. I could have been here, and not missed so much already. And how much more will I miss?"

28

"You were not happy with that. And you were certainly better than it. And after all that business with...well, you know who ..." He trailed off, and a cold shudder worked down Elsabeth's spine at one particular ghostly face she had no mind to recall. "And leastwise I think you make more now than I could pay you," he continued instead.

"But is that really it? Or is it just an excuse to not be tied down, to freely go wither I will? I could not with him, you know. But was it for him or me that I left him behind?"

"Look, Elsie," he said, "'Tis not my place to judge. If 'tis a confession you want, you shall want to have a word with Father Ottin up the hill, if you have not already."

"I know. I know. And he has already given his counsel." Elsabeth took another long drink. Her brows grew heavy, and she mopped her face. "'Tis late, and the room is spinning mightily. I really ought to sleep. If I don't go to my room I might even drop right here and now."

His features twisted with concern, and he reached out to touch her hand. "I can be missed for a bit, if you don't want to be alone."

Elsabeth looked up at him, and ordinarily she might have melted at the earnestness in his expression. It was such a rare thing; too many looked upon her for their own gratification, and from any other man in these circumstances she would have her sword at his throat. Instead, she simply offered a mournful shake of her head.

"Not tonight. No, not tonight. I want to be alone." She offered him a small smile. "You are a good man, you know? You have done so, so very much for me. It still amazes me that you have not found a good woman to settle down with and put me from your thoughts."

29

Wernhart offered a smile in turn. "'Twould be a tall order to find your match round here. Come on now, I'll have Brid help you up to your door."

Elsabeth drained the last of her tankard, and clasped Wernhart's hand lying on the table. "You are a lovely, lovely man, love. I really do love you, thank you."

IT TOOK BRID SOME EFFORT TO GET HER UP THE STAIRS TO the private rooms at the back of the inn. Elsabeth's feet stumbled beneath her, and the whole world spun quite alarmingly. She leaned heavily against the smaller woman, who bore her weight with a great exertion, but not so much as a grunt of complaint. Her arm draped across Brid's shoulders, and Brid put one arm round her waist to support and guide her. Elsabeth did not laugh, nor did she sing (much to the relief of her companion of the moment, for rumor of her unmusical voice preceded her).

All the doors looked alike — most leading to communal sleeping areas, but a few to the odd private room for the more affluent guests — each branching off the long hallway running the length of the inn, and without Brid to guide her she mused she might have stumbled into the wrong one and given quite the surprise to its proper tenant. They reached her room without misadventure, however, and Elsabeth sank against the door.

"Will there be anything else tonight, Frau Soesten?" Brid said pleasantly.

"No, no, 'twill be all. I think I'll have a bit of a sleep. Thank you."

Brid lifted her skirts for a polite curtsy, then hastily retreated, leaving Elsabeth alone in the hallway.

She fumbled for a moment with the door, but soon had it open, and stumbled inside. The room was plain, though comfortably furnished, and one of the nicest in the establishment. A boon of maintaining a close friendship with the proprietor. There was a trunk at the end of the bed for her baggage, and a table occupied the floor between the bed and the door. Lamps lit the room and cast flickering shadows that filled the corners and crannies, and a closed window looked out onto the darkened streets.

Elsabeth fumbled with the hooks of her doublet upon shutting out the rest of the inn behind her, and let it drop to the floor. It landed with the sharp rattle of its concealed metal plates. Her sword leaned against a wall, and her jacket lay upon the bed. She took a deep breath and mopped her face as she stumped with one leaden foot in front of the other to the bed beckoning her with siren song.

But before she reached it, she felt a sudden hand on her shoulder from behind.

All at once the cloud of drink fell from her eyes, and Elsabeth sprung into motion. She seized hold of the hand, spun round to face her assailant, and caught a momentary glimpse of a cloaked and hooded figure. However, it darted quickly around her and twisted free of her grip. Elsabeth stumbled across the room and struck the door hard, driving the breath from her lungs with a grunt.

She turned and reached to her back, and her rondel flashed from its sheath. The hooded figure stood before her, straight and without even taking up a fighting stance. Her face heated at that cheek, and she charged in an ungainly rush. Elsabeth leveled a stiff thrust at the intruder's middle, which he casually brushed aside, and stepped wide around to her side and out of her reach.

Elsabeth turned again, and a furious exchange of blows ensued. She struck with her hands and rondel. She shifted her weapon from hand to hand, and between overhand and underhand grips. Yet most of her attacks were wide and clumsy in her inebriated state, while the few that came near enough to threaten her assailant were bat aside with casual disregard. That just made her hotter, and her attacks became wilder. She stomped across the floor after him, bumped the table, and struck the walls raising an awful racket. And yet no one came to investigate. She was alone with her adversary, and no help seemed forthcoming.

Finally, after much staggering, swinging, and flailing she managed to seize hold of her adversary by the front of his cloak, and slammed him against the wall with her rondel at his throat.

Elsabeth's breast heaved with every labored breath, and her rondel trembled in her hand. Her assailant did not move, pinned as he was against the wall with the point pricking his bare flesh. The only sound in the room was their panting breaths. She seized hold of the hood shadowing his features and tore it off, and a gasp mixing surprise and annoyance escaped her lungs.

There before her stood Cuncz von Leyen, smirking at her with infuriatingly calm and confident eyes despite the knife at his throat.

"You!" she breathed, as her drink-addled brain struggled to process what she was seeing.

"Good evening, my dear! 'Tis wonderful to see you again," he said, in that unfailingly and frustratingly polite manner that exuded control despite his circumstances.

Elsabeth glared balefully into his eyes, and for a passing moment the fancy of thrusting her rondel into his windpipe crossed her mind. But it was only a passing moment, and once the rush of the fight and the shock of finding him beneath the hood faded, she twisted her lip into a scowl. She buried her rondel into one of the wooden slats of the wall next to his head (Cuncz did not so much as blink or shrink away from the blow, denying her the satisfaction of shaking his confidence).

"Fuck you," she said, then seized his face in both hands and pulled him into a kiss.

Cuncz kissed her back fiercely. Their tongues met and intertwined, and he sucked and nibbled on her upper lip. He gripped her firmly by the shoulders, and Elsabeth stumbled backwards when he leaned his body into hers. His hands slipped down the length of her side, first to her waist, then to her hips, and around to cup her bottom and pull her tightly against him. Her heart raced, and her breath came in desperate gasps in the brief moments their mouths parted. She twined her fingers into his hair, and one of his hands left her backside to brush the hair back from her cheek, before gliding up and down the length of her neck. Her flesh tingled under his touch, and a warmth she could not attribute to drink spread through her.

Then his lips left hers, and a low moan escaped her throat when they landed upon her neck. He traced a line of nibbling kisses down from her jaw to her shoulder. Her knees buckled beneath her, and she staggered backward. Her hip struck hard against the table in the middle of the floor, and a loud *bump* echoed through the inn, accompanied by the thudding of their booted feet on the wooden floor in an unbalanced rush across the room. Another solid *thud* broke the silence when Elsabeth's back struck the far wall. Between the impact, the thrill over Cuncz's lips on her neck, and the length of his body pressed against hers, she struggled to draw breath.

She clutched his head to her, and he suckled and nibbled her flesh. The hand holding her head went to one breast. His strong fingers fondled her through her shirt, then wandered to the waistline of her hose and worked round to the lacing in front. The other left her bottom to brace himself against the wall. Another ragged gasp rattled in her throat when he reached down and grabbed between her legs. Elsabeth's back arched when Cuncz's lips found the hollow of her throat, and she moaned again at the fingers rubbing the inside of her thighs. Then, he let slip one of the lacings securing the front flap of her hose, and reached his hand down and into her braies.

His hand was hot against her flesh. Her moans grew more insistent, and she leaned her head back against the wall. Searching fingers reached the space between her legs, and she squealed delightedly as he stroked and probed, seeking for that one special intimate place he had discovered during their last encounter which set her body on fire.

Elsabeth cupped his face and pulled his lips from her neck so she could kiss him again, then raced to fumble with the lacings holding his codpiece closed. First one, then the other, came free after some moments of blind tearing, while her legs wobbled and threatened to give way under his fingers probing and teasing her. His hand left her breast, and the fingers between her legs slipped out again to tug her braies aside. She seized hold of him round the shaft and pulled him free of his hose.

Elsabeth's breath left her in a rush as he filled her, lifting her off her feet and forcing her back against the wall. She wrapped her legs around him, and clutched the back of his head. He feverishly pumped his hips against hers, and she grunted in time with the rhythmic bumping of her body against the wall.

Her grunts stretched into pleasured moans at the sensation of him moving inside her, an exquisite fullness that left the void she had felt growing all night long forgotten. Cuncz, however, withdrew from her before she could slip entirely into that welcome, pleasurable oblivion, and pulled her away from the wall. He spun her around, took hold of her hair and pulled it aside, and his lips found the back of her neck. His mouth wandered the length of it from the corner of her jaw to the end of her shoulder, and his touch set her bare skin on fire. His other hand then seized her neck with a firm but gentle grip, tilting her head just enough that his lips could find the hollow of her throat from this new position. He released her hair and freed the tail of her blouse from her hose, then slipped his hand once more down her braies to fondle the space between her legs. She reached behind her to seize him by the hair. A shudder coursed through her, and a ragged moan escaped her throat at the sensation of his probing fingers teasing her with the promise of what was to come.

So intertwined they stumbled across the floor to the table. The front of her thighs bumped hard against it, and she felt the length of him press against her bottom. His hands left her neck and, to her momentary disappointment, slipped out from between her legs. Instead, his thumbs hooked through the waist of her hose and braies, tugging them down with no delicacy until they fell to her knees and bared her backside to him. He pressed the length of his belly against her back and filled his hands with her breasts for a moment as he craned his neck around her for another kiss that sucked the breath from her lungs. Then he bent her forcefully over the table, scattering everything atop it across the floor. Elsabeth squealed when he entered her again, the movement nearly lifting her from her feet.

The table groaned in protest under their weight. Its feet squeaked as it skidded along the floor with every sturdy thrust of his hips. All the strength drained from her legs, and without the table to support her she would have sunk to the floor. Elsabeth gripped the edge and squeezed her eyes tight. Ecstatic moans escaped the back of her throat.

She threw back her head, and the more unrestrained her cries of pleasure, the more feverish and intense Cuncz's efforts grew. His hands wandered from the front of her thighs to her hips, and then to her waist. He seized hold of her shirt, and whipped it off over her head to expose her body to the winter chill permeating the room. He filled his hands with her breasts. The cool air was forgotten beneath the heat of him pressed against her, and the intense warmth radiating from within her with every stroke. He kissed her neck again; long, sucking nibbles from the corner of her jaw down to the top of her shoulder and back again.

Cuncz pushed her back down onto the table with one hand between her shoulder blades. The soft whisper of fabric joined the steady bumping and squeaking cadence of the table slowly being driven across the room as his shirt joined hers on the floor. He laid his hands atop the backs of hers, twining his fingers through them. He sucked her earlobe into his mouth, licked and nipped at her neck, and kissed along her shoulder.

Elsabeth cried out as her whole body spasmed in ecstasy.

Cuncz uttered a ragged moan and shuddered in response.

The table groaned.

A sharp *crack* filled the room.

And suddenly she and Cuncz were tumbling face-first to the floor with a deafening crash as the legs of the table gave out beneath them.

But for a time, at least, all her troubles vanished from her thoughts.

4

COLD LIGHT SPEARED ACROSS THE ROOM, AND BY some wicked contrivance of the Dark One struck Elsabeth square in the eye.

She moaned pitiably and tossed one arm across her face in a vain effort to shield herself from that infernal beam. A fog of sleep and drink clung tenaciously to her mind, the former evaporating under the luminous assault, the latter expanding rapidly within her skull until she thought it might burst under the pressure. Elsabeth lurched upright, allowing the blanket pulled up round her shoulders to fall across her lap, and she wrapped her arms around herself reflexively when the morning chill smote her naked breast. That shocked her into alertness, and with it the pressure building in her skull threatened to tear it apart bone by bone. She mopped her eyes with one hand.

Elsabeth shifted to stand, but the moment she moved a hand shot out from behind her and caught her round the wrist. Cuncz raised himself up on his other elbow, and looked up at her with that infuriating, self-satisfied smirk.

"Good morning, Tetty," he said.

She screwed up her lip and glowered down on him with a look of feigned annoyance. "Oh dear God, and here I thought last night was merely some awful nightmare in my drunken stupor," she said flatly.

Cuncz chuckled softly and dragged her back down onto the bed. "I am not one to take advantage of a woman in such a distressed state—"

"Of course not."

"—but you did kiss me first. I merely came up for a pleasant chat."

"Does anyone really believe a word that comes out of your mouth?"

He leaned over her and kissed her. Elsabeth's breath caught in her throat at the electric jolt coursing from her lips and down to more intimate places, and she curled her toes into the mattress beneath her. When he parted from her again it was with a lingering, sucking nibble on her upper lip, and Elsabeth gasped in a desperate breath.

Cuncz brushed the hair back from her cheek. "I would ask much the same of you, but you and I are both much too accomplished with our tongues to be so easily caught."

"Well, I'll grant you that your tongue certainly is talented, though more so on a few particulars of my anatomy than at spinning lies. Don't let this go to either head, love, but I was desperately in need of last night. The past few months have been somewhat wanting."

One of his hands slipped down the length of her torso, and glided across skin stretched tautly over the sheet of muscle at her belly on its way down to her hip. "Missed me, did you?"

"After a fashion," she said.

"And yet you were in such a hurry to leave bed this morning."

"The sun was in my eye. Be a dear and have Conrat go up and blot it out."

Cuncz reclined onto the pillow once more, and Elsabeth nestled down into the crook of his arm. "Conrat, I am afraid, remained behind in Leyen to manage things while I am away and keep up appearances. Quite the worthy man; no one will ever know I am gone."

Elsabeth grunted. "Still playing your little intrigues I see."

"My dear, the games never end. And where, may I ask, is the good Brother? I noticed his horse was not in the stable last night."

"If you must know, Brother Hieronymus winters at some stronghold or other of his Order. Every year that I have known him; and good for me, because once the first snow falls he shan't stop complaining about the cold until I leave him there.

"I meet him again come the spring thaw, but I am really of no mind to discuss him further. And that bloody light is still in my eye."

With a suddenness that recalled his agility during their scuffle the night before, Cuncz had her under him again, blocking out that intrusive piercing ray with his own body.

"Better?" he said.

"I don't know that the view has improved, but at least the light is not trying to bore a hole through my eye sockets."

Cuncz leaned down and kissed her again, and Elsabeth moaned softly. *God! Why does he have to be so bloody good at this!* One hand explored her body from her breast to her thigh, while he supported himself with the other. With much greater reluctance than she wanted to admit, she put a hand against his chest and pushed him away. Again he drew out the kiss for as long as he could, before releasing her upper lip with a last, parting nibble.

"What are you doing here?" she asked, holding him at bay with one hand, and trying very hard not to think about how nicely his skin stretched across the muscle beneath. His hand came to rest on back of her hip, and pulled her lower extremity close against him. It took a great deal of effort not to think about that *other* bit of his anatomy now poking her in the base of the thigh.

"Why, enjoying all the pleasures your company offers."

Elsabeth fixed him with an impatient glare.

"What are you really doing here?"

Cuncz heaved a sigh and rolled off her again. He flopped onto his back between her and the shaft of light burning through the window.

"I had hoped we might have a brief time to enjoy one another this morning before we got to business."

"Tch. I knew it. You want something from me."

"I already had something from you. Quite a few times last night, in fact. I must remember to pay the innkeeper for the table ere I depart."

"That is not what I meant, and you know it!" she snapped, and blushed fiercely as memory of the table collapsing under the raucousness of their tryst returned to mind.

"All right, I have a spot of work for you."

Elsabeth threw off the covers and jumped out of bed. "Oh! I bloody knew it."

Cuncz lifted himself up on one elbow, and his eye shamelessly wandered her naked figure from head to toe. "And this is why I hoped to broach the matter in due time."

Elsabeth snatched up her braies from the floor and slipped into them again. "What difference does it make if you broach the matter now or in due time? It does not change the fact you are just here because of some new plot you seek to draw me into."

"I'll not lie about your usefulness to me in this matter, but 'twas not the only reason I am here."

She stepped into her hose and glowered at him. "So you intended to fuck me into the job, then." She made it a statement of fact.

Cuncz merely shrugged offhandedly. "Rather I considered that a not-inconsiderable bonus."

"For me or for you?"

"Why not both?"

Elsabeth popped her head through the neck of her blouse and slipped her arms back through the sleeves. She did not bother with the ribbons that pulled them snug against her upper arms, but stuffed the tail into the top of her hose and knotted the flap closed.

"Don't flatter yourself. I really don't know what infuriates me more: That you actually think I would fall for it, or this bloody act like nothing ever bothers you when it turns out wrong."

Cuncz casually fluffed a pillow and stuffed it behind his head. "The job pays a thousand *pfunde*," he said, and Elsabeth froze halfway through fastening her doublet.

"Say again?"

"One thousand *pfunde*. That is the import I place upon this task. And not just for myself, but for His Imperial Majesty."

Elsabeth stared at him, and gawked as if he had sprouted an extra head. Her half-fastened doublet went forgotten. "One thousand *pfunde*. From the Emperor himself?"

"His very own seal is stamped upon the order and upon the papers of account. But I do have other agents, if you have no need for such coin."

She flushed, and a part of her mind screamed warnings at the strange tone of voice with which he spoke that last part. "'Tis a hefty sum. And no small honor, I should think."

"I could not, of course, bring your name directly to His attention should you carry out this service for Him, such is the secrecy."

"And what is this service?"

"In due time, as I said," he said with a mischievous glint in his eye. "First, I think we should go down to breakfast."

LSABETH AND CUNCZ ARRIVED IN THE COMMON ROOM TO find it suspiciously empty.

The fire crackled on the hearth and the aroma of fresh bread mingled with the fragrant perfume of burning wood, but though it was well into the morning, every table but one was empty. That was occupied by Cuncz's three favorite guardsmen — Clement, Jacobus, and Thaddeus — who took their breakfast with large tankards of ale. Wernhart looked up from refilling Thaddeus' tankard when she entered, but if he thought anything of what transpired between her and Cuncz after she declined his company the night before, he wisely held his tongue.

Instead, he finished his task and bowed deeply to Cuncz.

"Your men are being fed, Herr von Leyen," he said, "and I'll have your breakfast along presently."

"Thank you," Cuncz said. "I have heard good things about your kitchens and drink, so I most look forward to it."

Wernhart bowed deeply again, then inclined his head to Elsabeth in turn. "Good morning, Elsie. How are you feeling?"

"Better, I suppose," she said, and nursed her temples. "Though I think I could do with a platter of rollmops, if you have any."

He offered her an understanding smile. "I'll see what I can do for you. I always have something on hand for just such a malady."

"Thank you, love."

Cuncz directed her to a table in the corner and pulled out a chair for her so she might sit with her back to the wall. She eyed him sharply at that display, but Cuncz merely weathered it with an affectation of innocence she did not for a moment believe.

Elsabeth and Cuncz broke their fast in awkward silence, with Wernhart hovering round them in case he was needed. Cuncz did not say a word more about what had brought him to Pruck while he ate, and before long Elsabeth's impatience began to get the better of her. She did not press him, however, and restrained herself to a bit of fidgeting and nervously popping rollmops into her mouth. The dainties were rolled round gherkins pickled with dill, and went a long way towards easing her belly in the aftermath of the last night's drinking. Her head still pounded something fierce, however, and would not be so easily nursed.

Finally, Cuncz finished, and drained his tankard in one final draught, thumping it down harder and louder than Elsabeth's throbbing temples liked.

"My compliments to you on your table," he said, and Wernhart's face brightened at the praise. "I may have to see about stealing you away for my own kitchens."

Elsabeth spit him with a glare. "Don't even think it."

Cuncz shrugged innocently. "I merely suggest a man of his talents ought to be plying his trade in far loftier places! I wager even his Excellency the Prince-Bishop would not boast of so fine a table."

Wernhart flushed, and bowed. "'Tis welcome to hear such words, Herr von Leyen, seldom as I hear them from the regulars. Though doubtless they are no less appreciative, else I would not be able to call them such. Nonetheless, my own small kitchen is all I desire."

"Suit yourself, though I may have a man sent to learn what secrets you would be willing to part with."

Elsabeth glowered at him from across the table. "In the meantime, you and I have more pressing business to discuss than the culinary art of the worthy Wernhart."

"Indeed we have." Cuncz rose and directed her towards the door with exaggerated flourish. "My dear?"

She spared Wernhart a distressed look, but if any rescue was at hand, it would not be coming from that direction. So she stomped out, with Cuncz and his guards behind her.

The morning was already late, and the sun well above the eastern horizon, when she set foot into the streets of Pruck. Snow clung in deep drifts beside the collection of half-timbered houses and shops, and piled high on their peaked roofs. Elsabeth shielded herself against the sunlight dazzling her eyes on the snow blanketing the fields and road, and her skull threatened to split open in protest. The monastery frowned down behind its walls from a hilltop a mile to the north, and smote her heart with a fresh anguish that had not yet been drunk away the night before when her eye strayed unwillingly in that direction. She bowed her head and tightened her jacket against the winter chill.

Cuncz directed her around the inn, and Elsabeth found the streets of Pruck no less suspiciously empty that morning than she did the common room. Cold as it was the sun was bright, and at the very least the children of town ought to have been out sledding on the slopes, or throwing snowballs, or skating on the iced-over ponds, or doing their chores and tending to the animals put away in the barns for the winter. Instead, all was empty and silent. Not eerily so, but the windswept peace of a winter's morning after a gentle snowfall. But conscious as she was of Cuncz beside her (he now threaded his arm through hers to lead her whither he willed) she held little doubt there was some mischief at play.

Around the back of the inn was a wide yard. In one corner, far from the back door leading to the kitchens, stood a brick oven where much of the baking was done, alongside a tall smoker. There were also trestle tables, which in warmer days would be occupied by those who wished to take their meals in the open air, or for the celebrations and feast days hosted at the inn for the community. Elsabeth frowned when she spied a heavy canvas tarp spread out upon one of these tables, surrounded by servants in Cuncz's livery and, more to her growing concern, an armed guard far larger than she deemed appropriate for Cuncz's clandestine sojourns. At the far end of the yard, opposite the inn itself, were sections of log stood up on end in a line. Atop each was set a large melon, just about the size of a man's head.

"All this mystery for a bit of dessert?" she said.

Cuncz chuckled. "You shall see. And of course, I expect everything you do see shall be kept in the strictest confidence."

She eyed him sidelong. That knowing smirk was plastered across his lips, and Elsabeth wished for nothing more than to wipe it from his features.

"'Tis been a few years since I cut only melons or hog-carcasses in Master Paulus' training yard, but I know such a gauntlet when I see it."

"Oh, you shan't be cutting, I can assure you. Now then—" they reached the table, and at Cuncz's direction the tarp was rolled back slightly in dramatic fashion. Elsabeth frowned at the contraption that was concealed beneath; it consisted of a long tube of iron fixed to a wooden handle, not unlike the tiller of a crossbow. But there were no prongs, or nut, or trigger, or any other mechanism she could see. "—this is what 'tis all about."

Cuncz picked it up off the table and set it in Elsabeth's hands. Then he took a burning slow match from a servant near at hand and directed her towards the line of melons at the far end of the field. She turned the tube this way and that, puzzling over it in a manner that left her feeling maddeningly uneducated in front of Cuncz and his servants.

"Are you enjoying your game? I have no idea what it is I am even looking at."

His features were suddenly grave, and if anything, the loss of his façade of good humor unnerved more than satisfied her.

"'Tis no game, my dear. Or if it is, 'tis one of a most deadly sort. Now—" Cuncz sidled up behind her, and with his arms round her, guided her in lifting the contraption in her hands. Elsabeth's face heated at his proximity when he hugged her close, with his chin resting on her shoulder, his lips nuzzling next to her ear, and his lean frame pressed against her, all shamelessly done in front of his servants and guards. "—there is a hole in the top of the barrel, see? Take aim as best you can at the melon upon the left, then touch the match to it like so."

He wrapped the fingers of her right hand round the match, leaving her to hold the handle in her left. Elsabeth looked between her target and the thing in her hands, and frowned when she found no expedient means of both pointing it and safely doing as he instructed. So, she took a breath, and with her best guess directing her aim, touched the match to the hole.

A sharp *crack* like thunder shattered the stillness of the morning. White smoke erupted from the hole, and belched from the far end of the tube. The whole thing bucked in her hand.

Elsabeth let out a yelp, jumped a foot into the air, and dropped the wicked bit of devilry as if it bit her hand. The report echoed across the hills, and in some corner of Pruck horses squealed in fright. Elsabeth's heart was in her throat, but no one dared make any remark about her reaction.

Cuncz casually stooped, retrieved the fallen tube from the ground, and brushed the snow from it. A good three feet of soot covered the ground in front of her, but the melon stood unharmed on its section of log.

"What in God's name is that thing?" she stammered, as Cuncz held it out for her inspection.

"This, my dear, is what the Navarrese call a *hand gonne*. They have been spreading among armies the world over the past hundred years, though are not yet common. The secret of their operation is a blasting powder, whose provenance lies far east in Chang'an, though I am told they use it mostly for noisemakers, rather than practical weapons of war. Here, I daresay, *gonnes* stand to revolutionize battle as we know it."

Elsabeth looked sharply at him at mention of that name, and the parlor tricks of Girart and his two strange co-conspirators months past sprang to mind.

"'Twould seem to me it has little practical use beyond noisemakers. I could not both keep my eye on the target and touch the match to it at the same time, and there is no practical means of aiming it beside."

Cuncz nodded and smiled. "Quite astute. But this is only a rude example. Still in use, but already obsolete."

He turned back to the table, and when the tarp was drawn back, Elsabeth peeked round Cuncz's shoulder to look upon a collection of arms more familiar in form to her eyes. They were more obviously akin to a crossbow, with the wooden tiller shaped to better fit against the shoulder, and an iron lever as a trigger.

47

Once again there were no prongs, nut, or string, only a long tube of iron. These *gonnes*, however, also possessed an S-shaped piece of iron pinned to the tiller just behind a shallow pan and linked to the trigger beneath, so that when it was depressed the whole assembly tipped forward. Cuncz slipped the end of his slow match into a jawed assembly at the end of the serpentine bit of metal, and primed the pan with a small measure of powder from a flask handed to him by one of his servants. He then offered this new *gonne* to Elsabeth. She frowned doubtfully at it, then sighed and exchanged it for the one in her hand.

She lifted it to her shoulder and took aim along its barrel much as she would a crossbow. This she found much easier, as she no longer needed to concern herself with the placement of the match, and at the far end of the tube was a nob of iron aligning with another at the near end for a rude sight. Elsabeth braced the contraption against her shoulder, prepared now for the recoil when the infernal thing ignited.

The *gonne* discharged promptly upon squeezing the trigger, and she shielded her eyes against the flash of powder in the pan. Smoke and fire roared from the end, and set as she was it still kicked quite fiercely. She still did not hit her mark, but this time at least the melon to its right exploded in a shower of juicy fragments across the snow. The scent of expended powder hung thick and acrid in the air, and the smoke slowly dissipated under the wind.

"Marvelous!" Cuncz said, and snatched the *gonne* back from her. "Now, 'tis not without its flaws. The accuracy is not what it ought to be, and the burning of a slow match would give away your position, but here we see something that can change the face of war itself!"

Elsabeth brushed some soot from her jacket and leaned her hands on her hips. "Perhaps, though I still don't see how this would be all that superior to the crossbows the Navarrese already have in abundance, or even a good Coventrish longbow."

Cuncz made a show of sighting along the *gonne's* barrel. "'Tis the old way of thinking that clouds your head, my dear Tetty, along with perhaps a bit too much drink last night."

Elsabeth heated and clenched her fists.

"As it stands," he continued, ignoring her pique, "the crossbow and longbow certainly do have their advantages in accuracy and range. But I have seen tests that will put shot clear through the stoutest cuirass at over a hundred yards; not even the finest craft of the bowyers of Coventry could boast of such a feat! But more to the point, it takes a lifetime to train a skilled bowman. And crossbows are not without their own difficulties in loading and firing. Imagine being able to raise a whole army armed with tools such as this, and being able to do so in a matter of weeks!"

She frowned again as Cuncz's words sunk in. "I suppose you could put an entire kingdom at arms. If you could manufacture enough."

Cuncz smiled again, and the gleam in his eye chilled her through to the bone. "And that is also the beauty of the *gonne*; it takes a skilled and seasoned bowyer to make a proper bow, yet while I will not say any blacksmith could turn out a working *gonne* — for there are indeed unique tolerances and quality of material if you don't wish the whole to explode in your face — but near enough so that I see them made in mass quantities; thousands, if not tens of thousands!"

Elsabeth swallowed and shivered a bit, but not from the stiff winter wind billowing along the tops of the snow-clad fields. "And what has this to do with me?"

He returned the *gonne* to the table and stepped up to her side. With one hand round her shoulders Cuncz led her away, so he might speak with none of the others hearing.

"I have learned, through one of my agents, that there is a clockmaker in Carcassonne who has devised an even more advanced *gonne* than this, one with no need for a match to fire, and that would be a profound improvement indeed, for as I have said there are still a great many flaws in these models."

"For one I wonder how your... *gonners* would not light themselves on fire or blow themselves up."

"Quite right. And that is what this has to do with you. I need someone — someone I can trust to see the job done — to meet with my agent and secure me one of these new *gonnes* for His Excellency the Prince-Bishop, who shall then present it to His Imperial Majesty."

"Along with your name, I imagine."

"So it should be expected. But consider this: Navarre has only recently concluded a very costly conflict with Coventry. A war that ended on her terms, but one which will take much time and further expense to heal the scars. Imagine what a resurgent Navarre, armed with such a weapon as this, might do in vengeance."

Elsabeth looked sideling at Cuncz. "Love, I have rarely set foot in Coventry since I was still chasing at my mother's skirts. As much as you have seemingly pried into my comings and goings, I would think you would know that already."

"True enough, but 'tis also important that my name not be known for its involvement in any such intrigues. Thus, I cannot rely on any other agent in my employ." Cuncz seized her by the hands. "I need you, Tetty."

"So, I am distant enough from you if I am caught I can't lead back to you. Your best argument was still the one you gave in my chamber." She forestalled the smirk forming on his lips. "And you know to what I am referring, so don't try to misconstrue. One thousand *pfunde*, you said."

Cuncz squared his shoulders. "Yes, I did. Upon securing an example of this new *gonne* and returning with it here to Pruck. I'll not deny 'twill be a most dangerous escapade, and as you yourself noted, should something unfortunate befall you I won't be able to help you and you will surely be taken for a spy, whatever fair guise you might wear."

"All right, then. One thousand *pfunde* for one *gonne*."

He smiled and clasped her hand. "Wonderful! Now, you shan't be alone in this venture. My agent is already in Carcassonne and awaits only instruction on how to proceed. You will meet with him, and I am sure between the two of you, you can come to some plan."

"And how am I to know him?"

"You don't need to," Cuncz said. "Wear the ring I gave you, and he will know you."

Elsabeth spit him with a suspicious look. "And how do you know I have not sold it? 'Twas a fine bauble and would have been worth a pretty *pfennig* in a pinch."

Cuncz tsked her. "Come now, Tetty, I have seen something of your vanity in action, and I doubt you would readily part with any such trinket given in good faith."

Her face heated.

"One *gonne*, brought here to Pruck for one thousand *pfunde*," she said instead.

"And the sooner 'tis done, the sooner you shall have it." He bowed deeply. "Now then, I'll leave you to it. I hope to see you again soon."

With that he turned and strolled off through the snow, as casually as if he were walking the gardens of his own stronghold away to the southeast. Elsabeth watched him go, torn between the desire to throttle him over his smugness, and leaping for joy at the promised windfall.

51

She cast an eye to the monastery frowning down on them from a distance. Perhaps here was the answer to her troubles after all.

THE CITY OF CARCASSONNE STOOD AMID A WIDE swath of farmland east of the Ain River, and some sixty miles northwest of Pruck. A great stone wall encircled it, with a well-fortified gatehouse centered in the southern face. Clusters of hamlets sprung up in the fields surrounding the city, and in the spring, summer, and fall would be a hive of activity as laborers worked in the fields to plant, tend the crops, and carry out the harvest. Now, in the deep of winter, all was still and silent, and the ordered fields slept beneath a white blanket of snow.

Elsabeth clutched the fur-lined hood of her cloak closer round her face against the biting winds, and shivered from her perch on the bench of the wagon trundling along the narrow road leading towards the gate. Very few folk were abroad, with only an occasional wagon or horseman on the morass of clinging mud approaching the city gates. Those who had more sense remained huddled in the local inns and taverns of their home villages and left the roads to the foolhardy.

She glanced sidelong at the driver of the wagon; a fellow with a face tanned to the consistency of leather by cold and sun, and with weather-beaten garb to match. She could not risk bringing Felis on such a venture under the circumstances. Nor, she suspected, would the old Lizarran *jennet* have appreciated being forced out into the cold and wet, and away from the comfort of Pruck's stables. Cuncz would only allow his guard to take her as far as the crossing of the Ain, so she was left to find her own way to Carcassonne. Fortunately, she chanced upon this enterprising fellow heading that direction hoping to take advantage of the paucity of trade in the dead of winter to corner the local market, and bartered passage on his wain. She even needed only occasionally to fend off a wandering hand along the road.

Now, after nearly a week's journey, they approached the gates of Carcassonne. Guards, bundled up in heavy cloaks over their armor and more concerned about returning to the fires in the watch-houses next to the gate, spared them only a cursory looking over and the briefest inspections of her ride's cargo (which Elsabeth distracted from a more thorough examination with a batting of her eyes) before waving them through.

Traffic was just as light within the city as it was upon the road, and most of the residents confined themselves to the warmth of their homes, or the inns and taverns dotting the many market squares. Nonetheless, Carcassonne was alive with the echo of voices, or the barking of dogs in the many yards. The south gate was the only hub of appreciable activity within sight; warehouses lined all sides of the square within, with inns catering to the travelers and merchants crowding among them. There was also a stable and a barracks for the gate guard built up against the inside of the wall. Laborers hurried to unload the few wagons that braved the quagmire of the roads, taking as much care as haste allowed in their hurry to finish their work so they could return to the warmth of fire, ale, and the bawds plying their trade in the inns.

Elsabeth jostled in her seat and laid her hands on her lap. She idly fingered the ring on her left hand, and swept her eyes across the crowd of workers, travelers, and the few pedestrians loitering outside. Cuncz had left her no clue as to *whom* to look for, and she ground her teeth in frustration. A city of such size could take days to search, and she had no mind to scour every inn or tavern for her contact.

The wagon came to a stop, and its driver hopped down while a few boys rushed forward to take his horses. Representatives from the warehouses charged into battle over the destination of the cargo beneath the tarp covering the wagon bed. Elsabeth rose from the bench, gathered her bags, and accepted the hand down offered by her driver.

"Here we are, safe as I promised, Mademoiselle," he said. His Navarrese was heavily accented with a touch of Boehman.

"Thank you very much," she said, in her own clean Navarrese as she stepped down to the street. Her escort held her hand a moment longer than one would deem appropriate, and she slipped her fingers from his grip.

"Are you sure I can't be of further assistance? Perhaps a warm drink and a bed yonder?" He nodded towards the signboard of the nearest inn, depicting a rather comically exaggerated figure of a naked woman carousing on the back of a bucking horse. One hand hefted an enormous frothing tankard, the other a sword — or rather a particular bit of anatomy drawn in mockery of one — while her outsized breasts bobbed wildly.

Elsabeth forced a bit of color to her cheeks, and straightened to stare indignantly down on the man.

"I have already paid you quite well for you to deliver me here, and endured quite enough pawing on the road with as much courtesy as I could manage."

He blushed fiercely and shrunk from her glare. "I beg your pardon, I meant no offense. But 'tis a rare sight to see a woman travel alone, and if I might offer some advice, 'tis easy for a man to draw the wrong conclusion."

Elsabeth carefully softened her tone. "Your concern is appreciated, but I am due to meet someone here, so I shan't be alone for long. Good evening to you!"

And with that, she turned from the wagon, and started off with purpose towards a much more respectable-looking establishment on the far side of the square. As Cuncz instructed she kept her ring in plain view for all to see, and a frown tugged at her lips. Though she affected an air of deliberateness on her way across the square, she still had no idea where to go, whom she was looking for, or how they would even make their presence known to her. She eyed the sparse knots of people in the market in search of some clue, but few spared her more than a passing looking over; though she had carefully chose her dress to flatter her shape, the heavy cloak hid the particulars of her figure from view, and her hood shadowed her face. Her pattens clacked on the cobblestones and kept the end of her skirts out of the slush. Only the ring weighing down her fourth finger was exposed to view.

Elsabeth swept her eyes across the city as she walked. Much of her view was blocked by the buildings crowding the edge of the square, but she spied the towers of a large church or cathedral away to the northwest, nearer to the heart of Carcassonne, and the walls of a castle occupied a rise further around to the northeast.

"There you are!" a man's voice suddenly called out behind her. Her heart leapt up into her throat; the only weapon she carried with her was her rondel, and it was stowed away in her bags where she could not reach it.

Elsabeth turned, and before she could lay eyes upon her caller, he threw his arms around her and mashed his lips against hers. Her muffled cry of protest died in his mouth, and he bent her backwards nearly double. Her cowl fell back. One hand seized her by the hair, and the other pinned her arms to her side. She heated in spite of herself and her heart hammered against her breastbone, but her mind raced for a means of escape; her arms were pinioned, and off balance as she was she could not use her legs in her defense. The man was about her height and very strong, and all but crushed the breath from her lungs with his grip. Something hard and unyielding jabbed her in the belly, and unless he had been quite gifted by the Lord of All, Elsabeth knew he was almost certainly armed with a weapon he could quickly bring to hand if she resisted.

With no other choice for the moment, Elsabeth forced herself to relax and endure the kiss. His tongue remained within his own mouth, however, and he kept his hands respectfully away from her backside, only supporting her weight at the small of her back so she would not topple over onto the street.

Then he lifted her back upright again and withdrew his lips from hers. Still too close for her to have a clear look at him, he nuzzled the side of her neck, and his mouth hovered uncomfortably close to her ear.

"Come with me quietly," he breathed, then pushed her away to arm's length and raised his voice for all to hear. "My love, let me have a look at you! 'Tis been much too long!"

Now Elsabeth had an opportunity to look him over in turn as his eyes swept her from head to toe. He was a handsome enough fellow, and she chided herself over the sense of relief that brought her over his assault. Black hair to his shoulders artfully framed a face that was too comely for the plain laborer's garb he wore. His hazel eyes were sharp and keen, and she blushed at the sense that they pierced through the cloak obscuring her figure to look straight through her.

His doublet and hose were all well-worn and somewhat threadbare. A cape thrown round his shoulders hung to his knees. It stirred when he pushed her away, and before it settled she spied the long knife hanging at his belt that had formerly been jabbing her in the stomach.

"I came as quickly as I could," Elsabeth replied, matching his enamored tone. Her assailant held her tightly by the shoulders; a posture that left him open for a knee somewhere sensitive. However, the crowd in the city streets now watched the display with amusement, so any attempt to escape would attract more attention than she liked.

Bugger it. There is no other choice now but let this play out and chance an escape later.

"Well, now you are here, and all is right again. Come on, let us get out of the cold where I can warm you up properly. 'Tis not far."

The suggestive lilt in his voice left little doubt how, precisely, he intended to warm her up. He stepped up beside her and threaded an arm round her waist, leaving her with no room to maneuver. His other hand disappeared under his cloak, and he turned her towards one of the streets leading away from the gate square.

I best continue on as if he has that knife in his hand. He won't strike here; 'tis too public. But if he thinks he can draw me off somewhere private and prick my belly at his leisure he is in for a surprise.

However, he did not take her off the main thoroughfare and into one of the narrow alleyways where a murder could be carried out quietly and without suspicion. He chattered amiably about the news of the day, none of it particularly consequential; the weather, the doings of the neighbors, the trivia of a day's labor. Elsabeth interjected a short word or two here or there as appropriate, dismissed his questions over her journey, and swept her eyes up and down the street.

There were only a few folk abroad further from the gates, and a cold wind rolled along the street, funneled by the half-timbered buildings rising up like a cliff on either side. Shops gave way to houses and apartments. Most of the faces she saw peered out from doorways filled with the welcoming glow of fire and lamplight. A few neighbors greeted them pleasantly and dismissed their passage with friendly disregard. Elsabeth refrained from giving any sign of distress; her companion pressed closely enough against her side that he could strike quickly, and she doubted she could respond in her defense. Even with a fatal blow he might be able to drag her along for some time without suspicion.

They slowly drew near a block of apartments not far from the castle. The inner wall reared up some ways ahead of them, obscuring much of it from view. They entered a more affluent section of the City; in summer there would be gardens and flower boxes, and birds singing in the parks. But now everything slept under the white blanket of winter. The streets were clear, though wet slush filled the narrower sidewalks and paths leading off the main thoroughfare and up to the doors of the houses and apartment buildings looming over them. The temperature continued to drop as the sun set, and by the time they reached their destination there was little light to see by other than the golden glow of lamps flickering behind the windows gazing out onto the street.

They passed through a small market square, empty of all but a few pedestrians making their way between a tavern on one corner and their private dwellings. A few guards milled about in front of the door, and Elsabeth suspected the establishment was likely a popular hangout for off-duty soldiers (she spied one woman among them, who let her cloak slip from her shoulders, and risked the chill to advertise the goods she had for sale). She was led to an apartment building on the opposite corner. It was plainer than some of the other homes clustered around it, but still projected an air of opulence lacking from the poorer sections of the City.

Her companion ushered her through the door, and Elsabeth found herself in a small antechamber lit by lamps. Down a short hallway was a common room where a few of the residents gathered. Voices echoed off the walls, but the conversation was too muted for her to make out what they were saying. A fire crackled in the hearth of a fireplace providing a welcoming wall of warmth the moment she stepped in from the street.

Her companion stepped out of his pattens and managed to scoop them up without lowering his guard. Elsabeth did the same, before she was directed up a stairwell on her right. The man followed close behind her, and for a moment she considered rounding on him with her bags. However, the narrow confines meant she would not be able to swing with much force, and he could easily beat past the blow to strike her with his knife. Assuming she did not unbalance them both and send them on a fatal tumble together. So again she allowed herself to be led on, but a growing sense of panic gnawed at her belly. While her captor may not have been inclined to act on the street, here was a much more suitable place for a quiet murder; a cut throat from behind, or a knife in the kidney with a hand across her mouth, and she would not be able to call out.

But the strike never came. They climbed first one level, then a second, and finally a third. Her captor turned her off the landing and directed her to a door bracketed by iron lamps.

"Here we are at last," her companion said in her ear, and stepped up close behind her. At this proximity Elsabeth braced herself for a blow that never came. Instead, he reached passed her, slipped a key into a lock, then turned the doorknob. The door slowly swung open, and he gently guided Elsabeth inside.

Elsabeth stumbled forward a few paces into a darkened entryway. There were no lights and no fire in the hearth, and the apartment was chilly compared to the warmth of the stairwell. Freed of her companion, she lunged forward an extra pace to clear some distance between them, dropped her pattens to the floor with a sharp clatter, and spun round to face him from a defensive crouch with her bag gripped tightly in both hands. He was unimpressed, however, and casually hung his cloak on a hook before turning towards the lamps bolted into the wall on either side of the door. He lit them both, and soon golden light spilled into the antechamber.

"All right," Elsabeth finally said. "I have played along with this charade long enough. So now you have me alone, but whatever you have in mind you shan't find me dying quietly."

He dismissed her threat with an amused click of his tongue.

"You are certainly no less spirited than I was led to believe. And please, you shan't be needing that." He motioned towards Elsabeth's bag raised between them like a shield and raised ready to strike at need.

And with that, he raised one hand with his palm inwards, and revealed a ring identical to the one she wore.

Elsabeth's breath caught in her throat, and she narrowed her eyes suspiciously. "Just who are you?"

"Kilianus," he said. "Michael Kilianus, in the service of Freiherr von Leyen. And you and I have business to discuss."

6

ELSABETH STOOD AND STARED, DUMBFOUNDED, and for a rare moment at a loss for words. Kilianus stepped around her into the room, but she remained rooted in stunned silence, staring at the door. Then she shook off her stupor and spun round to face him. He crossed the floor with several long strides to a window peering down briefly into the darkness of the alleyway below, before closing the shutters.

She remained tense and ready to spring into movement at the slightest threat, but her captor merely made the rounds of the room lighting the remaining lamps inside, until slowly the shadows rolled back, revealing a modest living space that occupied the entire floor on this side of the building. It was sparsely appointed, with a hook near the door on which she could hang her cloak, and a threadbare rug laid out on the wooden floor in front of the hearth. A couch sat facing it with a chair on either side. Other than the door out onto the landing, the only exit from the room led to another chamber further towards the rear of the building, which Elsabeth suspected housed the apartment's sleeping quarters. A supply of firewood was stacked neatly next to the hearth, along with all the accoutrements needed to tend to the fireplace.

"Well," Kilianus said as he worked on lighting the lamps, "Herr Baron said he would be sending help, but I did not expect it to be so lovely."

Elsabeth flushed and folded her arms beneath her breast. "And how do you know who I am?"

Kilianus casually lifted his hand and flashed his ring at her again. "You and I bear a common mark. The Baron likes for all of his agents to be able to identify one another quickly, and without too many dangerous questions."

She gritted her teeth and glowered at the ring on her finger. "You mean this ring?"

He glanced over his shoulder at her while he finished with the last of the lights; a simple brass and glass lamp set atop the mantelpiece.

"He did not tell you?"

Elsabeth spit him with a glare. "No, he most certainly did not. He led me to believe 'twas a token of his affection. Well, let me say I don't exactly find myself affected to learn the whole thing was just a bloody ruse this entire time, and just a way to mark me as one of his."

Kilianus grunted and shrugged.

"'Tis not for me to question his ways, though he can be a queer one at times. He certainly fancies the games he plays."

"That, at least, I am quite aware of."

"He spoke highly of you in the last instructions he sent me, so at the very least you made an impression. One for which I am grateful. I have been stuck in this God-forsaken post for half the year and was afraid I would have to do the job on my own."

Elsabeth dropped her bag in an out of the way corner and rubbed her arms against the chill slowly working through her body.

As the rush of adrenaline over her capture subsided, she was suddenly reminded of just how cold it was without the fire downstairs warming the building.

"So then you know why I am here."

Kilianus busied himself at the fireplace, and soon had a small blaze going. The fragrant scent of burning cedar soon filled the apartment, and wary as she was, Elsabeth shuffled towards the fire to warm herself against the chill clinging to the room.

"Of course. You are here to help me steal a *gonne* and return it to the Baron."

"As quickly he can seem to get word around, I am amazed he sent me here half blind. I had no idea who I was even supposed to be looking for."

"Well, I did. At least I knew to be looking, and about when to begin. The ring told me all I needed to know."

Elsabeth looked down at the ring on her finger once more, and her face heated indignantly. "Well, I shall have to have a word with your Baron the next time I see him."

Kilianus finished his work with the fire and stepped up beside her to take her cloak. Elsabeth backed away defensively, and he raised his hands, palms outward.

"I assure you, I am who I say," he said.

"I don't necessarily disbelieve you," she retorted, and narrowed her eyes dangerously. "On the other hand, I am seldom of the mind to go off alone with a man who grabs me off the street in such a manner as you did. You should count yourself fortunate 'twas a busy street and Cuncz wanted me to be discreet. Any other time I would have had that knife at your belt before you could have laid another finger on me."

Kilianus rubbed the back of his neck in chagrin, and Elsabeth was satisfied when his face colored in embarrassment.

"And I assure you, I am not one to go grabbing and kissing random women on the street. But I needed a way to make contact without drawing suspicion." He quirked a lopsided grin that was much more predatory than Elsabeth liked, but still managed to look at least passably endearing. "And sometimes the best way to avoid suspicion is by calling attention to the very thing you want to hide. Just not in a way someone would be looking for."

Elsabeth heaved a sigh and wearily pinched the bridge of her nose. "And of course, a kiss between long-parted lovers in the middle of the street will draw attention, but of the sort that would be dismissed just as quickly. Usually out of embarrassment. And such intimate proximity is also an ideal means of passing information in confidence."

"Precisely. Though even then, one must be wary of what one says in public. Still, it served its purpose, for here we are!"

She folded her arms and peered at him levelly. "And 'twas also an opportunity to sample the goods since we shall be working quite closely together for the foreseeable future."

His face turned an even brighter shade of red, and he straightened indignantly. "I thought I acted with restraint and respect, under the circumstances."

Elsabeth rolled her eyes and waved him off. "Oh, don't deny it. I have had more than a few take advantage. I know the trick quite well. Just be assured there shan't be so much as a peek beneath my chemise from here."

"A man can at least exercise his imagination."

"I shan't be stopping you short of my rondel in your belly, so imagine what you will. Where are we, anyway? I don't know

Carcassonne, though I did notice the castle nearby, and would be able to find my way back to the gates at need."

Kilianus dropped into one of the chairs next to the fire and crossed his legs at ease. Elsabeth slipped off her cloak as the room began to warm and lowered herself with exaggerated grace onto the seat opposite him. *Nothing like a bit of teasing over what he shan't have as revenge for that kiss earlier.* If Kilianus caught on to the purpose of her movements, however, he did not show it.

"These are the apartments and boarding houses for the day laborers who work at the castle," he said. "I am set up as a carpenter doing minor repair work around the grounds. Fortunately, it pays rather well, so I am able to afford nicer lodgings than most."

Elsabeth considered the largely bare room. In the light of the lamps and fireplace she could now see that, though plain, the apartment was in good repair, and constructed of fine materials. "Well, 'twould not do for a lowly craftsman to be living in luxury. Did Cuncz have any role in securing this lodging?"

Kilianus laughed. "Of course not! Once he turns us loose, we are largely left to our own devices. I recall a past assignment I spent an entire summer sleeping in a stable. I made quite the stink — literally — of the whole affair. No, all of this is paid from an honest day's labor."

Elsabeth managed a small, amused laugh. "Well, your Baron has nothing if not a sense of humor. So, you have access to the castle. What, then, is my role in this? I hope you don't expect me to cook your meals, as I have it on authority from a particularly gluttonous friar that my cooking is not even suitable as waste for hogs."

"No, much to my relief meals are provided in the common room, twice a day; once to break our fast, and again in the evening. Once I learned a few of the particulars about my partner in this enterprise, I took the liberty of arranging you work as a maid in the castle, helping out the staff there."

Kilianus leaned forward onto the chair, and his expression turned grave. "I do hope you are up to this. This is no recalcitrant Abbott we are dealing with. The Baron shan't be coming to our rescue if things take a wrong turn."

Elsabeth twitched her lips into a smile and draped her hands lightly on the arms of her chair. "Don't you worry about me, love. I know the game we shall be playing. Let us just focus on the task ahead, and how to see it done."

"Right down to business, then?"

"'Tis what I am here for."

He gave a short nod and leaned back in his chair once more. "Well then, to start, 'twill be best if we continue the ruse that we are man and wife, now that a substantial part of the town witnessed our little show."

Elsabeth grunted. "'Twas quite the public spectacle, and I agree, too many I suspect saw it to change this now. Though in the future I expect to be part of any further decisions about our identities in advance. Oh, and let us be clear if 'tis not already; this marriage is strictly for public show, and I shan't be performing any wifely duties in the marriage bed. You can sleep on the floor."

"I'll try not to be disappointed. But I would not think of it, as I am sure Herr von Leyen would take a rather dim view of anything so untoward on my part. You can trust my courteousness where that is concerned."

She felt her face heat at the insinuation in his voice, but did not press the matter further.

"What can you tell me about Carcassonne?" she said instead.

"The City is ostensibly ruled by Ethor Odson, the Graf de Carcassonne. I can't tell you much of him, as he is often away on business elsewhere in his lands or attending to the King. The real power here is the Marshall of the City, Robin de Sens."

Elsabeth considered with a tap of her chin. "I don't know that name."

"Well, 'tis a good one to get to know; the *gonnes* under development here fall under his command, and he is directly overseeing the project. Not a particularly joyful man, and he keeps his oaths to the Graf de Carcassonne very seriously. He is also the only man in the castle with regular access to the *gonnes* and their maker."

"It sounds like Herr de Sens may be the best source of information, then." She quirked a grin. "Perhaps a little too much drink, and a friendly smile might loosen his lips."

Kilianus shook his head. "I doubt it. I don't think I have ever seen Herr de Sens touch a drop of drink other than small beer, or shown much interest in any woman in the castle, as I hear he has a wife tucked away on lands granted to him by the Graf de Carcassonne."

Elsabeth tsked. "'Twould hardly be the first man I lured away from his wedding vows."

"I suspect not, but those men were not Herr de Sens. The one vow I have ever heard of him placing above that of the Graf de Carcassonne is that which he made before the Lord of All on his wedding day. As I have heard the guards say, there was a feast one night some years back, and de Carcassonne partook a bit too heavily of the wine. De Sens's wife was in attendance — a pretty thing, too, by all accounts — and de Carcassonne in his stupor lay a hand where he ought not to. De Sens challenged him to a duel on that very spot, despite his oath of fealty. De Carcassonne apologized, and de Sens's holdings grew by a third the next morning."

"Tch. I may have never met the man, but I have known my share of knights. No one is ever that good." No sooner were the words out of her mouth than a dull ache began to gnaw at her belly as the memory of Ain rose unbidden to mind, and she tightened her hands on the arms of her chair. *One, perhaps, was nearly so, but even he fell short.*

Kilianus shrugged, showing no sign of noticing her sudden distress, and Elsabeth forced the unwelcome thoughts back down into the dark recesses whence they came.

"Believe the tale or not as you like," he said, "but I have seen enough of the man to have no reason to doubt it."

Elsabeth grunted, and folded her arms and crossed her legs in a huff. "Well, then this affair just became a great deal more difficult."

"Then I suggest retiring for the night and starting afresh tomorrow. Perhaps once you have had a look at things for yourself we can come up with something better."

7

MILLE D'ALLE PEERED THROUGH THE MAGNIFYING glass suspended over his workbench. He bent low and hunched his shoulders. His back ached and his fingers cramped from his long hours at work. He strained his eyes under the lamps filling his workshop with a dim golden light, and at times his vision faded until he blinked the haze away. He delicately turned the lockplate in his hands. A wheel was fixed to the plate by means of a metal shaft, with a squared nut on the outside of the plate and an eccentric forged onto the inside. V-shaped grooves with transverse cuts at regular intervals were struck into the rim of the wheel.

He slowly rotated the wheel on its shaft and satisfied himself it turned freely and without catching despite the tight tolerances within the mechanism. He then fit a short length of fine chain to the eccentric, and connected the other end to the tip of the main V-spring secured to the plate by a bracket at one end. He attached another metal bracket to the inside of the lockplate to secure the wheel in place and obscure the chain from view. Next came the main sear, fitted onto a post riveted to the inside of the plate, with a secondary sear fixed to the trigger itself.

D'Alle took a spanner, placed it against the nut on the outside of the lockplate, and as he turned it the wheel rotated until the end of the main sear fell into a blind hole in the inner face of the wheel, locking it in place with a sharp *click*. The chain fixed to the eccentric wrapped partly round the shaft and put the main spring under tension. He pulled the trigger, and with another satisfying *click* the secondary sear released, the main sear then pivoted in turn releasing the wheel, and the mainspring snapped back into its rest position, rotating the wheel quite forcefully on the shaft. The entire process unfolded within less than the blink of an eye.

A knock at the door interrupted him before d'Alle could begin assembling the dog and its mechanism. He heaved a sigh, carefully placed the incomplete lock on his workbench, and sat back in his chair. It creaked under the shifting of his weight — or perhaps it was the creaking of his own tired bones and joints — and he mopped his face with both hands, heedless of the oil and grime coating his fingers.

"Yes, yes, come in!" he grumbled, injecting just enough irritation at the interruption into his voice that he hoped the intruder would have second thoughts.

There was, of course, to be no such luck. The door swung open, and in stomped the visitor he was most disinterested in seeing.

Le Chevalier Robin de Sens, Marechal de Carcassonne, was not the most handsome of men — though not, if the gossip of the rare maid sent down to service his quarters in the bowels of the castle was anything to judge by, altogether displeasing to the eye. He was certainly tall and strongly built, as one would expect of a man of his profession. He kept his dark hair cropped short, and his features were clean-shaven. These, however, were of decidedly odd proportion; a mouth slightly too big, a nose too small, and eyes set too far apart for their size. Still, they were symmetrical, and had done him no ill favor in the pursuit of his wife, by all accounts a rare beauty even if she was seldom seen in Carcassonne.

De Sens dressed, as was his wont, in a light brigandine beneath a tabard emblazoned with his arms — *Quarterly 1ˢᵗ and 4ᵗʰ chequy Argent and Vert; Quarterly 2ⁿᵈ and 3ʳᵈ Argent, overall a hawk recursant Sable* — but no other armor. He did, however, wear his sword at his side, in a scabbard covered in green leather and decorated with silver inlay in a floral motif interspersed with hawks with their wings outstretched. A green cloak wrapped around his shoulders and warded off the chill of the castle's lower levels that D'Alle had largely forgotten while engrossed in his work. Now that his attention was forcibly diverted back to the practical world, he shivered in his thin shirt and doublet at the reminder. He made no move to stand as would ordinarily be expected upon the entry of a man of de Sens's station.

With him came two armed guards bearing halberds, who took up flanking positions inside the door while de Sens was within. D'Alle idly wondered just who, precisely, they were protecting; de Sens, or himself and his work.

"Good evening, Master d'Alle," de Sens said pleasantly upon entering, and swept his widely spaced eyes across the dim interior of the workshop. D'Alle had neglected to light more lamps than he needed at his desk, and the fire on the hearth had long since burned out. "How might I ask goes your work today?"

D'Alle folded his arms across his chest. "'Twas going much better before the interruption, Monsieur. Do you know how much time it takes to make every adjustment and have each piece in order?"

"I never do, but I suspect you shall soon be reminding me again. And certainly longer than if you were to use the apprentices Monsieur de Carcassonne has provided."

"Feh!" d'Alle let the grunt of dismissal hang in the air between them, and snatched a soiled and greasy scrap of cloth from the table. He uselessly mopped his hands with it; the cloth was already so saturated with grease and grime it was of little help any longer for cleaning. "I would hardly call them apprentices! They are barely fit for stoking a smith's furnace, much less the delicate work that needs doing here."

He leaned back in his chair and folded his arms across his chest. De Sens slipped his thumbs through his belt, and patiently awaited the rant to come. And it came like clockwork.

"Do you know just how much work must go into each lock? Each piece carefully fitted — by hand, no less! — with little tolerance for being even the slightest fraction of an inch out of adjustment! Too much oil and it will collect the dust of this cave—" he waved a hand around his workshop "—and gum up the entire works! Too little and it mayn't function at all. If the links of the chain are not fitted properly 'twill be too long, or too short, and the wheel mayn't turn when the trigger is released. A spring not fitted exactly so and it mayn't come under tension when the wheel is turned!

"This is master's work, and as I am the only master, 'tis me and me alone to assemble everything!"

De Sens heaved a patient sigh and weathered the assault as he always did. Just once d'Alle would have liked to see the man lose his temper, but he remained frustratingly stoic.

"I understand the difficulties you are facing, Master," the Marshall said. "But what you are crafting here is quite far beyond the experience of any other craftsman Monsieur le Comte can muster. Especially as you decline to explain the particulars of your design."

D'Alle grunted. The chair let out a squeak of protest as he eased himself to his feet, and he stretched out his lower back. Just how long, precisely, had he been sitting?

"They would not understand it, anyway. 'Tis hard enough explaining to the smith how to craft the parts I need. And as you said: 'tis my design. Mine. I devised it, and I shan't let some half-witted court artificer profit from my work! Certainly not for the pittance Monsieur le Comte has seen fit to pay me."

De Sens looked to the guards standing beside the door and gave a subtle wag of his head. The door creaked on its hinges, and the two men filed out of the room before shutting it behind them, leaving them alone. D'Alle feared nothing untoward by the dismissal of the guard; he had no written plans for his masterwork, after all.

"I thought the terms Monsieur le Comte offered were more than generous." Secure or not in his position, d'Alle did not miss the warning edge in the other's voice.

"If it were just for an example or two, made in my own time, perhaps. But this demonstration Monsieur le Comte insists upon ..." he sighed and raked his hands back through his thinning white hair, now stained grayish-black from the grime and oil covering his hands. "Two weeks is not nearly long enough. I still don't have the barrels back milled from the smith, or the stocks from the woodworkers. 'Twill certainly not be time enough to make sure everything is fitted well. If any part is too loose the *gonne* may not set right. Too tight and it shan't fit together at all. These are precision instruments, not crude munitions."

"You promised Monsieur le Comte your *gonnes* would be ready."

D'Alle glowered at the other and planted his hands on his hips. His heavy leather apron was perhaps no match for de Sens's brigandine, but the Marshall now stood in his battlefield, and D'Alle bore it as proudly as any man-at-arms. "I promised no such thing! The first *gonne* worked, but there is always room for improvement. I merely told him given the proper resources I could make the next one better, I never told him when. 'Twas Monsieur le Comte who set the time, not I."

"And you agreed to it," de Sens said pointedly. His armor rattled as he folded his arms across his broad chest and glared him down. D'Alle waved a hand dismissively.

"I could never resist a challenge, foolish though it was to accept. And that was when it was just one improved *gonne*. Now he wants four. And he wants a public demonstration on top of it all! Two weeks is not even time to properly train a *handgonner* in its use. And I suppose now I shall have to do the demonstration myself, even though I could never shoot straight."

"Master," the other said, and his voice softened in a most conciliatory manner, "Monsieur le Comte places high expectations only because he trusts that they can be met. You should consider it a compliment he holds you in such regard."

D'Alle grunted again. "Monsieur le Comte is better with the flattery, Monsieur, I suggest you leave it to him."

"All right, but let me tell you this; I have already spoken to Monsieur le Comte, and he has agreed that should the *gonnes* be ready in time, and performed as you have promised, there shall be a bonus in your pay. An extra five *livres* for each."

He sighed and pinched the bridge of his nose. "I'll do my best to have them finished in time."

"Thank you, Master, and if there is anything Monsieur le Comte can offer to help speed your work...?"

D'Alle rounded on him. "Yes! Fewer interruptions to start with! And light a fire under the smith's arse to have the barrels ready. And if fire alone is not enough for him to jump to it, sit him on his forge if you must. I need the barrels forged and the rifling cut so I can start putting them all together. I would like at least a couple days to test fire each *gonne* before the demonstration."

De Sens inclined his head. "I shall see what I can do, but bear in mind the smith has other responsibilities beyond this project;

horses must be shod, and swords must be forged. Monsieur le Comte sees a certain potential in your work, but I still don't see these contraptions as any more than a passing fancy."

He offered de Sens a wicked little grin. "'Tis just what they said about the mechanical clock. I suspect ere long the chevalier shall go the way of candle clocks, and with my *gonne* 'twill be sooner than later."

LSABETH'S BACK ACHED. HER SHOULDERS BURNED. Her fingers cramped. And no matter how hard she scrubbed, a particularly stubborn stain in the linen bunched in her hands would simply not come clean.

Today was the fourth day of what had become a daily routine: In the morning, she and Kilianus made their way to the castle for work. While Kilianus busied himself repairing railings, or floorboards, or installing a new wooden mantle on one of the many fireplaces warming and lighting the keep, Elsabeth found herself assigned as a laundry maid.

The laundry was a large building on the northern end of the castle bailey, opposite the gates leading back into the City. An open hearth dominated the middle of the floor, where water could be heated for washing (along with providing a respite from the winter chill). The whole place smelled of ash and lye, and Elsabeth's nose wrinkled at the overpowering odor of ammonia from the pots of urine collected from around the castle for cleaning. Finished garments hung on lines out of the way to dry, and there were flat wooden wash boards where dirt could be beaten out with washing beetles.

And of course, there were the mountains of linens, bedding, underthings, and overclothes gathered from the apparently bottomless closets and wardrobes for washing.

There were three other laundry maids on the staff, though only one was in the laundry with her that morning. She was a short and squat woman a few years Elsabeth's elder named Rapine, and the most senior (having boasted of coming on to the staff some ten years prior and working her way up to the laundry). With it came a smug superiority in her eye as she handed out the most arduous tasks. Unfortunately, spending all her time shut away in the laundry up to her elbows in piss and lye gave Elsabeth little opportunity to learn anything beyond the consistency of the castle diet, and how it interacted with the residents' braies.

The things I am doing for a thousand pfunde.

Elsabeth mopped her eyes with the shoulder of her dress in a vain effort to brush away the stray hairs that worked out from beneath her cap under the furious effort of scrubbing. Her sleeves were rolled up past her elbows to keep them out of the brew while she rubbed and twisted the garment in her cramping hands. She lifted it out of the tub and held it out for inspection. It was a curious contraption consisting of two soft linen pouches attached to a band that laced up the back, with narrow shoulder straps supporting the entire garment. The whole was then decorated with sprang and lace trim. Its purpose was, of course, quite obvious once she sussed out how it was worn, though Elsabeth could not recall having seen such a thing in her mother's or sisters' linens, or even in Boehm.

I suppose it must be a Navarese invention, then. Seems quite the useful way to avoid too much bounce and jostle. 'Tis much more supporting than a chemise, without mashing things together like binding. I really ought to have one for beneath my doublet.

Unfortunately, the faint pink stain — wine that soaked through after a spill, she suspected — running down one cup stubbornly remained.

Elsabeth heaved a sigh and thrust the garment back into the tub in frustration.

The sudden splash drew the attention of her companion, who set aside her own scrubbing with an exaggerated roll of her eyes, wiped her hands on the apron tied about her waist, and stumped towards her.

"What is it now?" Rapine said, making no effort to disguise her impatience.

Elsabeth lifted the garment from the tub again and turned it to present the wine stain for inspection.

"I have been at it for a good half hour now, and it simply won't come out!" Elsabeth replied, injecting a measure of helpless frustration into her voice that was only partly feigned.

"Let me have a look." The woman snatched the offending thing from her hand with no great delicacy, and flattened it out for a better look. She clicked her tongue in annoyance. "Oh! You daft girl! Four days on and have you not learned a thing yet? For this you need to soak fuller's earth in lye, apply it to the stain, and let the whole thing dry before trying to rub out! And use the feathers, 'twill be easier on the linen than those clumsy hands of yours!"

Rapine roughly shoved the garment back into her hands, hard enough that Elsabeth stumbled back a pace. The woman planted her hands on her hips, and slate eyes peered down her nose at her (which was quite a feat, considering Elsabeth all but towered over her).

"I swear to the Lord of All I don't know why they saw fit to send you here, as I can't imagine you being of any better use in the scullery! Earned it on your back, I wager. Or maybe while

Mademoiselle Oudine was on hers from what I hear. Why your husband puts up with you I can't imagine."

Elsabeth clenched her teeth in a valiant effort to restrain herself from dunking the woman's head into the nearest urine pot. "I assure you I manage quite well enough at home, but 'tis the first time I have seen something as delicate as this—" she hefted the garment "—much less tried to clean one."

"Hmph. Well, you must be some rabble from the countryside, then, because all the fine ladies and even some of the well-off women of town have them to hold up their bosom. So you best learn and learn quick, because if 'tis not cleaned good and proper or if 'tis damaged, well 'tis worth more than your useless hide."

And with that, she turned and stomped off again.

Elsabeth watched her go for a moment, and if her eyes were a rondel she would have stabbed the woman four times over. She forced her musings over how much lye it would take to dispose of the corpse from her mind with an irritated huff, then went off in search of fuller's earth while mentally gauging the fit of the garment.

RILIANUS HID HIS LAUGHTER BEHIND HIS HAND AS BEST HE could, but the effort quickly proved fruitless, and he buried his face in the crook of his arm while he supported himself against the mantle.

Elsabeth's face heated, and she crossly watched his whole body shake from her perch on the couch fronting the fireplace. She folded her arms and crossed her legs in a huff, but neither posture nor glare made much impression on him, and for several long moments she endured the guffaws.

"Are you quite finished?" she asked, and speared him with her most withering "if I only had my sword" glare.

He raised his head from his arms and wiped the tears of mirth from his cheeks. His face, too, was red from want of air, and it took him a few breaths to regain his composure.

"Sorry, quite sorry," he said, but his voice continued to tremor in an effort to restrain himself from further laughter at her expense. "'Tis just with the esteem the Baron placed on your skills, I am rather amazed to find you so easily stymied by so simple a task."

Elsabeth drummed her fingers on her bicep in annoyance, and did not let up with her glower. "Well, as I have never been the domestic sort myself, I have never had the occasion to learn the finer points of laundry. Either the girls in my father's employ or who kept my host's house in Soest managed it, or I simply paid to have it done. I certainly have a newfound pity and respect for the laundry maids of my father's household, given all the mud and dirt they had to scrub out of my dresses when I was a child."

Kilianus cleared his throat with one last chuckle, then folded his arms across his chest. "And thus far you have overheard nothing?"

She sighed and sunk back into the couch, and let her hands fall into her lap. "Nothing, though I have spent every moment from the time I arrive at the castle in the morning elbows-deep in piss, ash, and lye, and matters of war are hardly in the realm of the laundry maids' gossip. So unless you have an interest in the scandalous predilections of the Housekeeper, this whole bloody business is a wash, so to speak."

"I confess 'tis not much better on my front. I have had an eye on the security arrangements, but have noticed nothing out of the ordinary for a castle or town of this size."

Elsabeth shrugged. "I imagine anything more would draw too much attention."

He nodded his agreement. "I thought as much as well. Unfortunately, I am not exactly able to slip away to poke around. I had hoped as a maid you might have had better luck in that regard as you would be much more likely to escape suspicion for turning up out of place."

"They have to let me out of the bloody laundry, first. What all do you suppose they would need to make a *gonne* in the first place?"

Kilianus considered a moment. "I don't know for certain what sets this particular type apart, but if 'tis a *gonne* like any other, I imagine 'twould start as an iron tube on a wooden handle or some such."

"If 'tis like the examples Cuncz showed me, I imagine they could simply modify a crossbow tiller for the purpose. The barrel would need to be forged anew, however."

"I've already poked around the blacksmith as best as I was able — fortunately, it seems I am always in need of more nails — but if he is working on it, 'tis not being done in the open."

Elsabeth wearily pinched the bridge of her nose. "Which leaves us about where we started. And even knowing who is helping make them does not tell us where the finished ones are stored. If I have learned anything from my past encounters with Cuncz, I suspect they may not even be telling them more than they need for their own part in the job."

Kilianus chuckled and nodded his agreement. "You must admit it has the advantage of preventing any one person from being able to ruin the entire enterprise."

She grunted. "It also means you never know when you are just being played for a fool. What about the clockmaker himself? You have already said de Sens might be immune from a little friendly persuasion, but what of him?"

He cleared his throat again at the suggestive lilt in her voice, and Elsabeth took satisfaction when he shifted on his feet in discomfort at the insinuation. *Serves him bloody right for his amusement at my expense.*

"In all honesty, I cannot even say who he is. I am familiar with most of the guards and staff, and all of the guests and household are accounted for, so I can't recall having ever seen him leave whatever hole they have him stashed away in. There is no apartment for him on the grounds that I can suss out, either."

She frowned thoughtfully. "It sounds like he may as well be a prisoner, then."

"Like as not, but the dungeons would be too inaccessible for us to search."

Elsabeth leaned against the arm of the couch and propped her head on her hand with a sigh. "If I did not need the windfall so badly, I would almost call this a fool's errand and cut my losses before the game was up. I don't think I can keep up the laundry charade much longer. Someone is bound to decide I ought not be let anywhere near a wash beetle, lest I break it over that arrogant and insufferable quim's head."

Kilianus' eyes hardened, and an indignant scowl passed across his features. "Some of us don't have the luxury of a mercenary. But if you find the venture so disheartening, perhaps you ought to leave."

"I may be a mercenary and my obligation may not be to Cuncz, but that does not mean I am not bound by one nonetheless." Elsabeth tightened her hands into fists and her voice turned dangerous. "Unless you want to come to an argument with me on the point, I warn you not to suggest otherwise. I may not have my sword, but don't think for a moment I am clawless without it."

For a moment Kilianus did not respond, and surprise flitted across his features at the unexpected threat in her voice.

"I'll take you at your word; your reputation does proceed you, and I have no need to put it to the test. Though my curiosity is certainly piqued over what has you so driven."

She fixed him with a level gaze, and a small pang stabbed at her belly at the earnest curiosity in his expression. "And it can go on being piqued; my business is my own, particularly when it has a chance of finding its way back to your master. I don't need him meddling in my affairs."

Kilianus did not give her the courtesy of reacting to the veiled insult of Cuncz, and merely raised his hands in a conciliatory fashion. "All right." He sighed and mopped his face. "The common room shall be serving supper soon, so I think it best we keep up appearances. I don't know about you, but I for one think better on a full stomach and with a pint of good beer in hand."

The mention of food started Elsabeth's belly to rumbling, wiping away the guilty pang that had been poking her and reminding her she had not had a proper meal since breaking her fast that morning.

"At the very least, I am suddenly in need of a good pint, thinking or not. You go on down without me, and I'll be along shortly. I have something to try on, first." Elsabeth then reached to the neckline of her dress, and pulled out a bit of linen tucked safely out of sight beneath. Kilianus quirked an eyebrow, and his mouth turned down in puzzlement.

"What is that?"

A playful smile tugged at the corner of her lips, and Elsabeth twirled the curious undergarment she slipped from the drying line around on her finger.

"Never you mind, just a little something I picked up from the laundry today."

THE NEXT MORNING BROUGHT ABOUT A WELCOME respite from the fruitless tedium of leaning over the wash tubs, and a much-needed change of fortune. Upon her arrival at the laundry, Rapine shoved a basket of clean linens into her hands and shooed her away.

"Take these up to Monsieur de Carcassonne's chambermaid," the woman ordered, as she darted about gathering up sheets and bedlinens and blankets. "He'll be back tomorrow by nightfall and will surely want to lay himself down on clean linens after his journey."

Elsabeth allowed an appropriate measure of excitement to blossom on her features. "Monsieur le Comte is coming tomorrow? Oh! What is he like? He was away from Carcassonne when I arrived."

"Tch, never you mind. Though I suppose you are pretty enough he might have an interest were you to catch his eye, if you follow me." Rapine added the last with an envious look over her figure that Elsabeth could not miss. "I suspect you shan't have the opportunity, though, as there will be a great deal of washing to do. All the household is scrambling to put their nicest things in order; we only just got word he was coming this morning, so the entire staff is in a terrible panic! Now go on and be quick about it, there shall be a great deal to do when you get back. Off with you!"

Elsabeth now found herself making her way along the opulent halls of the living areas of the castle, and sure enough, the excitement among the household, guards, and staff was palpable. Maids and butlers scrambled to polish the wood and metalwork, dust the furniture, wash the windows, paint the walls, and beat the dust from the carpets, tapestries, and curtains. The guards on watch were all in their cleanest dress uniforms, and stood smartly at attention even in the deserted areas of the castle. Elsabeth ducked her head appropriately when she made her way past the lesser nobility resident of or visiting the castle. She bowed her head and cleared the floor for them, and none paid her any mind. She was, to them, just another domestic underfoot.

She delivered her bundle of laundry to the Comte de Carcassonne's chambermaid, a pretty but frazzled thing a few years younger than her on the verge of panic that she might not have her lord's chamber ready in time. Elsabeth considered offering a hand to the poor girl, but as this was her first opportunity to slip away from the laundry, she had to make the most of it.

The castle was not particularly large, and certainly not as grand as the castle at Ain. It took her little time to meander from de Carcassonne's private chambers to see the rest of it in a circuitous route. Kilianus was nowhere to be seen, like as not engaged in some work out on the grounds. Unfortunately, she saw little of interest to their mission on her walk beyond the chaos of a castle awaiting its master's return.

At least in the upper levels. Upon returning to the ground floor and making her way back to the laundry, Elsabeth drew near to a guarded door leading down into the basements of the keep. It first caught her interest from around the corner; the soft murmur of voices drew her ear, almost too quiet for her to hear clearly, but one word managed to rise above the background din of activity: *clockmaker.* Elsabeth's heart climbed up into her throat.

She glanced about and frowned. She was making her way down one of the major corridors. Although no one else was heading in her direction, there was nonetheless considerable traffic as the staff went about their business.

Well, not exactly the sort of place for discreet eavesdropping. Best I look for somewhere else to listen in.

She rounded the corner. Immediately upon sighting her the guards fell silent and snapped to attention with their halberds planted firmly on the floor; it was, of course, no display of respect, but a mere formality so as not to be reported for relaxing on duty.

She gave them each a surreptitious but thorough appraisal. Both were tall and well-built, as one might expect of the fighting men of the castle. They dressed alike in brigandine with blue velvet outer shells. Steel vambraces covered their forearms, and they wore steel greaves on their shins. Their heads remained uncovered, allowing Elsabeth a good look at their features. One wore a luxurious and neatly groomed black mustache, but his hair was thinning and the lamplight of the corridor reflected off the bare patch forming on his crown. The other was clean-shaven and wore his honey-colored hair neatly cropped.

Elsabeth hurried past them, as if she were on an urgent errand, and made for a cross-corridor two doors beyond them. This was deserted, so she ducked around the corner, and pressed her back against the wall.

For a moment her ear was greeted by silence, as if the guards feared someone might be listening should they resume their conversation. But after a few moments — likely long enough to assure themselves she had passed beyond earshot — they quietly resumed their conversation. This hallway was deserted of activity or traffic nearby from the other staff, and with no background noise to drown them out Elsabeth could hear them clearly.

"The man is a damned pain the arse," one said. "I swear by the Lord of All I can't stomach any more of his complaining."

"Forget his complaining, I can't say I have ever heard a man with a higher opinion of himself."

"Well, if I have to cater to any of his demands one more time I may go down there and give him a good thumping with the end of my halberd."

A sharp *thump* echoed through the hallway, and Elsabeth suspected he likely struck the floor with the end of his weapon to emphasize the point.

"Only if you want the Marshall on your arse."

"'Twould almost be worth it."

"I honestly can't disagree with you. I'll be glad when this madness is over, and they ship him off to Domme."

Elsabeth frowned. *Someone other than Cuncz must think highly of this project if they expect to send this fellow off to the King of Navarre himself. Of course, that will just make finishing this business all the harder if we can't make headway before that happens.*

"Agreed, as long as he is anyone else's problem but ours. So if God is with us, this demonstration will be the end of it and we'll be rid of him."

At that, Elsabeth strained her ears even harder, and a small smile tugged at her lips.

"I can hope. At any rate, I am due back at the garrison. A formal escort is being assembled for Monsieur de Carcassonne when he arrives tomorrow, and I drew one of the short straws. I'll be up all night shining every inch of metal in my kit!"

A sharp laugh echoed through the hallways.

"Oh, such a pity," the other said, and the sarcasm practically dripped from his voice. "What with all the girls of the town out to see Monsieur le Comte, and I dare say the fine regalia of his guardsmen."

"I'll try to save some for you, then."

"Meet me tonight at Isabeau's?"

"If I am released in time for dinner."

"Good. If not, I'll give Isabeau your love since you'll not be there to offer her a little of it yourself."

The last was added with a suggestive lilt of his voice that left no doubt as to his intentions. The other grunted dismissively.

"And you are welcome to it. 'Tis an over-tilled plot as it is, and not one I am in any great rush to plow. Especially with fairer fields awaiting me at home."

"Tch, you don't know what you are missing, Frederick."

"Bleeding sores on the member, for one. I swear, Pierre, one of these days your cock is going to lead you straight into trouble."

"That may be, but at the very least I shall die in much more pleasurable company than yours. Good day to you!"

The other laughed. "Go on, then, and try not to do anything too foolish before Monsieur le Comte arrives."

And with that the two fell silent. Elsabeth listened intently for a moment more, and straining her ears thought she heard the soft tread of boots heading the opposite way along the corridor.

The smile tugging at her lips broadened at the plan taking shape in her mind.

ND YOU ARE SURE THEY WERE TALKING ABOUT THE *GONNES?*" Kilianus said from the other side of the door.

Elsabeth stood in front of the full-length mirror tucked away in one corner of the bedroom. She brushed her hands down the front of her dress to smooth the fabric out, and admired her silhouette reflected back at her. The undergarment she swiped from the laundry the day before lifted her breasts, emphasizing their shape even more than the cut and fit of her dress alone, and deepened the shadow of her cleavage.

'Tis hardly sporting, really. I suspect every eye at Isabeau's will be fixed on my tits the moment I step through the door. I really must be sure to hold on to this contraption.

"Well, they did not speak of it in so many words," she said, and turned this way and that to check the fit of her dress. Satisfied, she seated herself at a dressing table against the wall and went to work on her hair in the small looking glass hung behind it. "But they were certainly speaking of your clockmaker. It sounds like he is being a right pain in the arse."

"I am more concerned about what you said about them moving him to Domme," Kilianus said. "Did they say when?"

"That they did not. But it sounds like 'twill be soon."

"That leaves us with little time, then."

"Which means we need to make headway in finding these bloody *gonnes*. I would not be surprised if this demonstration they have planned for the Graf de Carcassonne is to show him these contraptions work before he sends them on to the King. And once that happens, they will be out of reach. However, I think this does give us an opportunity."

Kilianus cursed under his breath, and she heard the solid *thunk* of him bumping the back of his head against the wall in frustration.

Elsabeth finished with her hair, letting the long copper tresses spill loosely down her back in a manner sure to catch as many eyes as her protruding breast. She carefully studied her reflection

"I can't argue with your thinking," Kilianus replied. "We shan't have access to them so long as they and their maker are kept so securely locked away. I know that corridor and the door you mentioned, and it leads down into the vaults and dungeon. I can't imagine a more well-guarded part of the keep. There is no other way in than that passage, and even if we could disable the guards at the entrance, we would not make it a hundred feet from the door before we were caught."

His voice turned thoughtful. "But if they are planning a demonstration, that means they must move the *gonnes* somewhere more accessible. Perhaps the regular armory? They'll want to do a few tests before they demonstrate them for the Graf de Carcassonne, and 'twill be easier to manage if they don't have to run all the way back to the vaults to retrieve them."

Elsabeth retrieved her Wheel pendant from the tabletop and hung it round her neck. She adjusted its hang to nestle in the top of her cleavage and gave herself a final looking-over, before pushing away from the table.

"What we need is more information," he continued, while she made her way across the bedroom and towards the door leading back out into the common room of the apartment. "When exactly do they intend to make their demonstration, and where might the *gonnes* be stored in preparation."

Elsabeth opened the door and stepped out of the bedroom. Kilianus leaned his back against the wall beside her, with his arms folded across his chest and his features twisted in concentration.

"Well, you can leave that to me," she said. "I have an idea where I might find some loose lips to tease a little more out of than is good for them. Now, tell me what you think!"

Elsabeth twirled about as she left the bedroom, letting her skirts float up a little, and turning to give Kilianus a good look at her. He stood away from the wall, and to her satisfaction his eye landed right on her bosom.

"Forgive me for being forward, but were those always there?" he stammered, and his face flushed in embarrassment over the remark and having so blatantly fixed his gaze upon her chest.

She offered him a playful laugh. "Since I was sixteen, and they have never failed me yet."

"I am almost afraid to ask what you have in mind."

"I would say don't, 'twill be better for you not to think about it, as you ought to know the dirty business of teasing information out of those loath to give it up. Now, husband, don't wait up for me, I shan't be back for some time."

And with that, she gathered up her cloak, wrapped it about her shoulders, and disappeared out the door before he could speak another word.

10

ISABEAU'S WAS, PER USUAL, FILLED ALMOST TO bursting that night. It was neither an overly large nor particularly opulent establishment, but cozy and rustic, befitting its usual clientele of the soldiers from the castle garrison, and laborers and craftsmen of the City. Nonetheless, it presented an air of sophistication and respectability sorely lacking from the common nunneries elsewhere in the City, so much so that even the odd member of the lower peerage or other functionary in the employ of the Comte de Carcassonne might make a discreet appearance among the common soldiery, and other folk with whom he dared not be caught socializing with in polite society. But here it was custom that any man who entered left his rank and title behind when he hung up his cloak and crossed its foyer. Carpenters rolled dice with barons. A chevalier shared a drink with a draftsman.

And of course, there were the girls. Isabeau's girls may not have been the *prettiest* whores in Carcassonne, but were still lovely, and Isabeau held them to high standards. Their ages were diverse; from younger women just come to marriageable age, to those showing the gray encroachment of middle age in their hair. They dressed in nice dresses and adorned themselves in what jewelry they could afford. Some could sing, or play some manner of instrument, or were learned in poetry or philosophy, and many could dance. All, of course, could fuck, and whether one loved music or dancing, or exercises of the mind, it was all a prelude to what went on in the private rooms upstairs. They were also clean and well-cared for, and every working girl in the City hoped to someday find her way under Isabeau's roof.

Pierre was already well deep into his cups, and Frederick had yet to appear. He sat at their usual table in a corner of the common room, which occupied much of the lower level. The door in from the street was guarded by two particularly large and imposing figures tasked with keeping order among the clientele, and even the nobles in their shadowed hoods dared not make a scene, lest they offend their host. Isabeau herself — an older woman with streaks of gray shooting through her raven locks, yet still striking and slim, and whose figure had not yet rounded with age — manned a counter at the door and made it a point to greet every guest upon their arrival. A fire crackled in the large stone fireplace in the back of the room, filling the common room with warmth, and light supplemented by the perfumed lamps on each of the tables occupying the floor danced on the walls and the faces of the patrons.

There were three other exits from the common room aside from the front door: a stairwell opposite Isabeau's counter led up to the private rooms above, where visitors could stay the night either alone or in the company of one of her girls, and two doors leading to the expansive kitchens and brewery backing the common room. The fragrant aroma of cooking food in the kitchens filled the air, fueling the appetites of the visitors. Men and women laughed, dice clattered across the table, and music — provided by Isabeau's own girls that night, though it was not uncommon for visiting minstrels to perform — rang out across the dozens of conversations all competing with one another in the enclosed space.

Pierre's companions that night were two strangers from the City. One was a miller bored from the lack of work in the depths of winter. The other a shoemaker seeking refuge from his wife after some inane squabble or other, who ranted between drinks and his turn with the dice. Pierre only half-listened as he drank and wordlessly gave thanks to the Lord of All that he remained comfortably free of such entanglements, and able to pursue the short-term diversions offered by Isabeau's house. Their coin, however, was as good as any others', and between pulls from his tankards of ale (a new one appeared at hand almost as soon as he thumped the empty one down) they rolled dice well into the evening.

Pierre heaped a not-insignificant pile of coin (a good bit larger than the winnings of the other two) in front of him, and chuckled. His companions cursed at his good fortune.

"I think we ought to check these dice," the miller grumbled into his drink. "You have had far too much luck tonight! 'Twas the second time you rolled the King!"

Pierre glowered across the table at him. "You don't dare accuse me of cheating, or I'll have your head!"

The miller scooped up the dice, and rattled them around his hand as if testing their weight. "We don't need to call Isabeau over, do we?"

"Fah! Why would I put bad dice in on a game like this, anyway, eh? We are passing them around the damn table, so I would just be helping you on your rolls."

The miller squinted at him. "Unless you were palming them and swapping them out when it came to be your turn."

Pierre drained his tankard, and thumped it down on the table. The coin bounced and clinked in response, though the sound did not carry beyond the table, for it was drowned out by the laughter and raucousness in the common room. He made a show of displaying his bared forearms, for his sleeves had been pushed up to his elbows most of the night. "And where do you think I would be putting them?"

"I can imagine one or two places," the miller grumbled, but offered no further argument. Instead, he took another drink, then made his cast to begin the game anew.

This went on for some time more, and Pierre was focused so intently on his dice (and the miller's complaints about his good fortune) that he was not quite certain whence she came. At first it was just him, the miller, and the shoemaker at their table, and the seat beside him was empty. One of the girls came with a fresh round of drinks she set out at the table beside each of them, and departed again with a wink and a swirl of her skirts. Pierre reached for his tankard, and just as his hand was about to settle on the handle it was taken from his reach. He rounded upon the thief and found his wavering gaze meeting the eyes of a most striking woman.

Her face was framed artfully by a cascade of hair — he could not quite be certain of the color — and the flickering light of the lamps cast a deep shadow between breasts determined to burst up out of the low neck of her dress. A silver pendant in the form of the Wheel nestled invitingly between them, and glimmered in the lamplight in such a way his eye was naturally drawn away from her features and onto her cleavage. Pierre for a moment stared open-mouthed; the venom forming on his tongue at the theft of his drink evaporated, and the miller and shoemaker were likewise rendered dumb. Finally he blinked, wondering if the apparition sitting beside him would vanish during that brief lidding of his eyes. But when they opened again she remained, gazing levelly at him with one corner of her mouth pulled up into a coquettish smirk over the rim of the tankard.

"I hope you don't mind me joining you," she purred, her voice a simmering, sultry contralto. The woman lightly put her lips to the tankard and took a sip. "You seemed so lonely with only these two for company."

A man not so deep in his cups might have been on his guard in such circumstances, but Pierre promptly forgot his appropriated drink, (especially as it was quickly replaced once one of the girls noticed his empty hand) and flashed her a toothy smile. "'Twould not be right and gentlemanly of me to mind, would it, lads?"

The woman turned her eyes on the others. The miller nodded eagerly and slurred his agreement. The shoemaker, for his part, blushed fiercely and ducked into the collar of his doublet.

"I had best be on home," he stammered. "The uh... the wife will be cross for certain if I am late to bed again. And I have lost quite enough coin for one night."

With that he raked his meager winnings back into his purse, nodded politely to the three of them, then rose and departed. He quickly vanished into the crowd, but neither Pierre nor the miller paid him any mind.

"What is it we are playing?" the woman asked, her eyes — like her hair, he could not make out their color through the fog of drink, the dim and flickering light, and the deep shadow of her cleavage tugging at his gaze — still watching him from over the rim of her tankard. She lounged at ease in her chair, with one arm draped along the back.

"'Tis House of Fortune," Pierre replied around a mouthful of ale, and motioned at the game board painted on the table.

"I don't think I have ever played that one. Could you show me? You seem like a master of the game." The woman leaned forward with interest, in such a way that allowed an almost unimpeded view down her dress.

"Why of course! Whose throw is it anyway?"

"I think 'tis yours, now," The miller said, no less able to tear his eyes from their guest's bosom.

Pierre fumbled for the dice. "Well, my dear, you see the board? Drawn up like a house?"

The groan of a chair scraping across the floor was followed promptly by the warmth of her body leaning up against his. She laid her hands atop his shoulder, and leaned her chin on them to watch. Pierre's body stiffened at the contact. "Why I do!" she giggled. The sudden warm exhalation tickled his ear.

"Well, you roll the dice, and match the numbers to the rooms in the house." He motioned back to the board with a flourish, which was divided into numbered cells.

At the bottom was a square marked with a Two and an exaggerated illustration of two pigs fucking. Above that square was Eight. Next were three squares, from left to right Six, Nine, and Five. Then another single square, Ten, and above that another set of three — Eleven, Seven, and Three. At the very top, in a cell shaped to form the "roof" of the house, was a Twelve. The Seven and Twelve were both decorated in a fashion similar to the Two; in the Seven a depiction of a wedding feast, and for Twelve a crown. The other squares, along with the rest of the board, were likewise decorated, all by men and women of exaggerated anatomy and engaging one another in various scandalizing positions, much befitting the establishment. Pierre noted with satisfaction that the woman was not the least taken aback by the graphic imagery.

"Why is there no four?" She screwed up her features in confusion.

"'Tis because ..." Pierre stumbled for a moment and frowned when no explanation sprang to mind. He twisted his lip and glanced across at the miller. "Why is there no four?"

The miller merely shrugged and took a drink from his tankard. "I have not the slightest idea."

"Well, whatever the reason 'tis a tradition at Isabeau's that whoever rolls a Four leaves a coin for the server."

Their guest took a long drink from her tankard. Some spilled down the corner of her mouth and dribbled towards her chin. She neatly wiped it clean on one finger, and sucked it off. "And what do the other numbers mean?"

"First," he said, and took a coin from his pile, and added it to the Seven square. The miller casually tossed his own coin onto the cell with it. "Everyone puts in their ante on the Seven — the Wedding Square, and the pot. And then, we roll!"

Pierre let the dice rattle around in his hand, then cast them onto the table, coming up as a three. "On anything but Two and Twelve, you put a coin on the cell if 'tis empty—" and he did as he spoke "—and if not, you take the coin. The roll then passes to the next player."

The miller scooped up the dice and made his cast — seven — and added a coin.

The woman frowned. "But that square was not empty!"

Pierre chuckled at her ignorance of the game. *She must be new, then, all the girls at Isabeau's know the game. I wonder where Isabeau managed to find her. Why, she ought to be warming the bed of some noble or other, not working on her back even in a place as fine as this!*

"Because that is the Wedding Square! When you go to a wedding, you bring a gift, not take one. There are two other special rolls: Two and Twelve. On a Two, you have rolled a Lucky Pig, and can claim every coin on the board but for the Seven. But if you roll a Twelve, you are the King, and the King takes everything."

The woman flashed him a smoldering smile that sent a thrill racing from his belly clear to the hair on top of his head. "And it seems you truly are the King of this table."

"I still say he is manipulating those dice somehow," the miller groused. Pierre harrumphed and picked them up for another cast.

"Don't blame your poor fortune on me, my friend!" Pierre shook the dice in his hand, then looked to the woman still leaning against his shoulder. From this close vantage he could not quite sneak another peak down her dress, but his nostrils were filled by the scent of roses and lavender. He fought to ignore the stirring in his braies, and opened his hand with the dice. "Would you care to make the throw, my dear?"

She lightly plucked the dice from his hands and shook them in a manner that — combined with the way she looked up at him from beneath her lashes — made him blush. Then she cast them lightly on the table, where they clattered about before landing on a Five. She made a pout, but Pierre added his coin to the board without complaint.

"No matter," he offered in assurance. "'Tis too early yet for someone to win. 'Tis best when the pot is a great deal richer."

She smiled lightly and leaned on his shoulder once more. "Some things certainly are better after a bit of anticipation and waiting."

Her voice lilted playfully, and for a time Pierre found it increasingly difficult to focus on the game.

11

HE FRIGID NIGHT AIR SNAPPED HER PARTLY BACK to awareness when she slipped out a back window once her business with the guardsman was finished. The world swayed and spun, and a light fog clung tenaciously to her eyes. Not so much she could not see or had abandoned all awareness of her surroundings, but she nonetheless wandered through a haze on her return from Isabeau's.

The night was already very old, and the streets of Carcassonne were deserted. Most of the men still frolicking at Isabeau's would spend their night there in the warm company of the girls, and only a rare few would brave the cold streets to find their way to their own beds. However, the lamps were still lit, so she need not grope her way in the dark, and guards bundled in thick layers of wool still made their rounds, watching for cutpurses and other villains who might prey on those without the sense to remain indoors. Elsabeth's dress and cloak, chosen carefully for the task of enticing her mark, were ill-suited to keeping out the bite of winter, and she shivered violently all the way back to the apartment.

The things I am doing for a thousand pfunde.

She reached it without incident and only a few minor stumbles, and threw the door open in her rush for the shelter of the entry hall.

The common room was dark when she stepped in off the street, but she was smothered by a blanket of relative warmth now that she was out of the wind. The potency of Isabeau's drink reasserted itself, and the fog around her eyes grew thicker. With her head beginning to spin quite fiercely, Elsabeth turned for the stairwell and started up to her apartments, with much of her weight supported on the railing as she concentrated on putting one foot in front of the other and made an unsteady ascent.

Upon reaching her door she flung it open and stumbled inside. Contrary to her recommendations otherwise, Kilianus had indeed waited up for her. He dozed stretched out on the couch in front of the fire blazing on the hearth, and all the lamps were still lit. Elsabeth blinked against the sudden brightness of the front room, and the warmth of the fire was welcomingly overwhelming after the icy streets and chill of the lower levels. Elsabeth kicked off her pattens and let her cloak slip from her shoulders, and made straight for the fire.

Kilianus stirred at the sound of her ungraceful entry and one eye popped open.

"So you are back, and the sun has not even risen. I expected not to see you until at least the afternoon."

"Love, 'twas a frightfully cold walk with my tits all but hanging out of this dress and a cloak that was much too thin, and I have had a great deal to drink besides. I am of no mind for this sort of conversation. 'Tis one I have had far too often with a certain meddlesome Olivian."

The couch creaked with the shifting of Kilianus' weight, and she found him standing beside her at the fire. Elsabeth ignored him — as the fog of drink encroached once more on her vision, he was now little more than an indistinct, wavering blur — and focused on warming herself.

"I trust you enjoyed yourself. I have not been to Isabeau's myself, but have heard quite enough stories about it from the other workers and guards."

"If you must know, not that 'tis any of your concern, but 'twas nothing of the sort. Nothing more than sharing a few drinks and rolling some dice — a not-inconsiderable bonus to my pay, I might add. I really must thank Hieronymus for showing me how he throws dice, though even knowing his secret damned if I could beat him in such games. Once I had the mark alone, 'twas just a matter of a little bit of flattery and stoking his ego, a little appeal to his baser instincts to keep his mind on me and not what he is saying, and plenty of drink to loosen his tongue. I did not even have to loosen the lacing of my dress. 'Twas really all too easy. And then a little something from my locket in his wine to put him to bed."

Kilianus laughed and shook his head. "The whole business sounds most unseemly, if you ask me."

She rolled her eyes. "Tch. Oh, please. And what would you have done had it been some chamber maid standing between you and our objective? Don't tell me you have never used a few sweet words and a little too much drink to pry the occasional secret from the opposite sex in service to your Lord."

Elsabeth turned to face him, and a playful smile crossed her lips as she looked him up and down. "Or perhaps I have misjudged you, and 'tis the same you weave your tongue against. The occasional groom or page, perhaps?"

Kilianus flushed indignantly. "I am quite aware of the sordid tricks of this trade, and yes, I have broken a few maids' hearts. But 'tis not my first choice, especially as their lives have at times been forfeit in the aftermath."

"And what might you have done differently?" she asked, the smile still on her lips. "Abduct him off the street, and bring him here for interrogation?" Elsabeth clicked her tongue again in scolding fashion, and shook her head. Kilianus's face reddened even more. "That, I am sure, would have had the whole household on alert and looking for him, and we would have a prisoner to contend with besides.

"But a guardsman who had a little too much to drink and passed out in a nunnery? Why, no one would be the wiser."

"And what if you were seen or recognized? You are not unknown in the castle. We are here as husband and wife, after all, and it would risk our cover."

Even through the fog of drink Elsabeth caught a slight hesitation in his response, and her playful smile twisted into something much more mischievous. Kilianus flinched back defensively at the sudden change, and she stepped towards him with her hands coquettishly folded behind her back and thrust out her chest. Kilianus' eyes flicked by their own volition to her breast in response before he mastered them and returned them respectively to meet hers. "I do believe that is actually envy in your voice."

"I don't know what you are talking about."

"Oh, I am sure you don't. But you see, 'tis no unusual thing — the esteemed Herr de Sens apparently aside — for husbands and wives to have other bedmates. In fact 'tis quite common in some circles."

"I am quite aware of that as well, in fact. What I don't see is where you are finding envy."

Elsabeth pouted and fluttered her lashes, and took another step forward. Her body now brushed against his. "Don't you find me beautiful?"

Kilianus shifted uncomfortably at the contact and raised his hands; either defensively or so they would not by instinct touch her somewhere socially inappropriate. "I did not say that. A blind man would not deny such a thing."

She spun away deftly and stepped a few paces away, allowing her hips to wag in exaggeration fashion. A sly peek over her shoulder betrayed the straying of his eye to her bottom. Kilianus dug his nails into his palms and promptly looked to the ceiling. His face now was a brilliant shade of crimson.

"After all, you did kiss me as a means of introduction. I could hardly blame you for wanting a deeper drink from the well after so brief a taste. That I might turn my attentions on another yet deprive you must be unbearable!"

Kilianus planted is hands on his hips and glared. "'Twould be a lie to say I have not had my fancies, but that does not make a man jealous. I am well aware of the needs this profession at times requires, and personal desire oft must be set aside for my sworn oath to my Lord."

"Tch, so 'tis your oath that holds you back?"

"That is not what I said!" he spit, almost too quickly.

Elsabeth laughed. "Oh, you very much just did, love. I have not had quite so much to drink that I don't comprehend. I must say now I truly am intrigued."

Kilianus laughed and shook his head in disbelief. "Oh, he was right to warn me about you. You have a manner of twisting words about that could drive a man mad!"

Now it was Elsabeth's turn to blush, and she crossly folded her arms over her chest. "Given the clever turns I have heard slip from that man's tongue he is hardly one to talk!"

A smile quirked his lips, and he matched her posture, but in amusement rather than pique. "Indeed. And I begin to see why Freiherr von Leyen is so enamored of you. In many ways, you two are quite alike. 'Tis little wonder that he considers you his favorite courtesan."

Elsabeth rounded on him, and the cloud of drink settling over her was forgotten in a blaze of wrath. Had her eyes been swords she would have run him clear through and impaled him upon the wall.

"Now you understand this and understand it well, Michael Kilianus: I am *no man's* courtesan!" she hissed, her voice dripping with such venom that Kilianus blanched at the threat in her voice. "Do you hear me? Not yours, not my dear Paulus', and certainly not Cuncz von Leyen's!

"'Tis a hard world for a woman living by her own means, and I must make use of whatever weapons God has given me to continue living as such. At times that means my sword — and if I had it with me, make no mistake that you and I would be having a very hard argument this very moment — and at others the particulars of my sex, which by the Lord of All's grace were made quite fair to look upon.

"Were I a man, the things I need do might have me labeled a rascal, a rogue, or a cad. But I am not a man. I am a woman, and so they have only one word for me: Whore!

"That is the great hypocrisy; a man may plow many strange fields for the simple pleasure of it, and few will think anything untoward of him. In fact 'tis often quite the opposite, and is to be expected of him by his fellows. But to be a woman and enjoy a good tilling makes me a whore. And there is no more devastating word the world may level against a woman. A man at least might clear his public disgrace on a fair field of honor. But no such recourse exists for me, and I have learned this through much pain since the first day a man laid hands to me uninvited."

She bunched her hands into fists, and strode forward until her face was nearly in his. Kilianus swallowed and flinched back, as if seeking any path of escape, but she had him backed now towards a corner of the room and the only way out was past her.

"They do not say Matthias Bock died honorably. Oh no, they say he fell at the hands of the *whore* Elsabeth Soesten. I was but sixteen and just come into womanhood, and God's truth I had not yet known a man's touch! But still they called me whore. And I am the whore that led Paulus von Soest to his death, no matter how dearly I loved him and he me. And I am now the whore who embarrassed Stemham Crosseby before the flower of Navarrese swordsmanship. There is no field of honor for me to expunge the name of whore, even if a man would dare face me on it. 'Twill follow me all my days, and all the days after the Lord calls me to His kingdom and my bones have gone to dust!"

Elsabeth jammed a finger hard into his breastbone, and Kilianus grunted.

"So do not *dare* to call me courtesan; for that is merely 'whore' couched in social niceties. I am no property of Cuncz. I am not his mistress. Not his courtesan. Not his *whore*." She jabbed him again and again in the breastbone as she ranted. "I have my reasons for taking on this venture, and none of it is for any love borne for Cuncz, nor any prowess of his cock. Am I understood, or need I send for a sword?"

Kilianus raised his hands in surrender. Elsabeth's face and neck burned, and her breast heaved in anger. For his part, he kept his eyes locked upon hers, though Elsabeth wished they would fall to her chest for no other reason than an excuse to strike him.

"Forgive me, but I meant no such offense. And if my remark was unwarranted I am truly sorry. I meant only that the Baron thinks quite highly of you; for your skills in subterfuge as much as your beauty, and perhaps 'twas his mistake in interpreting the nature of your relationship, or my own. There is no one, except perhaps Conrat, who knows his thoughts in all things.

"You have no need for your sword, or any other arms that might find their way to your hand."

Elsabeth held his gaze for a long moment, but there was no lie she could hear in his voice, and his hazel eyes gazed solemnly back into hers.

She kept hold of her pique for a few breaths more, then released it.

"So long as we understand one another," she finally said, and released him from her glare.

"Completely."

"Good, then." Elsabeth stepped away from him again and turned back to the fire. For a moment she said nothing, and merely gazed into the dancing and writhing flames, the only sound, the merry pop of wood crackling as it filled the room with warmth and light. "He truly speaks so highly of me, does he?"

"I confess I have only the message he sent me in advance of your arrival in Carcassonne, but yes."

"And what are your thoughts?"

"I think he spoke quite near the mark." Kilianus' voice trembled uncertainly, and a smile tugged at the corner of Elsabeth's lips. "You have great affinity for this work. And I don't mean the manner in which you wield your sex on unsuspecting guardsmen." The last he added hastily, as if in fear of repeating his earlier insult.

"Tch, 'tis hardly just against unsuspecting guardsmen." Elsabeth turned to face him once again, and Kilianus' features fell into some semblance of what she suspected a hart might affect as a fatal arrow sped towards its mark. "He truly does fancy me, does he? 'Tis not merely some affectation to manipulate me to his ends?"

"I... uh... do not have his ear in such personal matters, but his fondness for you by all accounts is no exaggeration."

Elsabeth clasped her hands behind her and stepped towards him once more. Kilianus shrunk away from her nervously. "Such a burden that oath of yours, protecting Cuncz's interests so intently, that you forget your own."

"I assure you, Freiherr von Leyen is more than generous in his compensation for my efforts on his behalf."

She continued towards him, and soon had him backed against the edge of the doorway connecting the antechamber to the bedroom. "Oh, I am sure. But here is the thing about me: I could not give a damn about Cuncz's personal interests in me. As I said, I am not his. I have never been, and never shall be. I may have taken this job for him, but my life is my own to do with as I will."

"I would not now intimate otherwise."

Elsabeth smiled slyly. "Good, you are a quick study. I do as I will, with whom I will. 'Tis my choice to make as a free woman."

As she stepped up closer to him, Kilianus laid his hands on her shoulders and gently pushed her back. "Frau Soesten, whatever 'tis on your mind, I don't think under present circumstances ..."

"What, because I have indulged a little too liberally of drink?" Elsabeth deftly slipped his hands from her shoulders and guided them to her hips. "Or because of some misplaced sense of loyalty?"

He swallowed visibly when she pressed against him. "I think both reasons would do."

"Tch. I have hardly drunk so much that my faculties are so compromised. And as I have already said, I do not belong to Cuncz. His thoughts about me could not be further from my own."

"But not mine."

Elsabeth smiled and tipped his chin playfully. "I must admit, I do find your integrity quite endearing, but I do so enjoy a challenge, as well. There is many a man I could have with but a batting of my eyelashes, and I sometimes forget what it is to have to make an effort.

"And perhaps this is petty of me, but I for one have had enough of Cuncz's intrusions in my life. Nothing would please me more than doing something to rankle him."

Kilianus, his hands still on her hips, attempted to push her away once more when she leaned the length of her body against his, but though he succeeded in moving her lower extremity, Elsabeth leaned in and delivered a sucking nibble to his neck. Kilianus allowed a moan to escape his throat.

"Please, Gnädige Frau."

Elsabeth pulled her lips from him and hung her arms round his neck. "What is it that *you* want, Michael Kilianus? As I have said, I am not his property, but a free woman. Does your oath to Cuncz preclude your own desires?"

Kilianus hesitated for a moment. Their eyes met, and Elsabeth felt his hands flex on her hips. Then he leaned down and kissed her. This was not the same as his distraction on the streets of Carcassonne. Instead, it was deep, desperate and urgent. Elsabeth kissed him back fully. The hands on her hips slipped around to her bottom and crushed her body against him. His tongue met hers, darting and dancing round it with the agility of a master fencer. Elsabeth moaned softly against his mouth as his hands flexed on her backside. He leaned his body fully against hers, now, and crushed her breasts against his chest.

Elsabeth stumbled backwards when he shifted his weight against her, and a loud *bump* filled the apartment when her back struck the opposite door jamb. Then they rolled off it back into the antechamber, stumbling across the floor until Kilianus toppled over backwards and pulled her down on top of him as he fell on the floor in front of the fire.

12

THE FIRST THING ELSABETH NOTED UPON awakening the next morning was that she was lying on something quite hard and unyielding. The second was a smothering warmth settling over her and drawn up above her shoulders. And the third, the fragrant scent of herbs, spices, and cooking meat filling the room. She did not open her eyes immediately, and for a moment lay still and braced herself against the agony of the headache to come. Then she let her eyes flutter open.

To her relief the room was darkened, and there was no light to spear her in the eye and rip open her skull. A small mercy. She found herself lying on the floor in front of the fire with little in the way of a pillow except her own naked arm, so now as well as a headache she had a pain in her neck and shoulder to contend with. She was also, for the moment, alone, with a blanket drawn up to her neck. Her dress, stockings, and other underthings were scattered discarded across the anteroom floor. The lamps were out, though a fire crackled on the hearth to keep the room warm. A small pot simmered in a corner of the fireplace out of the flames.

Elsabeth slowly sat up, wrapped the blanket tightly round herself against the morning chill, and leaned back against the couch. Her head throbbed in protest, and she nursed her temples with one hand while the other clutched the blanket to her breast.

"Bugger," she mewled pitiably, and lowered her hand from her head to the crick in her neck. "The things I am doing for a thousand *pfunde*."

Presently, the light tread of shoes on the wooden floorboards filled the room behind her, and Kilianus rounded the couch, dressed only in his hose and undershirt. He held a small clay bowl with a spoon in one hand.

"Good morning," he said, a little too loudly for Elsabeth's liking, and knelt beside the fireplace. He filled the bowl with something steaming and hot from the pot.

"You should know I have killed men for less than that," she grumbled, and held her head again. "What time is it?"

"'Tis not quite the ninth hour."

"Oh, bugger, I was supposed to be back at the laundry two hours ago. And why are you still here?"

"I was given the day off today." Kilianus settled onto the floor beside her and handed her the bowl. "Here, eat this."

Elsabeth accepted the bowl and looked doubtfully at the thick brown broth and diced meats and vegetables. While quite an unfamiliar sight, it at least *smelled* appetizing, despite her stomach tying itself in knots. "What is it?"

"The Izmiri call it *kishkiyya*. 'Tis something I learned to make while bodyguarding an ambassador there perhaps five years ago. The Izmiri swear by it for recovering from a surfeit of drink."

She sniffed the bowl, and her belly began to rumble as her nose was greeted by a fragrant blend of herbs, spices, onions, a few other vegetables, and a few cubes of beef. "I thought the Izmiri foreswore drink. I can't recall their word for it, but 'twas against their religion."

Kilianus chuckled. "There are many things against ours that you seem to have no regard for, either. 'Tis much the same with them. At the very least it sounds more appetizing to me than a plate of eels and bitter almonds."

Elsabeth grunted. "I hope you don't intend for me to be impressed." She thrust her spoon at him for emphasis. "Either by your worldly experiences, or your performance last night."

"I would not think of it."

"Good," she said, and dipped her spoon into the bowl. She sniffed it once more, then took a tentative sip. To her surprise the flavor matched the savory aroma, nor was it too hot, and she took the whole spoon in one bite. "Make no mistake, 'twas not out of a desire for anything more than something I can stick in Cuncz's face when all this is over. Don't get me wrong, you are a handsome enough man, and I did enjoy myself, but that is all there is to it."

His lips curled into a scowl, and she felt his eyes boring into her. "Do you willfully leave a trail of pain and tears in your wake, or is it something I have done to you personally to invite it upon myself?"

"You, love, are merely collateral damage. And as for pain and tears, I have lost much more to my everlasting regret than you can possibly know." Elsabeth glanced sidelong at him, her spoon halfway between the bowl and her mouth. "So don't try to match me stroke for stroke. A little bruise of your ego will mend in time, and I am quite sure I'll be forgotten ere long the next time you send a maid to the gallows."

"Well, just so long as we understand each other, then," he said, and there was no mistaking the acid dripping from his tongue. "I hope my ego and your headache were worth the price. It did not come up last night, but what did you find out?"

"Enough, I think, to formulate a plan, but 'twill be no small urgency in pulling it together. The demonstration is the day after tomorrow. The Graf de Carcassonne will be attending, but also a number of other lords from across Navarre. It seems 'twill be quite the spectacle. I suspect 'tis as much to sell them on these new *gonnes* as it is just to show they work."

Kilianus frowned and stroked his chin. "You are right, that does not give us much time. I suspect by now we both know the lay of the castle well enough, but if 'tis not just the Graf attending, 'twill be quite the circus here with so many attendants and bodyguards. What about the *gonnes* themselves?"

Elsabeth took another bite of her soup and chewed one of the pieces of cubed beef with relish. *Bugger him, but this is quite good, and certainly better than a platter of rollmops.* She swallowed before continuing.

"As we suspected, they are kept down in the vaults, along with their maker. Certainly quite inaccessible as they are; no one but de Sens and the guards assigned to safeguard the clockmaker and *gonnes* are allowed down there. But they are moving them to the regular armory tomorrow for final assembly and a minor test-firing before the demonstration."

"Well, that is certainly something. The armory is far more accessible than the vaults. I think there is an opportunity to make our move tomorrow night. But that still leaves us with a concern of getting in and past the guard. I was given tomorrow off, and I would not likely be getting onto the grounds."

Elsabeth considered for a moment and stirred her soup thoughtfully. "That I think you can leave to me. They already think me to be useless and clumsy. 'Twould be a simple matter to damage some of the woodwork, and no one would think anything suspicious of it. A little bit of a panic and a fright, and an assurance that you could fix it ought to do the trick."

Kilianus nodded. "So they are well acquainted with you then. Once I am in and able to go to work it should be a simple matter to slip away. I think it best to wait until near the end of the night. With guests due these next two days, they will want the damage fixed quickly. Thus our lingering after the day laborers have retired for the evening should go relatively unnoticed. That still leaves the matter of the guards at the armory itself."

She took another bite of her soup and considered her discarded underthings. "That should not be a problem. If you can subdue them quickly, I shan't have too much trouble making a distraction of myself."

He regarded her with a raised eyebrow, but Elsabeth did not favor him by meeting his eyes, and instead watched him from her peripherals. "Is that your solution to everything?"

"'Tis not, in fact, but under these circumstances I think it the best. There may not be many men who can take me in a straight sword fight, but we won't have the time for that. 'Tis best they be dispatched quickly and quietly. And I suspect I am far more likely to draw their attention and put them off their guard.

"Once into the armory, we secure one of those *gonnes*, and I think also a sample of their shot and powder. But then 'tis a matter of getting back out again."

Kilianus stroked his chin thoughtfully. "I don't know how large the *gonnes* will be, though I suspect not too dissimilar from the types I have seen in the past, if they are meant to be wielded by one man. My toolbox ought to be large enough for the purpose."

Elsabeth scraped the last of her soup from the bowl. Her stomach was now greatly settled, and the worst of the pain between her temples had subsided. "The powder and shot would be simple enough to secret away in my laundry basket. 'Tis just a matter of getting out. The guards have not been in a habit of searching me."

"Nor I. Well, it seems we have the workings of a plan," he said.

She nodded and set her bowl aside. "In which case, I best get dressed and to the castle. Maybe they won't notice I am late. 'Tis all I'll need to be released right before we finish this business."

Elsabeth pulled the blanket tight around herself and rose. She hurried about gathering up her dress and underthings, while Kilianus watched from the floor in front of the couch. "I'll arrange us some horses while I wait for you to make your move," he said. "I think it best for us to be gone and quickly once we finish in the castle. I imagine it won't take them long to notice if one of the *gonnes* goes missing."

"We should probably be packed and ready to leave, too. In fact, 'twould be best if we don't come back here at all."

"I agree. I'll make sure to have the horses loaded and ready for a quick exit." Kilianus took a wistful look around the apartment. "I must say, I shall miss this place. 'Tis one of the nicer lodgings I have had on a mission. Some of the better company, at that."

Elsabeth straightened, one hand holding her blankets closed, the other laden with her discard clothing. Kilianus looked to the floor, with his arms folded across his chest, and nudging one of the boards with his toe. She sighed at his expression and lowered her head.

"Love, I am sorry if I gave you any hurt over last night. In other circumstances, I might have even been interested in you on your own virtues. But I have little liking for how your Cuncz tugged upon my strings to involve me in this whole affair, or that he thinks to have a claim upon me. It may be a petty vengeance, but I shall take it nonetheless.

"I have made myself quite plain 'tis no mission of loyalty to me, and I desperately need the windfall. I have made many mistakes in my life, and the purse he has promised may allow me to make up for one of the worst. But you, I think, put too much stock in loyalty to the man. He has already used me once, and I don't intend to go on being used."

Kilianus looked at her sharply, and something hard passed behind his hazel eyes. "I won't deny he loves his little intrigues, and has an unerring knack for twisting one into a position where they cannot tell him no, but I have served him long enough to know that, machinations aside, he is a good man."

"Be that as it may, the more distance I can put between myself and him when this is done, the better for me. I am in no position to trust his games. You just had the misfortune of being another piece on the board."

He turned his eyes away again and nodded. "Best you get ready and go, and not tarry any longer. If you run into any trouble, make an excuse that I was unwell this morning, and you had to fetch a leech."

"You don't need to tell me how to lie, love. One thing at least your lord and I have in common, our tongues are one of our keenest weapons."

Elsabeth turned for the bedroom. Just as she retreated through the door and closed it behind her Kilianus' voice slipped through.

"I can surely attest to your skill with yours."

ROBIN MADE HIS WAY ALONG THE HALLWAYS OF THE castle, his hands folded at the small of his back. He ground his back teeth until he thought they might collapse into dust.

D'Alle's request came, unbidden but not unexpected, in the midst of the final preparations for de Carcassonne's return. All the castle was in chaos. Servants scurried hither and thither underfoot, and Robin had to sidestep several mobs frantically scrubbing floors and polishing any piece of metal sitting on a shelf or bolted to the wall. And some metal *not* bolted to the wall; more than once, Robin had to fend off some over-eager attendant insisting on addressing the lack of shine on his sword-hilt. The castle guards' helms and armor had not only been polished and shined until they gleamed like beacons, but done over thrice.

Robin idly wondered whether there was an ounce of oil or wax left in the whole of Carcassonne.

He cut a circuitous route through the maze of hallways, but his course inerrantly led him towards the doorway leading down to the vaults and dungeons, where his charge was kept safe, secure, and in no little comfort at de Carcassonne's great expense. And yet there was always something more the clockmaker had to demand.

Robin did not know yet what was the matter this time, but were it his decision to make, he would have the demanding little man loaded into the nearest *bombard* and fired from the grounds.

A commotion up ahead lulled him from his imaginings of the splatter the clockmaker's head might make as it was dashed across the paving stones of Carcassonne at the speed of *bombard* shot. He quickly recognized the new laundry maid, her hands knotting in her apron as she weathered a scolding from Rapine. She was not a difficult woman to notice, and he had overheard enough idle chatter among the guard to know she had caught the eye of much of the male staff. Wisps of burnished copper hair peaked out from her cap, and were it not for the shy hunching of her shoulders she might even have rivaled some of the guard in height.

"...don't know what you expect at whatever hovel you crawled from," the senior maid snapped, and shook her finger in the other's face, "but here we expect *punctuality*. I don't know why they don't turn you out!"

"And I am sorry! But my husband was ill, and it took all night and well 'till the morning before the leech could come with this dreadful cold snap."

"Ha! Like as not he spent the night face-down in his drink over having to deal with you all day. Were it up to me you would be out, but 'tis not my decision, and the castle is in such a shambles we need every hand ..."

Robin passed them by. As he did, he thought he caught a flicker of the maid's green eyes glance in his direction, but then he was past and continuing on his way and leaving the scolding behind him.

He turned down several other corridors, making a show as if inspecting the preparedness of the staff and castle, before finally reaching his destination. However, a frown crossed his features at the sight that awaited him. Only one guard stood at the door leading down to the lower levels, where there ought to have been two. For his part, the man on duty displayed no less consternation in his features, and he drummed his fingers on the haft of his halberd in irritation. As Robin rounded the corner and came into view he quickly snapped to attention.

Rather than making his way straight for the door and prepare himself for the clockmaker's demands, Robin checked his pace and instead turned his attention on the guardsman.

"Good morning, Frederick," he said.

"Good morning, Monsieur," Frederick replied smartly. Though he made an effort to mask his irritation at being left alone on duty, it still managed to slip into his voice. "You received our guest's message, I warrant?"

Robin nodded. "I did indeed. But I am more curious as to why I arrive to find you here alone. Is Pierre not supposed to be on duty with you this morning?"

"That he is, Monsieur."

"So I have two questions for you: The first, is why you neglected to inform me of his absence when you relayed Master d'Alle's message?"

Frederick swallowed visibly and shifted uncomfortably from foot to foot as Robin fixed him with a searching gaze.

"And the second, Monsieur?" he asked, instead of answering his question immediately.

"*Where* is Pierre?"

Robin stepped up to him and stretched to his full height over the hapless guardsman. Frederick, for his part, weathered his glare with more dignity than the poor cringing laundry maid.

"Well, in answer to the second, Monsieur, I don't know, else I would have dragged him to his post as he was scheduled. As to the first...I suppose I had hoped he would turn up before Monsieur arrived."

Robin sighed and folded his arms across his chest. The brigandine beneath his tabard rattled at the movement, and he drummed his fingers on his arm.

"And yet he has not, and I arrive to find him missing when my orders were that two men were to be on guard at this door at all times."

Frederick blanched but did not shrink away. "Yes, Monsieur."

"So tell me, when did you last see him?"

"Yesterday afternoon, just before I was relieved so I could prepare my ceremonial dress for Monsieur le Comte's arrival."

Robin nodded. "Ah yes, you were drawn for the escort. I pray 'twas not an oversight to grant you such a prestigious assignment."

"Of course not, Monsieur! 'Twas all in order. Every bit of metal polished 'till my own reflection was looking back at me, not a thread out of place. And I was still here at my post bright and early."

"Which is more than can be said of Pierre. Have you any thought as to where he might be?"

"No, Monsieur... well..."

He trailed off, and his face colored abruptly. Robin raised an eyebrow as he regarded him, and after a long moment it became clear Frederick had no intent to continue unprompted.

"Well, what?"

"Well, Monsieur, Pierre did mention to me he intended to visit Isabeau's after his watch yesterday. He asked me to meet him. But of course I did not. I had too much to do to be ready for Monsieur le Comte's return!"

The last was added hastily, and with a note of embarrassed panic in his voice.

Robin heaved a sigh and pinched the bridge of his nose. "Isabeau's..."

Frederick nodded. "Yes, Monsieur. I have told him time and again he ought not to waste his time in such a place, especially when he is due back on watch the next morning, but ..."

"Were it not for how much money the taxes bring Monsieur le Comte, I would shut that place down if 'twere my decision."

"Respectfully, Monsieur, I think you might have a rebellion on your hands if you were to try. Some of the guard might even join in."

"Nonetheless, I shall be taking this up with Monsieur de Carcassonne. For now, maintain your post. Master d'Alle will simply have to wait while I attend to this matter."

Frederick snapped smartly to attention again, and firmly planted the butt of his halberd on the floor in relief that no more chastisement was forthcoming. "Of course, Monsieur!"

Robin sighed, shook his head as he started away, and turned for the main guardroom.

ISABEAU'S WAS CONSIDERABLY QUIETER BY THE TIME HE arrived than the accounts of the guard would imply. Robin dismissed it as a factor of the early hour, for much of the establishment's business was not done so early in the day.

A few folk were present, however. A handful of laborers who worked overnight and just finished sat around a table, tossing dice and conversing in hushed tones over drinks. Two of Isabeau's girls loitered about the common room and waited for one of the patrons to bore of tossing dice and come in search of other diversions. Isabeau herself dutifully manned her counter as Robin stepped inside, leading a small contingent of guards behind him. She straightened abruptly as he threw the door open and stepped in out of the cold, and every head within turned in his direction.

"Monsieur de Sens!" Isabeau purred, though not quite able to mask her surprise at seeing him. "I must say I never expected to see you walking through my door. Have you finally despaired of your separation from that pretty little thing of yours, and come looking for companionship?"

Robin twisted his lip in annoyance at the insinuation and speared her with a glare. For her part, Isabeau weathered his glower with more steel in her spine than even a veteran soldier, and folded her arms beneath her breast as a playful smirk tugged at her lip.

"I am not here for your entertainments, Mademoiselle," he replied, "but on official business. One of my men is late to report to his duties this morning, and I am told he visited here last night."

"Well, you might need to be more specific than that, Monsieur, for many of the guard while away their off hours with my girls."

Robin leaned his hand on the sword at his hip, and the subtle threat in the gesture did not go unnoticed. The night laborers immediately returned their attention to their drinks, and his ears caught the soft intake of breath as the younger of the remaining girls gasped.

"I warn you I am in no mood for games. I have turned a blind eye to your business in the past because it has never interfered with the duties of the guard. I assure you, you don't want that to change."

Isabeau squared her shoulders and did not back down. In truth, Robin could do little about her establishment; de Carcassonne himself was quite enamored of the place, and she well knew it. "Well, we can always take that up with Monsieur le Comte," she said, as if reading his thoughts on the situation. "But I can't keep account of every man who passes beneath my roof. If you have a name to give me I can ask after him."

"'Tis Pierre."

She mulled over the name for a moment, and tapped her chin thoughtfully. "Pierre... Pierre... Ah! Yes, the fellow with the lovely mustache, though he has not fooled anyone with the way he tries to comb his hair over that bare patch atop his head. I have not seen him since quite early yesterday evening."

Robin nodded to the guards behind him. "If you don't mind, I shall have a look around myself. And I best not find that you are trying to cover for him while he sleeps off a surfeit of your drink."

Isabeau stepped away from her counter and rounded it to bar the path of the guardsmen as they started into the common hall.

"Now just one moment, Monsieur!" she snapped, and planted her hands on her hips. "I make it a point that whenever a man steps across my threshold he leaves his troubles behind him. And I'll not have you bringing them in with you!"

Robin strode up to her and straightened to his full height. Isabeau neither flinched nor shrunk from him, and instead stared him down.

"If Pierre is still here," Robin retorted, "he will be bringing more than trouble with him, now stand aside so we may do our duty."

"I have an agreement with Monsieur le Comte, and you shan't set another foot further! I shan't have anyone disrupting the peace beneath my roof, nor intrude upon the privacy of my clients!"

"Mademoiselle Isabeau," a voice interjected, and he and Isabeau both turned their heads to find the younger of the two girls standing before them. She knotted her skirts in her hands, and shrunk down nervously over addressing her superiors. The girl was a slight and pretty thing, and quite young, perhaps only just coming of age. "And Monsieur," she added hastily, and blushed fiercely.

"What is it, Nicole?" Isabeau asked, her tone softening to put the girl at ease.

"Forgive me for interrupting, but I saw Pierre last night going into Room Twenty-Three with the new girl, as I was finishing with a client further down the hall. I can't recall having seen him come out again."

Isabeau frowned. "What new girl?"

The girl faltered a moment. "Last night was the first time I saw her, so I thought you had brought her on new ..."

Robin peered at her, and she averted her eyes at the scrutiny. "What did she look like?" he demanded

"I don't know!" she squeaked, and flinched at the sharpness of his tone. 'Twas dark in the hall and I only saw her for a moment before she slipped into the room. But I know I had never seen her before!"

"And I say again I have not brought on a new girl for months!" Isabeau insisted, and her tone suddenly grew defensive.

Robin, however, was already brushing past her, and called the guard to his side with a snap of his fingers. Isabeau scurried to catch up to him. "Two guards with me, the rest of you take up postings here. And if I should come down to find any of you occupied with anything other than securing this room, then Pierre shall be having company in the stocks for the next week!"

"Now just a moment, Monsieur!" Isabeau pleaded. "I'll not have you barging up to the private rooms—"

Robin wheeled on her, seized her by the front of her dress, and pushed her up against the wall. He thrust a finger into her face. "One of my men did not return from your establishment, and it seems that you cannot secure your own house, if girls are coming and going right beneath your nose."

Isabeau raised her hands in a gesture of surrender and made no effort to free herself from his grip. "I assure you, Monsieur, that I take great care in screening everyone who steps through my door, and have always ensured the integrity of any girl I take into my care. You can ask for yourself; this is no common nunnery. I don't harbor thieves or charlatans."

"Then you have nothing to hide, and no reason for concern if I have a look for myself!"

He released her with a shove, and Isabeau collapsed into the wall behind her. Robin turned again on his heel and made his way for the stairs leading to the private rooms. By now the commotion in the common room had drawn the attention of those above, and as he emerged from the stairwell with armed and armored guardsmen trailing behind him, the faces of a few of the working girls or their clients poking out to investigate disappeared once more with the slamming of doors.

The upper level was no less opulent in its furnishings than the common room, and though the lights were kept low, it was nonetheless bright enough that he could see to read the door numbers and had no fear of being ambushed by someone lurking in the shadows. Robin made his way along the carpeted hallway and stopped at the door to room Twenty-Three. He hammered his fist loudly against it.

"In the name of the Comte de Carcassonne open this door at once!" he commanded. Silence greeted him in response, and Robin knocked once more. "I said open this door immediately!"

Again, he was met with silence. The only sound was the muted giggles and moans from the neighboring rooms as the girls went back to work once they were certain he had not come for them.

Robin tested the door, but found it locked. He took a firm hold of it, braced himself, and with a cry of protest from Isabeau drove his shoulder into it. Once, then twice, and finally on the third the lock gave way and the door exploded inward.

The room was dark, with only the light spearing through the window and around the edges of the curtains illuminating the space within. It was warm but not stifling, and a thick rug occupying much of the bare wooden floor helped insulate the room against winter's chill. Robin noted no sign of violence or struggle; all of the furniture was upright, which was more than he could say for Pierre.

The missing guardsman lay on the bed snoring loudly. He was stripped down to his undershirt, with his doublet and cloak hung from the back of a chair next to the dresser occupying the wall to Robin's right, and his boots stood next to the bed in the center of the wall opposite. Beside the bed was a small table, with a bottle of wine and two glass goblets. One was empty, and the other conspicuously full.

Robin strode into the room, with Isabeau and the two guardsmen following. He made for the bed and leaned over Pierre. His mustache shivered with each deep intake of breath, but otherwise the only movement was the rise and fall of his breast. Pierre lay atop the covers with one hand on his stomach and the other lying at his side. His linen undershirt was still tucked into his hose, and he had only just managed to undo one of the lacings securing the flap of the latter closed before he succumbed to sleep.

Robin ground his teeth, leaned over the prostate fellow, and shook him by the shoulder.

"Pierre!" he called in a commanding voice. "Pierre! Wake up!"

Pierre was not impressed, and continued to snore loudly. The noise sounded for all the world like the purr of some cat of truly gigantic proportion.

"Pierre!" He shouted again, when no response was forthcoming. "Pierre you damned fool, wake up!"

Robin slapped him hard across the cheek, but still Pierre did not wake. Isabeau frowned and stepped up beside him. She laid one hand to his brow for a moment, and then lightly stroked his cheek.

"'Tis not a fever," she said. "Is he normally a heavy sleeper?"

Robin rubbed his chin thoughtfully. "No more than the other guard, since they are always expected to be able to rise for duty at a moment's notice."

He leaned over Pierre again and shook him hard by the shoulders.

"Pierre, will you wake up!" he snapped. "Or God help me when you do 'twill be to find your head in the damned stocks!"

Isabeau laid a hand on his arm, and gently moved him away.

"If you please, Monsieur, I think perhaps you ought to allow an expert to address this matter. I have had to deal with more than my share of clients who have overstayed their welcome after a surfeit of drink."

She gracefully lowered herself to the bed, and gently ran a finger down Pierre's chest from his collarbones all the way down to his sternum. And then she kept going. Robin blushed and turned away before Isabeau reached the flap of his hose, and purposefully circled the bed to the table on the far side to consider the wine bottle and glass. There was only the one bottle, and when he lifted it from the table he found it still half full. The bottle was labeled with a vintage of modest potency from the Free City-States.

Robin removed the cork and sniffed it. It smelled strongly of blackberries and oak, but there was something else; a slightly bitter aftertaste that clung to the back of his tongue upon inhaling, and made his eyes water. He jerked his head aside out of reflex and recorked the bottle before returning it to the table. Robin then examined the glasses. The empty glass had been drained nearly dry, and only a faint red line betrayed the color of its former contents. The other was still, as he had noted earlier, nearly full. Robin lifted it and lightly wafted his hand over the top, breathing in just a hint of its perfume. It matched the aroma of the cork; blackberries mixed with oak, but underlying that pleasant flavor a slight bitterness. He suspected after a few drinks in the common room he might not have even noticed it. But here, with his faculties intact, it could not be mistaken.

Pierre suddenly snorted, sputtered, and muttered something unintelligible. Robin set the glass back on the table and retrieved the wine bottle, then rounded the bed to join Isabeau as she rose again. Pierre stirred and nursed his head as he rose weakly up on his elbows.

"Bloody hell, what time is it?" he slurred. Try as he might, he was not able to draw the strength to rise up much more than he already had, and sunk back down onto the pillow.

"Well past time for your duty shift, Pierre," Robin growled.

If Pierre's face was not already pale from his condition, Robin fancied it likely would have turned as white as newly fallen snow at the sound of his voice.

"Monsieur!" Pierre stammered. He shot bolt-upright, driven by reflex and adrenaline as much as his conscious will, and would have nearly sunk to his knees on the floor beside the bed had Isabeau not darted forward to catch him. "Monsieur, I assure you—"

Robin cut him off with an abrupt wave of his hand. "I don't want excuses. I want to know what happened."

"Monsieur?" Pierre asked, and frowned.

"You were seen leaving the common room in the company of a woman last night. Who was she?"

Pierre blinked and studied the floor as he searched his memory, and some color returned to his cheeks in embarrassment. "I did not catch her name, but she must have been a new girl, I had never seen her before that I can recall."

"There was no new girl, or so Mademoiselle Isabeau claims."

"And I insist upon it," Isabeau said. "I have not brought on anyone new in months."

Pierre's legs could no longer keep him upright, and he sagged in Isabeau's arms. Robin gave a short nod, and she gently lowered him to the edge of the bed. Pierre slouched and buried his head in his hands. "Are you sure? I know I have not seen her before, and I never would have forgotten if I had."

Robin narrowed his eyes at him. "Describe her. What did she look like?"

The guardsman closed his eyes as he strained his memory. "She was... she was..." Pierre trailed off. "I mean she... 'Tis the strangest thing, I can almost see her, but damned if I can get a clear picture, if you follow me, Monsieur."

"Well, what can you see?"

"For the life of me all I can think of is a low-cut dress, and the nicest pair of tits I think I have ever seen. I mean they were just jumping right up out ..."

He looked up as he spoke, and by chance his eye caught Isabeau's amused smirk. Pierre's face abruptly turned about the same shade as the wine.

"Forgive me, Mademoiselle! 'Tis barracks talk and I would never say such a thing in polite company."

Isabeau merely clicked her tongue. "Come now, Monsieur, I have heard far more vulgar talk from the cooking staff. There is not much that can come off your tongue that could embarrass me."

Pierre shrunk shyly into the collar of his shirt nonetheless, and would not look up at her again when he continued.

"Suffice to say, Monsieur, they were quite the distraction away from her face."

"So it would seem," Robin said dryly. "So you met her in the common room, then?"

Pierre nodded eagerly, glad for the change of subject away from the woman's anatomy. "Yes, Monsieur. I was rolling dice with some others when she joined us at the table. I... uh... had rather a bad run of luck afterwards. She says she did not know the game, but she rolled the dice like she has been casting all her life. And it did not help we had quite a fair bit to drink, I suppose even before we came up to the room I could hardly put a foot in front of the other."

"So you came up here with her?"

"Yes, Monsieur. After a few games of dice and a bit of drink, she suggested we could get to know each other better in private. And well, Monsieur, I may not be able to remember much of what she looked like—" with that he cast a glance aside at Isabeau "— but had it been you in my position I don't think you would have refused such an offer. No offense to Mademoiselle Isabeau, but I only hear stories of the sorts of girls at the nunneries all the noble folk frequent, and I imagine she belongs bouncing on Monsieur le Comte's or some other upstanding fellow's scepter rather than rollicking among us common lads. So I was not about to refuse the offer and kick myself come morning, so I followed her. We started on a glass of wine and that is the last I can remember."

Pierre's countenance turned troubled at the recollection; whether from concern over the sequence of events, or the thought of having missed or, even worse, *forgotten* a fuck well above his station Robin could not tell. Nor did he care, for his own growing worries gnawed at him. He hefted the bottle in his hands.

"Was this the wine?"

Pierre squinted at it and gave a nod. "I think so, Monsieur. I never did learn my letters properly, certainly not anything that is not crude soldier's talk. But the label looks familiar."

Robin turned to Isabeau and raised the bottle to her. Isabeau took it and examined the label with a frown and a low whistle.

"'Tis not the most potent, but this is expensive stuff nonetheless," she said. "It certainly did not come from my cellar."

"I suspect 'twas also drugged," Robin said. "Have a smell of the cork with care. There is a bitter scent under it all I can't place."

Isabeau did as he said, and recoiled her head after sniffing the cork. "'Tis definitely drugged."

Robin turned and fixed his gaze on Pierre. Hearing this, the color once more drained from the guardsman's face, and he wrung his hands nervously. "Drugged? Am I ..." Pierre trailed off ominously.

"I suspect 'twas only enough for the effects we have seen," Robin said. "Had it been intended to be fatal, 'tis almost certain that we would not be having this conversation now."

Isabeau corked the wine again. "But what happened to this girl? Perhaps she might have slipped in with a crowd, but I certainly would have noticed her leaving."

Robin nodded idly as he fit the various pieces together and started across the floor once more. He made to the window, pushed aside the curtains, and opened the glass panes. He found himself looking out across a narrow alleyway. In daylight he could clearly see up and down both directions to the main street fronting Isabeau's, and another major street on the other end of the block. He then looked down to the alley directly below the window.

"Someone has been down in the alley recently," he mused, noting the clear sign of footprints in the slush and snow below. Robin stepped away from the window again. "If I were to guess, our mystery woman slipped out this way once she was finished with foolish Pierre."

Isabeau frowned. "But why would she drug one of our guests? Was it just to rob him?"

Pierre shook his head. "If 'twas, she was content to rob me at the gambling table."

Robin snapped his fingers, and the two guardsmen accompanying him stepped smartly into the room.

"That is none of your concern, Mademoiselle. 'Tis mine. Clearly, she did not want to be recognized; She made use of her dress to draw attention from her face and made sure to have my man well into his cups. This is now a matter for Monsieur de Carcassonne, and I suggest you remain silent, or I will see to it that this establishment is shut down permanently, do I make myself understood?"

Isabeau swallowed and nodded. "Yes, Monsieur."

Robin turned to the guardsmen. "Take him to the company surgeon," he said with a nod to Pierre. "Take him directly there, and he is not to leave until the surgeon is certain he is fit for duty. I will give you the benefit of the doubt that you were not derelict in your duties but instead the victim of an organized plot, but make no mistake that you shall be disciplined, and I intend to see to it that this place is made off-limits to the guard henceforth."

Pierre, too, swallowed. "Yes, Monsieur."

"See to it!" Robin snapped, and started out of the room without waiting for them to reply.

Robin ground his teeth as he made his way back to the stairs. He suspected it was no accident that Pierre was targeted by this mystery woman. Whatever her identity, there was only one possible thing she might have come for.

The only question now was whether she was acting alone, or as part of a conspiracy.

14

HE NEXT MORNING ELSABETH WAS UP BEFORE the sun and arrived early at the servant's entrance to the castle. The day before the demonstration had arrived, and a small thrill worked its way through her bowels in anticipation of the pending action. That thrill quickly soured on her approach to the small side gate, for the guard had been increased considerably since the day before, and the moment she set foot within the bailey she felt their eyes upon her.

Workers and laborers went about their business in the yard. Wagons were unloaded, and everyone who approached the gate was searched and their goods inspected before they were admitted. Elsabeth hefted her laundry basket on her hip. Fortunately, she carried nothing incriminating on her person (and her rondel was safely hidden among the folds of her dress, where only the most concerted search could find it). But if the guard was as stringent upon her departure tonight as they were now...

This whole business could be for nothing if they are searching everyone and everything coming in or out. Damn the luck!

Elsabeth approached the gate and waited patiently for her turn. Seven men barred the entrance; the watch captain with a sword at his side personally making the inspections, and six men bearing halberds flanking the gate. The captain's head was uncovered, and he was a handsome enough fellow with sandy hair and hazel eyes. The guard all wore kettle helms. All seven dressed in brigandine beneath tabards emblazoned with the arms of the Comte de Carcassonne. However, as Elsabeth stepped up, the captain halted her with a raised hand, and the guards nearest the door barred the way with their halberds.

"I am sorry, Mademoiselle," he said, "but under orders of Le Chevalier de Sens, no one without a prior appointment is being permitted entry to the grounds."

Elsabeth's heart clawed its way up into her throat. *Bugger, this is not good.*

She screwed up her features into an affectation of confusion. "But—but I am expected this morning!" she stammered. "I work in the laundry. I was late yesterday and they were frightfully angry with me and I promised I would be here early today!" She motioned to the basket balanced on her hip for emphasis.

"I was not told to expect anyone today, so I am afraid you will have to turn 'round and return home."

"No!" she mewled in her most pitiable voice. "Mademoiselle Rapine specifically told me to be here by the seventh hour. She will have me whipped for certain if I am late again! Please! I very much need the money; My husband has been ill and unable to work the past few nights, and the apothecary only gave us enough remedy to make it through this morning!"

The watch captain's shoulders heaved with a sigh, and he shook his head. "You have my sympathies, Mademoiselle, but my orders are explicit."

"But I am known in the castle!" Elsabeth forced a few tears into her eyes. "I—I am not some... some common woman off the street!"

The accusation had the desired effect, and the captain's face heated indignantly. "I assure you I meant no such insinuation—"

"Ask the guards!" she cried. "They have seen me!"

He sighed heavily and looked askance at the men flanking the entrance. One stepped up at the unspoken command, offered her a quick looking-over, and nodded.

"'Tis as she says, Monsieur," the guard said. "I have seen her most mornings the past week or so. Mademoiselle Rapine certainly does give her a hard time, as castle gossip puts it."

"See? I am known in the castle. Surely Le Chevalier de Sens would not bar me as if I were just a woman of the City."

The captain eyed her sharply, and Elsabeth clenched her jaw at the thought she might have pushed this too far. Bile boiled in her belly at the apologetic expression that passed across his features.

"I'll accept that you are known in the castle, but nonetheless I have only Le Chevalier de Sens's orders, and that is that no one should be admitted without a specific appointment. He offered no room for exception."

Elsabeth swallowed. *Damn it all if I can't get in...*

With the captain unwilling to budge Elsabeth lowered her head, and let the tears flow freely. She looked up at him from beneath her lashes and rolled her lip out into a small pout. "Please, Monsieur, I cannot simply go home. Surely there must be some arrangement we could make?"

He shook his head. "As I said, without instructions from Le Chevalier de Sens ..."

Elsabeth gave him a slight nod of her head, and he trailed off before leaning in at the invitation.

"I... I ordinarily would not say such a thing, and I am altogether embarrassed to even consider it, but 'tis truly desperate that I work today," she said in a low voice. The captain had to stoop his head almost to her ear for her to be heard, and she took advantage of the proximity to lightly play her breath onto his neck. "I... have other skills. Particular skills, and I would be terribly grateful if you would do me this service. I swear I would offer you my own services in return.

"The truth is money is terribly tight with my husband unable to work, and he is so ill, he has not been able to perform... other duties."

The captain's face colored, and Elsabeth crowded close to him in such a manner that even without that special garment she had swiped from the laundry he was afforded an unimpeded view down the neck of her dress. She caught the flicker of hazel stealing a glance at her bosom and smiled inwardly.

"Things are *terribly* tight," she added, with a playful lilt of her voice. For a brief moment the captain's legs nearly went out from under him, and he staggered a pace to maintain his balance. "Please, I would implore you from my knees here and now if I must, but surely 'tis a protestation best made in private?"

He choked on his own breath and tore his gaze away from her chest to look her in the eye. Elsabeth curled her lips into her most alluring smile and unleashed an unrestrained *smolder*. All the color drained from the captain's face, and she watched in satisfaction as his grip on his composure snapped. He glanced self-consciously at the other guards, but they gave no indication of having noticed his sudden distress or overheard what passed between them. Perhaps they might have guessed — and Elsabeth decided she would have been professionally disappointed had they not — but they said nothing and merely watched their confidential discourse with indifference.

"There are perhaps arrangements that could be made," he muttered when he finally found his voice, though Elsabeth caught a subtle but unmistakable hitch.

"For which I would be *most* appreciative," Elsabeth replied. *Another few moments and I'll have him eating from the palm of my hand, though I am certain he would rather be eating from other places. This garrison must be hard-pressed for women of my exceptional quality, 'tis almost unsporting!*

"And you will make good on your appreciation?"

"I am a woman of my word, Monsieur. I only ask your discretion about our... arrangement. My husband is frightfully jealous!"

The captain looked her over once more — his eyes fixed a moment longer than decent upon the neckline of her cotehardie — and then straightened.

"Very well," he said, loud enough this time for the guard to hear. He turned and offered her his arm, and Elsabeth accepted it. She slipped close enough to him that he would not be able to ignore the presence of her figure leaned against his, but not so close as to offer a hint of impropriety. He led her back to the entrance and motioned for the guard to stand down. They hesitated a moment uncertainly.

"Stand aside," the captain said. "As this woman is known in the castle, I see no further reason not to admit her."

The guardsman who spoke before bit his lip in consternation, but did not move. "Beg your pardon," he ventured, nervous at contradicting his superior in such a manner, "but Le Chevalier de Sens ordered we not admit anyone not resident on the grounds, even if they are known."

The watch captain straightened to his full height and glowered down on him. The fellow flinched back from the glare and returned to attention in the face of the rebuke to come.

"I am aware of Le Chevalier de Sens's command," the captain said, "but this gate is my responsibility, and he also trusts us to execute our own judgment. And I judge that this woman has valid reason for entering the castle. Am I understood?"

"Yes, Monsieur!"

"Good, now stand aside, and if there is any further question, I shall address it with Le Chevalier de Sens personally."

"Yes, Monsieur!"

The guards did as instructed, and, arm still threaded through hers, the captain led her past and opened the door to admit her. Elsabeth stepped inside with her basket balanced neatly on her hip, and the captain followed after.

'Tis almost unsporting.

ROBIN FOLDED HIS ARMS ACROSS HIS CHEST, AND SPIT D'ALLE with an irritated glare. The clockmaker slowly and deliberately fit the mechanism into the wooden tiller of the *gonne* and made a few adjustments. He could not begin to follow the turning of the screws, chains, bolts, and myriad other contraptions that made the entire engine work, nor name even one of its parts. A fact that d'Alle wasted no time in needling him over while he worked.

Four of the castle guard were posted within, doubled since the events of the day before. They would remain behind when he departed for other business to see to it that the clockmaker remained on task, and that no one entered without his authorization. Not even the maid who served d'Alle's meals (and, Robin suspected, provided other services not normally part of her duties in the castle) was permitted inside. He leaned against the desk and watched the elder man at work. That had certainly not been a pleasant directive to issue.

"You already keep me virtually prisoner down in this frigid dungeon, and now you deprive me of the only light and warmth I have had for weeks!" d'Alle had groused, and made a show of leveling the *gonne* on him when he checked the sights. Robin had been treated to an unwelcome view down the muzzle of the iron barrel, with the curious spiraling grooves carved into the inner surface just discernable under the dim lamplight.

"I apologize for the inconvenience," Robin had replied, with no genuine contrition in his tone, "but I am afraid you shall have to do without more than a warming pan for tonight."

"Bah! Don't punish me because your guards lack the discipline to resist a pretty face asking questions over too much drink."

"The measure is for your protection as much as the work. I don't know precisely what her plans are, but even you must agree 'twould be better to be cautious than to find your throat cut in the night."

That, at least, seemed to be enough to placate him, and d'Alle returned to his work. He fiddled now with some part of the *gonne* not working to his satisfaction, and largely ignored his intrusion on the workshop.

"How many have you assembled so far?" Robin ventured after a few long moments with only the clatter of d'Alle's tools to break the silence.

"The locks are all assembled, but I only just got the finished tillers and barrels back. This will be the first," d'Alle replied, far too nonchalant for Robin's taste.

He gawked down at the silver-haired little man, worrying over the baffling array of parts like some dwarven craftsman of minstrel's fancy. "You have not even finished *one*?"

D'Alle looked away and impaled him on an irritated glare. "The woodworkers you hired for the task cut the openings for the fittings too small, and some of the holes for the screws were out of place!" He mopped his face on a cloth so soiled with grime and oil it just left a long black streak across his features. "And the barrel did not fit its channel! I had to send it back to have it fixed."

Robin raked his hands back through his hair in exasperation. "The demonstration is tomorrow, man!"

The clockmaker turned the tiller in his hands and made a few more adjustments to the metal plate in the side. "Yes, I know." Again, the casual disinterest in his voice made Robin's finer hairs bristle in frustration.

"Monsieur de Carcassonne will not be pleased if these... contraptions fail to perform as you promised."

"And as I have told you time and time again, I am working as quickly as I can. But this is not work that can be rushed. 'Tis precision work and requires a delicate hand."

"And if they are not ready, you will have more than just your hands to worry about," Robin growled.

"Well, then perhaps you ought to go back upstairs to wave your authority around and let me work in peace!"

Robin's face heated at the dismissal. Unfortunately, he was well aware that he could do nothing to speed d'Alle's work, and trading barbs with the intractable fellow would accomplish nothing. He sighed and wearily pinched the bridge of his nose. Spies in the castle, the *gonnes* might very well not be ready as promised, and d'Alle's increasing demands on top of it.

"Just have it done. Everything is being moved to the main armory tonight."

ELSABETH PEEKED OUT OF THE CLOSET. SHE FOUND THE hallway deserted, so slipped out, straightened her dress and cap, and curled her lip distastefully as she wiped the corner of her mouth with her thumb.

The things I am doing for a thousand pfunde.

The watch captain, who followed her out before hastily returning to his post, had not been content to arrange meeting for later, and insisted on her demonstrating her "appreciation" immediately. So they slipped into the nearest convenient private place and she had appreciated him for a good part of the past hour, until he was satisfied and could no longer justify remaining away from his post. Fortunately, it got her into the castle, and she had more important concerns now than propriety and integrity.

Elsabeth quickly turned her attention back to her duties. Upon arriving at the laundry Rapine expressed surprise at seeing her not only admitted after the day before, but *early*, as well. But she gave no sign of finding her presence suspicious, and immediately sent her off to fetch linens still awaiting washing. She made her rounds of the castle and noted with growing apprehension it was not just the guard out in the bailey that had been increased, but within the halls as well. She made her way with her head lowered contritely, but her green eyes sweeping up and down the halls, taking careful note of the new postings and patrol routes.

I have confidence that I can create a sufficient fuss to put the plan in motion, but there are guards everywhere, now. 'Twill be much harder to get around without being spotted.

Of even greater concern, Elsabeth found her passage impeded on several occasions as she was stopped and both her person and laundry basket were searched. More than a few of the guard took liberties as they brushed her down, and Elsabeth weathered it as they expected of the frazzled and timid laundry maid run ragged by Mademoiselle Rapine. She also found herself restricted from a few areas and sent back whence she came. The guard was even heavier on the approach to the hallway leading to the dungeons where she and Kilianus suspected the clockmaker was kept, and today she was turned away immediately.

"There is nothing but trouble if you don't turn right around and go back the way you came!" said a stern-faced fellow dressed in brigandine, and a full array of steel poleyns, couters, vambraces, gauntlets, greaves, and sabatons, and carrying a halberd. He stepped to aggressively block her path, and Elsabeth was left with no doubt that any attempt to make it past him would be met with the blade of his polearm. Seeing such heavy armor on the castle guard set off warning bells in the back of her mind.

"Forgive me, Monsieur," she stammered, affecting a pitiable squeak of fright as she shrunk from his weapon. "I was told to collect washing from the guest rooms at the other end of the hall, and 'tis the swiftest way to that part of the castle! I have made this trip many times and 'twas never a problem before!"

The guardsman sighed patiently at the contrition in her voice and planted the butt of his halberd on the floor. "'Tis all right," he said, and his voice softened lest she lose her composure entirely. "But Le Chevalier de Sens has ordered this hall off-limits, and no one is to use it without his express consent."

Elsabeth chewed her lower lip. "I—I suppose I can go round. I did not know we were not to be going this way, truly! Do... do you know what 'tis all about? I have never seen the castle in such a state as this before! Is it because Monsieur de Carcassonne has returned?"

The guardsman leaned on his halberd and shrugged. "I can't say what 'tis all about. Certainly 'tis not because Monsieur le Comte is back, as I cannot recall the guard being called out in force like this when he was in residence in the past. Le Chevalier de Sens is aggrieved about something, though." He nodded his head back behind her. "Go on, now. I'll not tell anyone you were here, but you go on about your business."

She bowed her head deeply and scurried back up the hall again. As she looked for an alternate route to the far end of the hall and took note of the guards posted along the way, Elsabeth wondered if perhaps her actions at Isabeau's had roused some suspicion. She promptly forced such thoughts from her mind. Had she been recognized she almost certainly would have been greeted with an arrest when she arrived at the castle. And if the guard *were* on alert, she could not afford to let it interfere. No matter her concerns, all she could do now was learn as much as she could. They would simply have to contend with the change in the guard as best they could when the time came.

Nonetheless, Elsabeth could not shake off her disquiet over how much harder her job just became.

ROBIN LEANED AGAINST THE SWORD AT HIS HIP AND watched the train of workers crossing the darkened bailey. Above, the sky was almost black, and even the stars and moon were veiled. The bailey itself was lit only by widely spaced lamps, casting small islands of golden light that glittered on the churned-up slush and snow within. A chill wind whistled through the crenellations of the battlements and tugged at the cloak cast over his armor, and his misting breath hung in the air for only a moment before it was carried away in a tattered cloud of vapor.

D'Alle stood beside him, bundled up in several layers of wool and fur, and stamping his feet in a vain effort to keep warm. His boots squished into the snow and mud underfoot, and he huddled against the bite of the wind. Robin had offered the clockmaker to remain in his workshop or to warm himself in the armory while laborers moved his equipment, but d'Alle insisted on supervising himself.

A canopied platform from which de Carcassonne could watch tomorrow's demonstrations had been erected in one corner of the bailey, opposite an embankment of earth piled against the wall of the enceinte. Stands lined the makeshift shooting range on either side for other guests, all to d'Alle's exacting specifications.

Whether or not the *gonnes* actually worked, the clockmaker would at least have a fine venue to play in.

Guards — thrice the number normally required for such a late hour — patrolled the walls and flanked the entrance to the keep, armory, and barracks nearest the main gate. Robin ground his teeth. So far there had been no further sign of the woman who attacked Pierre, though he had ordered a thorough sweep of the City. Nor was there any further disturbance that suggested something untoward was afoot. All he could do now was wait and see if the spy made a move. The guards stopped each worker, including d'Alle's own assistants and laborers from the castle, and searched them and their payload before allowing them to proceed, but though it slowed the transfer of the *gonnes* and d'Alle's equipment, the move proceeded smoothly.

"I still say this is all unnecessary," d'Alle groused, as yet another of his apprentices was stopped upon emerging from the keep. He bore a long bundle wrapped in thick blankets which, Robin suspected, was one of the new weapons assembled that evening. The watch captain gave the bundle a good looking-over, then nodded and directed him to rejoin the train of baggage. By now a clearly-defined path had been trampled into the snow, and the bare, brown grass was visible through the slush. "If you would just wait for everything to arrive in the armory before inspection 'twould be finished by now."

"I assure you, Monsieur, that it is," Robin said. "There are any number of points between the vaults and the armory where your equipment could be intercepted, and I'll not take that chance."

"Hmph. It would be the coldest night of the year."

"And as I have already offered, you can always wait inside."

"Bah!" d'Alle barked. "And let one of these clumsy oafs drop another of my *gonnes*? I already had to take one apart to get the snow out of the mechanism, and will have to put it back together again."

"You can be silent, then," Robin growled, in no further mood to entertain the clockmaker's complaints. "The Lord of All knows that I could use a break from your grumbling."

D'Alle was just opening his mouth to retort when a guardsman forced his way through the door and hurried across the snowy bailey as quickly as his footing allowed. Robin stepped away from the clockmaker to meet him, as much for the excuse to escape the man's presence for a blessed moment as any eagerness to hear whatever news the messenger bore. As he drew nearer, Robin noted a bemused expression on a face quickly reddening from the bite of the winter chill. His breath escaped in great clouds of vapor, betraying the urgency which drove him out into the yard. A small thrill worked its way along Robin's spine, and his hand on the pommel of his sword tightened.

What the Devil is this? Some news of our mystery woman?

"Monsieur!" the guardsman panted upon reaching him. Apparently, he had been running even before he stepped out of the castle. He skidded to a halt, and his legs nearly came out from underneath him in the slippery mud and slush covering the bailey. Robin darted out one hand to catch him by the arm and steady him on his feet.

"Yes, Nouel, what is it?" He replied calmly, not allowing his sudden burst of anxiety to tell upon his voice or features.

"Monsieur, I think you had best come quickly. There has been something of a disturbance in the castle."

The sudden thrill turned into icy daggers lancing through him, and Robin looked at him sharply. "What manner of disturbance?"

"Ah, I think 'twould be best should you see it for yourself, Monsieur."

Robin sighed. *If there is trouble I would rather the fool out and say so!* However, he quickly mastered his frustration; it would do no good to berate the fellow here in the cold, or let the others see him give way to panic. He quickly made a sign to one of the other guardsmen supervising the move and waved him over.

"Monsieur?" the guard said from within the folds of his cloak. Robin could not see his face clearly between the dark and the heavy bundles of wool shielding him from the chill, but recognized the voice. He frowned.

"Pierre? What are you doing out here?"

Pierre shifted anxiously from foot to foot. "Ah, the surgeon cleared me, Monsieur. He can't say what it was that hit me, but it passed after a time. And I agreed to take Thibault's shift so he could be with his wife tonight; she is ripe and ready to burst, and I daren't keep the man away in a time like that. And since I missed my own watch earlier today I figured—"

Robin sighed and cut him off with a wave of his hand. "All right, all right. And I will at least consider your initiative when I decide what to do with you, but now is not the time. Take over here and keep an eye on things. I should be back shortly."

Pierre straightened suddenly and presented his halberd. Though Robin could not see his features, he nonetheless imagined the determined expression at being offered such an opportunity to redeem himself in Robin's eyes. "Yes, Monsieur!"

Robin shook his head and fell into step with the messenger. "Come on then, let us see what this is about."

HE CAUSE OF THE DISTURBANCE WAS IMMEDIATELY evident upon their arrival in the main hall. As the guard led him inside, he spotted the commotion near one of the delicately engraved panels decorating the wall behind the dais. A large crowd of onlookers had gathered around the Laurens household steward, Rapine, and another figure kneeling in front of the panel. A woman's sobs filled the hall, and as Robin drew nearer he could just make out Rapine glowering down with her hands planted on her hips, while Laurens, for his part, shifted uncomfortably at the spectacle.

Robin pushed through the crowd, and upon reaching the middle found himself looking down on the new laundry maid, shaking and wailing quite uncontrollably. Her copper hair peeked out from beneath her cap, and she buried her face in her hands. He frowned thoughtfully at finding her here; he had commanded the guard allow no one from town entry without prior approval, and if he remembered rightly, she made her residence outside the castle.

It seems I need to have another word with the watch captains as to the meaning of "no entry."

That thought gave him pause, and he scrutinized her carefully through narrowed eyes. She had, to his knowledge, only been in the city for perhaps a fortnight, and had been quickly placed with the laundry staff. However, she was also easily recognizable with her burnished copper hair, green eyes, and height. Her plain woolen cotehardie, though not unflattering, offered little fodder to the imagination unless one were to stand almost over her shoulder. Her figure was distinctly feminine, but though her bust was not particularly modest, she did not possess the abundance Pierre ascribed to his attacker.

Unless she has been binding herself to disguise her shape. But what little other description Pierre and Isabeau's girl offered is missing a few particulars.

Upon breaking into the middle of the circle, the root cause of the commotion became immediately clear: One of the decorative wooden panels had been smashed. A table was overturned, and the maid's laundry basket lay on its side on the floor with its contents of linens spilled across the dais.

"...stupid, useless, clumsy..." Rapine was saying, before trailing off at the sight of his arrival.

"Laurens," he said patiently. "What is the meaning of this?"

"Monsieur!" Laurens said, and bowed deeply. Rapine greeted him with a deep curtsey. The maid remained on her knees sobbing into her hands. "I am sorry for the interruption, Monsieur, but there has been an accident."

The steward unnecessarily indicated the smashed panel.

"What happened?"

Rapine, in her pique forgetting her station, clicked her tongue in annoyance. "Oh! 'Tis this stupid, useless girl!" she growled. Robin was half-tempted to chastise her over speaking out of turn, much less the fact that the other maid was only a few short years her junior. "I have said time and time again she is wholly unsuited to this posting, but Mademoiselle Oudette will hear nothing of it!"

"Laurens?" Robin inquired when Rapine had finished venting.

"Well, Monsieur," Laurens said, and glared at Rapine. The laundry maid's face heated at the unspoken rebuke and fell silent. "I was making the rounds to check on the last of the preparations in the hall for tonight's supper when I heard a crash, and I arrived to find the girl making quite the fuss on the floor, and the panel completely shattered. I confess I lost my temper, Monsieur, and that is when the poor thing fell into this fit. Well, I could not console her, and frankly I was unsure how to handle the matter, so I called Mademoiselle Rapine to take charge of her. But

Mademoiselle Rapine all but exploded on her and that just made matters worse!"

Laurens indicated the onlookers pressing in for a glimpse of what had stirred up so much excitement in the hall. "And that commotion just drew this crowd. I thought it best before things got out of hand that I call on you."

Robin sighed and pinched his nose against a brewing headache. "Laurens... 'Tis a single distraught woman and you could not manage that?"

"Forgive me, Monsieur, but Monsieur de Carcassonne is entertaining guests tonight in advance of tomorrow's festivities, and coming in and seeing the mess I... I am afraid I let a few words slip I ought not to use upon any woman."

He rolled his eyes and lowered himself to a knee beside the maid. "All right, now. All right!" he said sternly, but calmly. "What is this all about, Mademoiselle? What happened?"

The woman shuddered and continued to bawl into her hands. The only intelligible thing he could make out was her apologizing over and over again.

Robin turned away from her and fixed his eyes on his escort. "Clear this room. Get them out of here!" He swept his hand across the crowd in emphasis. The guard nodded and, with help from a few others loitering about the hall, went to work dispersing the onlookers. Robin turned back to the maid, and after a moment of hesitation laid a hand on her shoulder.

"Come now, that is enough!" he said sharply. "There is no time for that. What happened?"

She shuddered under his hand as she took a ragged, steadying breath, and wiped her face on her sleeve. Her green eyes were red-rimmed and puffy, and tears stained her cheeks.

"I am so, so sorry, Monsieur!" she wailed, and her voice trembled. "Please don't throw me from the castle. I desperately need the work because my husband has been ill the last few days. I did not mean to do it! I swear 'twas an accident!"

"What was an accident?"

"I—I had a load of linens to bring up from the laundry, including the cloth for the high table. I was just bringing it when I suppose I must have trod on a corner of it that had fallen from the basket. I tried to catch myself on the table, but all I did was trip myself up, and then I was stumbling into the wall and there was a horrible sound and I was on the floor and when I looked up again, I ..."

She trailed off into and inelegant and blubbering wail, and buried her face in her hands once more.

"You what?" he prodded.

The woman sniffled once she mastered herself again, and pointed helplessly at the damaged panel and the pieces of broken wood lying on the floor beneath it. "I saw that I had broken this lovely panel! Please! I swear 'twas an accident!"

Robin heaved a sigh. *I can't decide whether I would rather deal with this or d'Alle.* He looked up at Laurens, who fidgeted uncomfortably in the face of the maid's distress.

"When were Monsieur le Comte's guests supposed to gather?" he asked.

"A few hours," Laurens replied, and straightened with his hands behind his back in a most official-looking manner. "'Tis a somewhat late supper, but you know Monsieur le Comte."

"Yes, I do." Robin returned to his feet again and inspected the panel. It depicted a scene of the Comte de Carcassonne on the hunt in dark imported ebony over a lighter background, with many elaborately-graven trees, flowers, and beasts of an incalculable variety. The figure of de Carcassonne was among the many pieces lying now on the floor. "'Twould not reflect well on Monsieur le Comte if his guests should see it in such a state, and I am sure he would not be pleased if it were to be covered while he is entertaining. Can it be repaired, and in haste?"

Laurens shrugged helplessly. "I cannot begin to say, Monsieur. I only manage the house, and such craft is beyond me."

"I—If you need it repaired my husband could," the maid said from the floor with a trembling voice. Robin returned his gaze to her, and she now huddled hugging herself tightly. "He has been ill, but I am sure he could!"

"Your husband?"

"He is a woodworker, I think, Monsieur," Rapine replied, and folded her arms across her chest as she glared down at the other woman. "One of the craftsmen who has been working on the grounds the past few months, or so she says. She is always babbling on about this or the other, and says she has been late for her work in the laundry on his account more than once."

"I have seen them enter and take their meals together," Laurens offered. "He has been with the work crews for at least a month or so, and I have called on him once or twice with some odd or end that needed addressing."

"Has your husband a name, Mademoiselle?" Robin asked.

The maid nodded her head eagerly. "Yes, Monsieur! His name is Jacquemart. And I am sure he could fix the panel in no time!"

Robin pinched his nose in frustration. With the demonstration so near he was seeing spies in every cupboard, and another body in the castle was the last thing he wished to concern himself with. However, it was also best if Monsieur le Comte were never to learn of the damage to a panel he had commissioned at great expense. The dueling priorities of security and preventing a tantrum waged a war for prominence, but there was only one way such a battle would end. He sighed and shook his head.

"Laurens, with me," he said, and stepped away from the maid and Rapine. Laurens followed him so they could converse in confidence.

"Monsieur?" Laurens asked, once they had retreated from the dais and out of earshot.

"Have a messenger summon Monsieur Jacquemart and bring him here under my authority. He is only to bring whatever tools of his trade are required for the job. And I want him and his wife watched so long as he is present. Rapine can manage the woman, but have a guard posted. Once they are finished, they are to be escorted from the castle immediately. Am I understood?"

Laurens bowed stiffly at the waist. "As you command, Monsieur!"

"Good. Lord of All knows I have enough worries now without them adding to it." He clapped the house steward on the shoulder. "See to it."

16

T WAS PERHAPS AN HOUR BEFORE A MESSENGER
returned with Kilianus in tow. Elsabeth had been
helped up from the floor and put in a chair with a
cup of beer to steady herself by Laurens, the house
steward. She sat with it clasped between her hands and her head
bowed over it, sipping at it in an appropriately meek fashion while
watching the goings on around them from beneath her brows.
Rapine and Laurens, along with a single guardsman, waited in the
great hall. Elsabeth chided herself over this development.

*With how security has been tightened I should have known they would
not let Kilianus or me have a free run of the castle now. Fortunately, 'tis just
the one guard, but I don't know that he can be disabled quietly with the steward
and that irritating cow at hand.*

She considered her options while she waited, but had not yet
come up with a plan when the door was flung open and two
guardsmen escorted Kilianus into the room. He carried his toolbox
with him and bundled himself up under several cloaks. He coughed
and wheezed into his hand, as one ought to expect of an ill man at
this season. Nonetheless, when he briefly met her eye, his were
clear and sharp, and she read the tension in his limbs and body,
betraying that beneath the many layers of wool he was ready to
leap into motion.

"There you are!" he said, and nothing in his voice would give away his illness was but a feint. Elsabeth had to quietly admit he could play his part quite well. "I was expecting you home more than an hour ago, and instead I have the castle guard pounding at our door!"

He may cast a dim view of my manner of deception, but the man is certainly well-practiced in the game himself.

Elsabeth shrunk into the collar of her dress and hung her head, suitably chagrined, and did not respond.

"Are you this woman's husband, Monsieur?" Laurens asked, and stepped down from the dais to meet him with his hands folded behind his back in a most officious fashion. He tilted back his head to look down his nose on Kilianus, which was quite an impressive feat considering even *she* was nearly a head taller.

"I am, Monsieur. And what sort of trouble has she caused now? Lord of All knows how she manages to keep our lodgings in order without burning the entire building to the ground."

Rapine barked out a laugh. "If she keeps house as well as she manages the laundry 'tis a wonder you have not thrown her out. Or maybe 'tis not an illness of the season afflicting you, but a surfeit of her cooking!"

Elsabeth gritted her teeth and her face heated indignantly. *Hieronymus may scoff at my cooking but 'tis hardly poisonous! Oh! What I would not give to drown you in the piss bucket in the laundry.*

Elsabeth did not have to speak in her own defense, however, for Laurens interjected with a sharp glare that silenced her. "That is enough of that, Rapine. With the hard time you give all the new maids in the laundry 'tis a wonder that the entire staff has not been driven mad."

Laurens dismissed the two guards flanking Kilianus and directed him up the dais. "Here, Monsieur, you shall see the trouble. Monsieur le Comte is expecting guests within a few hours, and this panel was damaged after an accident."

Kilianus approached the damaged panel and its pieces lying on the floor and set his toolbox down. He stooped to pick up one of the broken parts and turned it in his hands.

"A pity. This was quite well-crafted, and by a master at that."

"Yes, and 'tis imperative it be repaired. Are you able to the task, Monsieur?"

Kilianus frowned at him and affected a dumbstruck expression. "Repaired?"

"Yes, repaired," Laurens repeated. "Your wife insists that you would be able to, though I imagine as much out of panic at the thought of what Monsieur de Carcassonne may do in retribution."

Rapine sniffed, and Elsabeth — still sitting with her head bowed shamefully — felt the looking over she gave her. "Oh, I am sure Monsieur le Comte could be persuaded to offer his forgiveness without this charade."

Laurens speared her with a warning glare, and Rapine fell silent again. Elsabeth clenched her fists around the cup in her hands to restrain herself from wrapping them round the maid's throat.

"Monsieur, this is the work of an artist," Kilianus said, not rising to the bait. "I am but a humble carpenter. I have carved a few trinkets myself for the local children, but this..." He lifted the piece he had been examining for emphasis. "Nothing approaching this quality."

"Monsieur, no one is expecting you to carve a whole panel to replace it. Certainly as there is not the time! But surely you could piece it back together from the fragments. At least well enough to last through supper."

Kilianus made a show of examining the panel again for a few long moments, then heaved a sigh and shrugged. "I suppose I could fit enough of it back together to pass muster, so long as Monsieur le Comte does not intend to show it to anyone too closely."

"That will be acceptable. However, I should advise you that you shan't be paid for this task. Le Chevalier de Sens has promised that so long as 'tis done quickly, he shall overlook your wife's behavior in recompense." Laurens very deliberately fixed his eyes on Kilianus'. "I do believe that is a more than generous offer."

Kilianus inclined his head contritely with a nod. "Yes, I would concede it to be so."

"Good. Then I shall leave you to it."

"You will not be supervising?"

Laurens straightened indignantly. "Monsieur, I have matters of greater import to attend to than keeping watch over such menial tasks." He motioned to the guardsman posted nearby atop the dais. "The guard will see to it you complete your task, and then escort yourself and your wife from the premises afterwards. Le Chevalier de Sens will then decide whether your wife may continue her employment in the laundry."

Rapine harrumphed. "'Twould be more than the lazy ox deserves," she murmured, loud enough for Elsabeth to hear but not so much as to draw another rebuke from Laurens. Elsabeth bristled.

Kilianus sighed and offered another nod. "Very well. Then if I may, Monsieur, I ought to get to work. 'Twill take some time to review the damage and see how it all fits back together."

"Very good. If you have need of anything, Rapine can send for it. Good night, Monsieur."

And with that, Laurens stepped down from the dais and made his way out of the hall, leaving her and Kilianus alone with Rapine and the guard.

"Agnez," Kilianus said, "Come here and help me pick all of this up."

Elsabeth made a show of finishing her drink and dabbing her mouth dry on a cloth, then slipped from her chair and crossed the dais to join Kilianus over the wood fragments scattered on the floor. She knotted her hands in her skirt and kept her head bowed, though she carefully considered Rapine and the remaining guardsman. The two were far enough away she would not be able to draw the guard's attention for Kilianus to deal with without the maid raising an alarm before she could be silenced.

Well, it seems we will likely have to manage them both at once. I don't like my prospects of wrestling with an armed and armored guardsman in naught but a dress and without my sword.

She reached Kilianus' side and lowered herself to the floor, making a show of gathering up the pieces and placing them in a compartment of his toolbox. Kilianus flicked his eyes between Rapine and the guard with consternation, and Elsabeth offered a subtle shrug. They dared not speak lest their voices carry, but this close to one another their hands were partly shielded from view.

Elsabeth slid two fragments of the carving beside one another, and quickly pointed between them, herself, and Kilianus. He gave a short nod of understanding.

This is us.

She then placed two other pieces roughly where the guard and Rapine waited for them to finish their task and pointed again.

The guard and the maid.

Kilianus motioned at the pieces and made a sign.

We will have to take them both together.

Elsabeth gave a short nod, and moved her piece to the maid's, and Kilianus' to the guard's.

I'll handle her, you take out the guard.

Kilianus nodded in turn, then swept up those pieces and added them to his toolbox. He slipped a hammer from the tray, stood, and offered her a hand up. Elsabeth accepted the help back to her feet. She brushed out her skirts before turning to Rapine. The maid watched her approach with unconcealed disdain, looking haughtily down her nose at her. Elsabeth did not immediately abandon her meek affectation, and drew nearer with her hands clasped contritely before her, and her head bowed. She watched Kilianus from the corner of her eye; he approached the panel with his hammer in hand and made a show of prying loose one of the damaged pieces still partly hanging in place.

"Pardon me, Mademoiselle Rapine," Elsabeth said, and stepped up to the other.

Rapine folded her arms across her breast and scowled at her. "What do you want now? Do you know how much of my own work you are keeping me from?"

Elsabeth lowered her hands to her side and bunched one fist. She straightened suddenly to her full height, and the disdain etched on Rapine's features melted away and was replaced by an expression not unlike that of a deer caught on a road with a speeding carriage bearing down upon it as Elsabeth's lip pulled up into a malicious smirk. "Sorry, love, but you are going to be kept from it a bit longer."

Her hand flew in a sudden and vicious right hook that connected squarely with the corner of Rapine's jaw. The maid spun into the floor with a loud *whump*. The guardsman called out and sprinted across the dais to break them up, but he did not make it more than a handful of paces before Kilianus turned and drove the handle of his hammer into his gut. The air left the guard's lungs in a sickening grunt as he was practically lifted from the floor, and his halberd clattered to the ground. A follow-up strike below the chin snapped his head back, and blood arced from his mouth. He went down in a heap and lay unmoving.

Rapine, moaning on the floor at Elsabeth's feet, had scrambled away on her hands and knees, far enough away to stagger back to her feet. A ferocious purple bruise marked the side of her face, and she swayed unsteadily for a moment before making an ill-advised attempt to rush her with an awkward and unbalanced swing of her fist. Elsabeth effortlessly guided the blow past her face, caught the maid by the wrist, and twisted her into an arm bar. Rapine yelped as Elsabeth jerked up on her wrist and pressed down against her elbow in one sharp motion, and used her leverage to drive the maid's face into the floor.

Elsabeth dropped heavily over her prostrate figure, and buried her knee into her back.

"You know, I have wanted to do that for a good two weeks, now," she said. "I can't say I have felt this good about punching someone in the face in a while."

"Bitch!" Rapine hissed impotently, and from the way her voice wavered Elsabeth suspected she knew just how powerless she really was. "Let me go!"

"Oh, shut up. Just be happy 'tis just your arm I have hold of, and that we are not in the laundry right now or I would have your face in one of the piss pots!" Elsabeth lowered her head next to Rapine's, and was satisfied at the fright in her eyes. "Now, love, I suggest in the future you might want to reconsider how you treat the other maids. I could snap your arm in two right now, and I would rather enjoy it. But I think I will leave you with the reminder of what 'tis like to feel so powerless yourself. Good night!"

And with that, Elsabeth knotted a hand in her hair, and slammed her face against the floor. Rapine let out a muffled yelp and lay unmoving.

"Are you quite finished?" Kilianus asked.

Elsabeth returned to her feet and flipped the maid onto her back with one toe. "Oh hush," she said. "I have been waiting two weeks for that. So what now? We did not exactly count on the guard being redoubled tonight, and it seems that we shan't get anywhere unescorted."

Kilianus returned his hammer to the toolbox and considered for a moment.

"I agree. I suppose you could fuck us into the armory, seeing as you much favor that strategy." She spit him with an indignant glare, but Kilianus paid her no heed and instead looked thoughtfully at the guard. "This fellow looks to be about your size."

Elsabeth's face heated. "I would be very careful about where that line of thought is taking you, love."

"Have a look for yourself."

She stepped up beside Kilianus and regarded the guardsman lying unconscious on the floor. His kettle helm had fallen off under the force of the blows, and she had a good look at his features now. They were youthful, and sure enough he was rather slight of build and perhaps only an inch or two taller than her. Elsabeth heaved a sigh and pinched the bridge of her nose as she pieced together Kilianus' intent.

"I am too broad in the shoulders to fit his garb," he said thoughtfully, "but you are slim enough it ought to work."

"While I appreciate you correcting yourself, you are also supposed to be the bloody professional. Instead, I think you have listened to a few too many minstrel's fancies. You ought to know this trick rarely holds up to scrutiny. The first guard we meet is sure to notice a few particulars of my anatomy that even a brigandine shan't mask. To say nothing if I must speak, or if they ask for a password."

"'Twill hold up well enough for our purposes so long as we can keep our distance and avoid a direct confrontation. From afar they ought not to notice your figure, and would just pass off your features as a youth. There is your hair, but that could be stuffed inside the helm easily enough."

Elsabeth twisted her lip irritably. "I still say 'tis not likely to get us far."

"Well, if you have a better idea I am waiting to hear it," he said. A soft and pitiable moan behind them drew their attention, and Elsabeth glanced over her shoulder to find Rapine stirring. "However, I suggest you offer it quickly or else we will lose our opportunity."

Elsabeth sighed again in frustration.

The things I am doing for a thousand pfunde.

17

ELSABETH GATHERED UP HER HAIR, KNOTTED IT AS best she could, and stuffed it into the kettle helm. It was just large enough that her long copper tresses piled neatly inside and helped the helm fit snugly over her head. She adjusted the fit of the armor and tabard — the former was long enough to hide her dress and chemise after tearing them off about the knee — stuffed her rondel through the belt at her waist, and, once satisfied her appearance would pass muster from a distance, snatched up the fallen halberd.

Kilianus busied himself using the torn off portion of her skirts to tie and gag Rapine and the guardsman before stuffing them into a cabinet just large enough to fit the two comfortably. The latter still lay unconscious with his back propped against one side, but the maid had regained her senses again, and now watched them both with frightened eyes wide as saucers. Elsabeth knelt beside Kilianus with the halberd stood upright in one hand.

"Be sure to make the bonds good and tight, love," Elsabeth said unnecessarily, but with a meaningful look at Rapine. "Especially the one round this one's mouth."

"I do know my business," he replied, in just the sort of conversational tone that would give Rapine little reason to doubt his word.

"I just don't want to have to come back and deal with her because she slipped a knot."

"We don't exactly have the time to dispose of them properly."

Elsabeth flashed a malicious smile at the maid, whose face promptly drained of color. "Fortunately, I have spent enough time running linens and garbage round this castle when I was not up to my elbows in piss and weathering all manner of insults to have learned quite a few places where a body might never be found. And there is always the lye in the laundry."

Kilianus finished what he was doing and gave Rapine a gentle slap of reassurance on the shoulder. "Perhaps if you are good. But for now, we have more pressing matters."

"Tch. Don't spoil my fun." She met Rapine's eyes. "Do behave yourself. I suggest you be nice and quiet for a time, you don't want to give me reason to come back for you, do you?"

Rapine hastily shook her head. Elsabeth chuckled and gave her a playful pat on the cheek. She levered herself to her feet with the halberd and stepped away so Kilianus could close and latch the cabinet. There was no key, but it could not be opened from the inside. Once finished, Kilianus gathered up his toolbox, and together they stepped from the great hall.

"We best be quick," Elsabeth said as they started off through the castle. "I don't know whether the steward will be back to check up on us, and even if no one lets them out it shan't take them long to realize something is out of sorts when they find both us and that guardsman gone."

They followed a circuitous route avoiding the more heavily trafficked areas and bore for a less used service door nearer the rear where they hoped to gain access to the grounds without being challenged. The rattle of her acquired brigandine and helm sounded deafening to her ears in the close confines of the hallways, and she expected to hear the telltale cry that would be their only warning they had been discovered at any moment.

Kilianus nodded his agreement as they walked. "I had not expected to see security heightened like this. Oh, a few extra guards once de Carcassonne returned, but nothing like this. Up 'til now their entire operation had been discreet, and I expected them to continue to rely on secrecy."

They rounded a corner and spied two of the domestic staff at the far end of the corridor. They checked their pace to let them pass without being too obvious about it. "I can think of a couple possibilities," Elsabeth mused. "At best, we simply underestimated de Sens's devotion to security."

"And the other I suppose is that he or someone else suspects trouble," Kilianus finished for her. There was nothing accusatory in his tone, but Elsabeth heated nonetheless in chagrin.

I have not seen the fellow from Isabeau's today, and that damned powder is always so finicky. Especially if someone has been drinking to excess already. If he was out too long and someone came looking for him 'twould like as not stir up suspicion. A dead guard would almost certainly.

"There is nothing we can do about it now," she conceded with a short sigh. "We best be ready to improvise further. Fortunately, it seems we both have the same gift for it. At least well enough to play on one another. Have you any mind how we'll actually make it *into* the armory? I don't want to dwell on the negative, but I would like to remind you this disguise shan't hold up at more than a few dozen paces in anything other than total darkness. And not at all if I have to speak."

"I am still working on it. As you say, at this point we may need to improvise."

Elsabeth glanced sidelong at him, but Kilianus' expression was frustratingly unreadable and uncomfortably like Hieronymus' confessor's face, which had contributed no small amount of her traveling allowance to his pots at the gaming tables over the past four years.

After a few minutes they reached a small side exit not far from the kitchens. The door stood open allowing the staff to slip in and out with trash destined for the midden heap. And though there was light traffic passing through, Elsabeth noted with satisfaction it was unguarded.

If I recall the layout rightly, we are not quite all the way round back by the laundry. Like as not the guards are content anyone trying to slip in unnoticed would be intercepted long before they could get this far.

She kept her helmet pulled low over her face and they waited for a momentary break in the flow of people moving in and out. When it came, they quickened their pace and hurried through. Fortunately, anyone nearby was too concerned with their own business to give them more than a cursory look.

They probably think I am escorting Kilianus out after his day's work. Well, the new security may at least be working in our favor for the moment.

A sudden blast of cold struck Elsabeth as she and Kilianus stepped out into the partly melted slush piled around the door. Though it was only a small service door, it was heavy and a good two feet of solid oak timbers thick, framed and cross-braced with iron, and its hinges were buried deeply into the stonework to reinforce it in the case of an assault. Lamps hung on either side and cast a dull circle of flickering golden light around the entrance, but beyond was darkness broken only by widely spaced lamps on the inner surface of the enceinte ringing the bailey. Elsabeth shivered as the biting winter gusts clawed through the thin woolen lining of her armor, and within moments her ears throbbed and her hands on the wooden shaft of the halberd went numb. Her breath hung in the air momentarily before it was shredded by the wind.

"Well," she said in a low voice only just audible over the mournful howling of the wind. "The first stage is over; we are out of the keep."

"The second ought not to be too trying," Kilianus replied in kind. "I have not noticed the bailey to be heavily watched. Most of the guards are on the walls, or at the armory and barracks."

Elsabeth frowned at him, but in the darkness all she could see was a dark shadow against the faint greyish light reflecting off the snow-swept bailey. "Need I remind you that so happens to be our destination."

"If it makes you feel better to nag. Though it has been my foremost thought."

She spit him on her glare, but the sharp look was lost on him in the darkness. They reached the corner of the keep and turned again. Ahead, a long space with a berm of dirt piled high at one end and flanked by grandstands occupied a space fronting the wall, and beside it was the barracks and main armory. A fire burned outside the barracks beneath a sheltered awning, with a number of men gathered round it. Others stood watch both on the walls, and in front of the outbuildings themselves.

"If you have worked up a plan I am listening," she said, unable to mask her impatience as it escaped in a sing-song lilt in her voice.

"Half a moment, just keep walking towards them." Again, Kilianus' thoughts were masked from her, and her finer hairs bristled when she recognized Cuncz's flippant cavalierness at any little change in fortune in his tone.

"'Twill not be half a moment before they see us and someone comes to find out what we are doing out here."

No sooner were the words out of her mouth, then someone at the fire stood up and pointed in their direction. There was no call of alarm — at the very least reassuring Elsabeth that it was only curiosity over what would bring anyone out of the castle in such dreadful cold and not wariness that something was amiss that caught their attention — but nonetheless the sentries on duty broke away from their post and started towards them.

"Bugger," she grumbled. "We won't make it within a sprint of the armory before someone notices a few particulars of my anatomy that will betray this whole gambit."

"Just be ready to move. Get to the armory. Grab one of the *gonnes* and get out any way you can."

The matter-of-factness in Kilianus' instructions sent a chill lancing down Elsabeth's spine, and her stomach began to knot around itself.

"What do you mean, 'be ready?' What are you planning to do?"

"We need a distraction. I do apologize for this, but we don't have a lot of options."

Elsabeth frowned. "Apologize for w—"

She never had a chance to finish. With speed belying his size, Kilianus dropped his toolbox, seized her roughly by the arm, and yanked her around to face him. Elsabeth let out a sharp yelp as her body twisted helplessly in his grip; the movement came so suddenly and unexpectedly she did not have time to set her feet, and even then, the wet slush blanketing the bailey cheated her of her footing.

And then her vision flashed, and she felt her body lifted up into the air.

Elsabeth came down hard on her side in the cold and wet, and for a moment she could not decide what surprised her more: The icy shock of snow on her face, or the sharp and throbbing pain where Kilianus' fist had connected with her jaw.

It was a masterfully placed blow, just enough to daze her and put her on the ground, and yet not one that would have put her out entirely. Her vision spun and for a moment Elsabeth could not decide whether the stars across her eyes were from the force of the hit, torchlight on the snow, or wheeling in the night sky above. She furiously shook her head to clear her eyes and spotted Kilianus speeding across the bailey and melting into the darkness. The guards were in two groups: Most charged after Kilianus in pursuit, while another knot of three or four rushed to her side.

Elsabeth scrambled against the slush but only managed to get to one knee. Her halberd was still in hand, so she propped it against the ground for support. Fortunately, her wits cleared enough to piece together Kilianus' intent, though she little liked the lack of warning, and she hastily waved the oncoming guards off.

"Don't worry about me!" she called out, trying to lower her voice as best she could and hoping that the sudden confusion would distract them enough they would not question its pitch. "After the intruder! Quick! I think he means harm against Monsieur de Carcassonne!"

"Come on!" a rough voice barked, likely a veteran of the guard. "You see to him, you with me, the rest get after him with the others!"

Elsabeth peered up from beneath the brim of her helm and watched him point to the men gathered round. Most sped off in the direction Kilianus fled. He and another turned for the castle. The last remained behind and crossed the remaining space between them in a few long strides. He was not armed that Elsabeth could see, and was bundled up against the cold with a cloak, hood, and several layers of clothing. She did not hear the rattle of armor.

The fellow rushed to her side and held out a hand.

"Come on lad, up we go, and we best get you to the fire ..."

He trailed off when Elsabeth took his hand and met his eyes as he helped her to her feet, and the mustachioed man from Isabeau's mouth dropped open in shock.

"You!"

"Thank you, love," she said. "But I must be going."

And before he could cry out a warning Elsabeth struck a hard rising blow with the butt end of the halberd right between his legs. All the air rushed from his lungs in a sickening wheezing grunt, and he doubled over clutching his manhood in agony. She reversed her strike in a sharp falling cut with the halberd shaft that caught him at the base of the neck across the shoulders, and he went down in a heap with a wet *squish* into the slush.

"I am sorry, but you really are having a bad run of luck."

His only response was a pitiable grunt muffled by the wet snow in his mouth.

Elsabeth considered the dazed guardsman for a moment, then hastily relieved him of his cloak and tossed it round her shoulders. It was already soaked through and covered with a dusting of snow, so did little to offer her warmth, but it would help to better disguise her figure from prying eyes.

She quickly surveyed the bailey. All around her was quiet but the ruckus Kilianus' flight stirred up echoed across the grounds. Nor did she note anyone else near at hand. It seemed that for the moment everyone had been successfully drawn off, leaving her alone in the bailey. She considered the guardsman lying crumpled in the snow and sighed.

I don't quite have the heart to leave the poor bastard to freeze to death. And 'twill only raise the alarm that much quicker if he is found lying out here. So I best get this fellow out of sight.

Elsabeth dropped her halberd and bent over to grab him beneath the armpits. With a grunt and a curse over his weight she lifted him up as best she could, and dragged him as quickly as her uncertain footing allowed towards the armory and barracks.

18

OBIN PASSED THROUGH THE HALLWAYS AT A BRISK pace with d'Alle close at his heels. The summons from de Carcassonne came just as the last of the *gonnes* and the clockmaker's equipment had been secured in the armory. Fortunately, no time was lost despite his distraction with the laundry maid and her husband, and for that Robin considered loosening his hold on the noose round Pierre's neck.

'Twould be a waste as he is indeed a good man when he has not had too much to drink. And perhaps keeping him away from Isabeau's will be enough to straighten him out.

Nonetheless, Robin gritted his teeth at the thought of yet another disruption of his duties. He was certain there was still a spy about, and he would not be at ease again until d'Alle and his *gonnes* were off to Domme and in the care of the King's men.

His path through the castle led him up a winding stairwell to the second level, and back through a series of passages connecting to private quarters for guests staying within the keep itself, rather than guest houses elsewhere on the grounds or within the city. Guards stood sentinel at important junctures, so that no one could pass unchallenged, and servants scattered out of his way. They bowed their heads when he passed, but he paid them no mind.

The furnishings here were more luxurious: plush carpeting and decorative hangings, chairs with velvet cushions, paintings, statues, and other works of art. D'Alle considered the décor on their hurried walk, but remained, for the moment, mercifully silent. The hallway they followed ended at a large suite of rooms. Four guards flanked the elaborate double-doors granting access to the private quarters of de Carcassonne, and he and the clockmaker were admitted with little fanfare.

He found himself in the spacious solar, through which all traffic into de Carcassonne's private rooms passed. A fire crackled in the fireplace on the right as he entered. It filled the chamber with the fragrance of perfumed and burning wood, and dancing golden light. Gilt lamps were lit to chase away the flickering shadows cast by the fireplace, so that every corner and cranny was bright, cheerful, and welcoming. A couch and several padded leather chairs formed a conversation circle in front of the hearth, and there was also a table where meals could be taken in private. Tapestries depicting scenes of the hunt and war adorned the plastered and painted walls, and the molding was richly carved and gilded, and gleamed under the lamp and firelight. The floor was of polished wood, with a round woven carpet bearing the arms of de Carcassonne — *Purpure, on a chevron inverted Or five roses Gules* — dominating the central space.

Doors opposite the entrance leading to de Carcassonne's private offices and bower stood closed.

Monsieur Ethor Odson, Comte de Carcassonne, stood in front of the fireplace with three other people. He was a man of considerable height (and girth to match). His graying hair fell to his shoulders and lines creased his face. In his youth he would have been a formidable man, but as old age encroached and he became more accustomed to riding than walking — and lounging in the hall of Carcassonne or Domme than exercising in the yard — his strength failed, his belly expanded, and his limbs grew heavy from disuse. Nonetheless, he still carried himself with a semblance of his former majesty, and stood tall and straight-backed, so that he nearly towered over his guests that evening.

He dressed richly in a brocaded blue silk doublet of a style growing popular further west in Arras, and golden hose cut so closely to his lower extremity that Robin's face heated at the sight of the bulging codpiece, (which, if rumor held, was filled mostly by padding) and legs that reminded him much of overfull sausages stuffed into casings too small to bear them. He alone of the retinue (but for Robin himself) was armed, with a magnificent longsword that served more for ceremony than a practical weapon of war. The scabbard was covered in carved purple leather graven with interlacing golden vines, and dotted with roses of gold and garnets. Lamplight sparkled on the golden plaques riveted to his sword belt, which Robin suspected served more to restrain his ample gut threatening to burst the gilt buttons of his doublet than to support the sword at his hip. A golden chain round his neck and rings on his fingers completed his outfit.

The other three were unknown to Robin, though he suspected they were courtiers or functionaries come to witness the morrow's demonstrations. They laughed politely at some jest of de Carcassonne; their tone just strained enough to betray they did not share their host's humor but dared not admit it. All cupped crystal glasses of deep purple-red wine.

Robin approached the gathering with d'Alle in tow, and upon reaching his side bowed deeply.

"Ah! Monsieur de Sens," de Carcassonne said, pausing his current tale upon sight of him. Robin glanced up from beneath the hair falling across his face at the genuflection, and watched the others take a relieved drink from their glasses now that they were released from the clutches of his storytelling. "I am glad you have made it at last! You are a damned hard man to track down."

Robin rose and leaned his hand on the sword at his hip. "Forgive me, Monsieur le Comte, but there was a minor disturbance I needed to address, and a few other matters regarding the demonstrations for tomorrow needed my attention."

A frown crossed de Carcassonne's features. "A disturbance? Here? I have heard nothing of trouble in the castle."

"Yes, Monsieur le Comte," Robin said, in his most soothing tone. "'Twas nothing you needed be troubled with; a small bit of excitement with the new laundry maid."

The other's face lit up at mention of the maid, and a smile immediately returned to his features. "The red-haired one, yes? I passed her in one of the halls when I returned to Carcassonne. Quite the striking creature; I had a mind to send for her myself for a better look ..."

Robin cleared his throat. "It seems she has been something of a handful for Mademoiselle Rapine. I am not sure she is worth you troubling over."

De Carcassonne clicked his tongue in playful admonishment. "Now, now, my lad. 'Twould be a dereliction of my duty if I not take a personal interest in the well-being of the staff of my home! But perhaps there is another position she is better suited for, eh?"

The last he added with a wink, and Robin's face heated again.

"I would not know. I have not had much occasion to see her for myself, and 'tis not my place to manage the staff. I leave that in Laurens' more capable hands."

De Carcassonne laughed out loud, and the rest of the company laughed with him. "Ah! My dear man!". De Carcassonne turned to the others, but motioned to him with his glass. "Here I think we find the one man in Carcassonne who keeps the Lord of All's word on fidelity close in his heart. Not once since he wed has he let his eye stray. Not that I can blame him; his wife is such a lovely creature. I for one feel there is much more to be appreciated in a variety."

Robin shifted uncomfortably at the scrutiny and mirth at his expense. "Respectfully, Monsieur le Comte, I do believe there are greater concerns than the incompetence of one of the staff's laundresses, and my lack of wandering eye."

"Oh! You are not on about security again, are you? I should think the preparations you have made are more than sufficient!"

"I would remind you that I do have good cause to believe that there may be a spy in Carcassonne," Robin said.

De Carcassonne shook his head and sighed, before turning to address his guests. "All because one of his guardsmen was found drugged in a local nunnery." They all laughed politely into their drinks, and Robin gritted his teeth. "I say again, Monsieur, that you are merely paranoid. I have never seen security in the castle so tight; I suspect not even an ant could sneak into the larder with how you have the entire guard marching up and down the halls at all hours, making a frightful racket and disturbing my guests.

"Now, I have left the disposition of the guard in your hands because I trust you, but I daresay I did not intend for you to jump at every little shadow!"

"I am merely doing my duty, Monsieur le Comte."

"And what say you, Master Clockmaker?" de Carcassonne asked, with a look past Robin's shoulder at d'Alle, who had been mercifully silent to this point. "Do you feel that Monsieur de Sens's preparations have been adequate?"

"Excessively so, Monsieur le Comte," d'Alle groused. "Why I could hardly even visit the privy without an escort. 'Twas a miracle I could even finish my work at all. And mind you 'twas not helped at all by the rush I was being placed under!"

Robin squeezed his eyes shut tight and pinched the bridge of his nose in exasperation as d'Alle unleashed the rant he had spent the past weeks crafting on his patron. *Oh! If only de Carcassonne would lose his patience with the man and end this farce!*

But there was to be no such reprieve. De Carcassonne merely stood with his wine in hand and listened to d'Alle's every minor complaint. From the constant presence of the guard, to the austerity of his workshop deep in the bowels of the castle, and the demand for a demonstration as quickly as possible. For his part, de Carcassonne took the tirade in stride, and in the end brushed the matter off with a wave of his hand.

"I assure you, Master Clockmaker," de Carcassonne said, taking on that peculiar buttery quality Robin found him wont to affect when seeking to guide his subject to a particular end, "that if everything works even half as well as you boast that you will be more than adequately compensated for the troubles."

"I should hope so, Monsieur le Comte!" d'Alle replied, and folded his arms in a huff. Nonetheless, his tone softened, and he appeared suitably mollified. "I assure you, you shan't see a mechanism like it for another hundred years!"

"Good! Good! His Majesty is eager for his own demonstration, but I daren't send you on your way without seeing it myself for assurances. I have not had the occasion to drop in on you before now and see your work, but might you tell me something of these contraptions and their mechanism? Of course, I fought in the wars with the Coventrish myself, you know, and had quite a bit of experience with the *gonnes* and *bombards* fielded by the King, but what sets these apart?"

D'Alle straightened to his full height, and a satisfied smirk crossed his lips at the prospect of an audience upon whom to unleash his self-aggrandizing genius. Robin sighed again and closed his eyes with a small shake of his head, and braced himself for the lecture to come; one that was certain to soon dazzle de Carcassonne and his guests, yet leave them no less perplexed over the complexity of gears, springs, and other gizmos.

This time, however, there was a reprieve. Before the clockmaker could delve too deeply into his mechanism, they were interrupted by hurried footsteps in the corridor outside. D'Alle trailed off, Robin turned and flexed his hand round the handle of his sword, and everyone stopped to watch as the doors were flung open, and in burst two of his guard; Aimery and Baulduin, if he recalled rightly. Both were red-faced and gasping for breath, and were bundled up in cloaks and with their halberds still in hand. Boots and trousers were both wet from melted snow.

"Monsieur de Sens!" Aimery, the larger of the two, gasped in a rough voice. "Pardon the interruption, but there is trouble down below."

Robin released his hold on his sword and stomped forward, spitting them both with a stern glower. "Trouble? What sort of trouble? I left the armory in your charge, what are you doing up here?"

"That is it entirely, Monsieur, there is an intruder on the grounds!"

Robin gritted his teeth, and an oppressive silence fell across the chamber. De Carcassonne stomped forward, and both men tensed as they hastily bowed their heads.

"What do you mean an intruder?" de Carcassonne demanded.

"'Tis just as I said, Monsieur le Comte!" Aimery stammered. "One of the guard had the fellow in custody, but he broke loose and struck him before fleeing across the bailey. I sent part of the guard to run him down while Pierre remained behind to help the lad."

"Damn!" Robin snapped, heedless of the company in the chamber, for he was already in motion without even bothering to beg his leave.

"My *gonnes*! My *gonnes*!" d'Alle exclaimed. "They are sure to be after my *gonnes*!"

"I know that, you damned fool! Aimery, where was he headed?"

"Not for the armory, Monsieur," Aimery said, as he fell into step with him. "He took off along the wall, I think headed for the main gate."

"Alert the guard and seal that gate, and every other way out of the castle! No one leaves without my express permission. Redouble the guard on the armory at once."

"Yes, Monsieur!" Aimery replied, and saluted sharply before hurrying off with Baulduin to see the orders carried out. Robin strode with measured purpose down the hall, with d'Alle scrambling behind him and tearing at his hair over the safety of his precious *gonnes* as they rushed to join the pursuit.

19

ELSABETH DRAGGED THE GUARDSMAN'S PROSTRATE body through the open door of the armory and shut it behind her. The dusting of snow covering the two of them quickly began to steam and melt under the warmth of a fire crackling in a hearth near the entrance, and it soon became rather hot within the confines of the structure. A brief search turned up enough spare crossbow strings to serve as bindings, and she made them fast around the hapless guardsman's ankles and wrists, tying them both together so he could neither stand nor use his hands to free himself. A balled-up wad of wool secured with a short strip torn from her cloak provided a serviceable gag.

Once finished, she quickly surveyed the interior of the armory. It was a sizable structure built up against the inner wall of the enceinte. Munitions-grade arms of all sorts, from crossbows to halberds and even a few swords, were stacked in barrels or stood in racks running in several long rows along the length of the packed-earth floor, or hung from pegs and wall-mounted racks, and a number of *pavises* stood in one corner. There were a few hand *gonnes* of the sort that required manually touching a match to the touchhole, and even one of the more sophisticated type with the lever-driven mechanism. Old suits of armor — most of them brigandine with simple kettle helms, vambraces, and greaves much like those worn by the rest of the guard, but here and there she spied full suits of articulated plate armor — were hung from floor stands, like rank upon rank of silent soldiers standing in formation. Though none of the arms stored here were of high quality, all were serviceable and in good repair, and she judged that de Carcassonne could outfit a good thousand men beyond his standing guard in a crisis. In a far corner stood several barrels of wax, oil, tallow, and, she suspected, powder for the *gonnes*.

There were also workbenches, most near the fireplace in the front corner directly opposite the door, or running along the inside walls where barred windows gazed out onto the bailey. During the day the windows, along with the open door, would help let in light for the armorers to work by. Now the only light came from the fireplace, casting muted red and gold light onto the floor.

She made her way down the aisles, and carefully felt along the racks, stands, and shelves in the dim light, mindful not to jar anything loose that could make enough noise to draw attention back to the armory. Then, on a workbench in the corner furthest from the door, Elsabeth found what she was looking for: four *gonnes* of unusual manufacture.

One lay in pieces upon the workbench, and she gave it a cursory study. Elsabeth could discern little of its mechanism, which had been removed and partly disassembled for repair or maintenance, or how it operated. All she could make out was a mass of springs and gears with all the complexity of a mechanical clock. *'Tis little wonder, then, that 'twould take a clockmaker to devise such an apparatus.* The most notable feature was a grooved wheel that would turn upon the outside face, and a jawed lever in place of the iron serpentine which held the slow match of the lever-operated *gonnes* Cuncz had showed her.

In a floor rack nearby, however, were three complete examples. Elsabeth snatched one up and turned it in her hand. It was perhaps slightly heavier than the other *gonnes*, owing to its mechanism, and while the inside of the barrels of the former were smooth, this one had twisting parallel grooves painstakingly cut into the barrel walls. A small wrench was tied to a tiller shaped to butt against the *gonner's* shoulder, rather than tuck beneath the arm, and after a moment's fiddling Elsabeth worked out that it turned the wheel on the side of the *gonne*. A piece of flint was gripped in the jaws of the lever, which could be lowered to rest against the grooves on the wheel. There was also a pan beneath, covered by a spring-loaded door, which she suspected held a measure of powder like the match *gonnes*.

Well, I know the purpose of flint on steel well enough. 'Tis quite clever, in fact, if I am not wrong about how it works.

Elsabeth quickly bundled up the *gonne* in a tarpaulin from the stores, and also secured a bag of powder. A small pouch of round lead balls and a leather wallet with extra flints went into the bag as well, along with any other tools on the bench she mused might be of use in the maintenance of the contraption, and the disassembled bits and pieces of the fourth *gonne's* mechanism. She doffed her cloak for a moment to sling *gonne* and bag at her back, then covered herself once more. Her cloak did not quite mask the misshapen lump of her hidden cargo, but in the darkness it might perhaps be missed on a cursory examination. Satisfied there was nothing more of use, she retraced her steps to the armory door.

Her prisoner had not yet regained consciousness, but she paid him little mind for the moment. Instead, she peered around the door and into the bailey. A blast of cold air caught her face and Elsabeth shivered. Nothing else moved within the grounds, but she could hear the commotion caused by Kilianus' flight further around the keep.

Bugger. With all that racket he could have the entire garrison on alert!

Elsabeth considered a moment. If Kilianus did not draw his pursuers to the servants' gate that would offer the quietest means of escape. However, it would also mean a flight on foot into the City; there was no stable or picket for horses there, and she might not reach those Kilianus secured for their escape. At the main gate she might be able to find a horse herself, but without a password the guard or master or horse would almost certainly see through her disguise, and any attempt at flight would surely be noted by the night watch. And even if she were not scrutinized closely, when the alarm went up they would almost certainly follow.

I shall need transportation one way or another. The hunt is sure to be on ere long, and I can't run all the way back to Boehm from here.

"Bugger," she murmured.

She turned back inside the armory and nudged the hapless guardsman with her foot. After a few moments he moaned pitiably and stirred, and slowly his eyes blinked open. Despite awakening trussed and gagged Elsabeth credited him for not crying out or thrashing in panic as she knelt over him with her hands on her knees.

"Good morning, love," she said in a low voice. The guardsman murmured something through his gag that needed no translation. Elsabeth clicked her tongue. "There is no need for that. I truly am sorry, but you just happen to be having a terrible run of luck. Under other circumstances I would make it up to you — and I can certainly be quite creative in demonstrating my gratitude in such matters — but, unfortunately, I am in a bit of a hurry."

Elsabeth leaned around him and undid the ties on the gag, but before he could call out, she pressed her hand across his mouth and held the cloth in place. "Now, I need out of the castle and the City, and quickly. I am more than capable of finding my own way out, but as I said, I am in quite the hurry. I need to know if there are any passcodes among the watch tonight. Seeing as you shall have need of your mouth, I shall remove my hand. Utter so much as a syllable of alarm and I shall cram this so far down your throat you will be able to wipe your arse from the inside. Nod if you understand."

The guardsman glared up at her, but gave a short, stiff nod of acknowledgement. Elsabeth removed hand and gag, and gave him a pat on the cheek. "Good boy, we seem to have an understanding. Now then, what sort of challenge can I expect at the gate at this hour?"

He worked his mouth for a moment and spit out a few loose threads trapped between his teeth. "It shan't matter. All of the guard are known to each other, and they shall know you for an imposter before you can get close enough to challenge."

"Tch. And yet you were almost right atop me before you grew wise. I rather like my chances of avoiding recognition on such a dark and cold night."

"Then you will be bobbing on a halberd shaft. And do as you like to me, I'll not betray Monsieur le Comte to any spy."

Elsabeth sighed. "Well, I had hoped to make a quiet escape, but if you really insist on making things difficult..."

She rocked to her feet and made her way over to the hearth near the door. The fire was still crackling merrily, and a stack of wood was piled up nearby and ready to fuel the fire. Elsabeth searched through the stack for a small brand and poked it into the embers. A few sparks shot up from the coals at the bottom, and the flames licked a little higher in response. After a few moments of this the end of her brand caught, and she held it aloft like a torch.

The defiance in the guardsman's voice faltered as he craned his neck to see what she had in mind. "What... what are you doing?"

"Creating a bit of a disturbance," Elsabeth said, and held her brand up to one of the canvas tarpaulins covering the stored arms.

At first it only smoldered and smoked, but then with a *woosh* one corner caught flame, and gold-red tongues began to spread.

The guardsman squealed and began to thrash against his bindings as Elsabeth watched the tarpaulin catch alight. She lit a few other places, then tossed her brand into the corner nearest the powder and dusted off her hands on her way back.

"Are you mad, woman! There is powder and oil stored in here!" he shrieked. "God in Heaven you can't do this!"

"So there is," she said casually, and crouched behind him to undo his bindings. By now the flames were beginning to leap up among the stores and climb the wooden post supporting the roof in the corner, and smoke filled the ceiling. "I really am not overly cruel, and bodies do tend to complicate things, so I shall be letting you go now. You could, I suppose, try to stop me from leaving, but I reckon you shan't have much time, and if you discount me as a fighter you are in for a rude surprise. I suggest instead you go for help before the fire reaches the powder. I'll admit I don't know quite what to expect; I have had only scant experience with it of late, but it might take a good chunk of the outer wall with it."

The guardsman strained against his bindings. His feet came free first, and he kicked and scrambled in an effort to stand. Then she released his hands and he rounded on her, intending to surprise her with a sudden blow to her temple. Elsabeth, however, anticipated the attempt. She deftly guided his fist past with a raised forearm, seized him by the wrist, and used his own momentum to slam him face-first into the floor.

Elsabeth dropped her knee into the small of his back, and twisted his arm until he yelped in pain.

"I warned you about that, love. Please don't make me regret my softer nature."

By now the fire had spread to engulf much of the corner across from her, and the crackle and roar of the flames overwhelmed the gentle popping on the hearth. Everything within was bathed red and gold. It was now quite hot, and every breath grew laborious. Much of the smoke coiled round the timber uprights and filled the space between the beams in the ceiling, but it was already growing thicker and nearing the level of the ground. She suspected before long that thick, glowing tendrils might soon be visible within the castle.

Elsabeth hauled the guardsman to his feet, snatched a sword from one of the racks nearby, and bodily dragged him out of the armory. The cold of the night air blasted her face, and she gasped in spite of herself. Behind her the flames were spreading to the space in front of the hearth; she had left with her prisoner just in time.

She sprinted across the snow with the guard's tabard clutched firmly in hand, practically dragging him behind her in a mad scramble to get clear of the armory. They did not quite make it halfway to the keep before a roar like thunder split the air. Something struck Elsabeth hard from behind and drove all the breath from her lungs. She felt a vague sensation of being lifted from her feet and flung forward through the air. Fragments of charred stone flew past her face, accompanied by splintered wood and flaming debris. The muddy slush rushing up to meet her face was blanketed by a carpet of black soot.

They hit the ground hard, and for a moment Elsabeth's vision blackened. Her head spun and she gasped desperately to draw a breath. Her ears rang, and her whole body ached.

"Bugger!" she mewled, when her head cleared enough to get her elbows beneath her, and she managed to force herself over and onto her bottom.

The armory had been ripped apart from within. Shattered and scorched stone lay in crumbled piles for yards in all directions. Cracked and splintered timbers littered the bailey, along with debris from the arms, munitions, and other stores kept inside. Flames leapt into the sky, and thick black smoke poured from the ruins. The wall on the far side was lit in flickering oranges and golds, and though the stone was blackened, it was still intact. More smoking and flaming debris continued to rain down around her, some falling very near the keep itself. It continued to burn on the snow, and the sharp stench of burning oil and pitch joined the acrid smoke filling the bailey.

Frantic voices filled the courtyard, and beside her the guardsman moaned. Elsabeth staggered to her feet and gave herself a quick patting down; fortunately, she found her limbs and other particulars of her anatomy still where they belonged, and the blast had not damaged her stolen cargo. The guardsman, however, was not so fortunate. A large splinter of wood, driven with the force of a quarrel from a crossbow, speared through his thigh. However, before she could make any move a column of bodies rounded the corner of the keep hiding the main gates from view. Someone shouted frantic orders as men rushed to throw snow on the flames.

Now for it. If I wanted a distraction, this is it!

Elsabeth jumped into motion, breaking away from the wounded guardsman and running to the first man she came across. She seized him by the sleeve, shaking and jostling him so he could not get a clear look at her.

"Hurry! This way! We have a wounded man over here!"

Without waiting for a response, she dragged him a few steps towards where she and her erstwhile captive had landed, and all but flung him onto the man's prostrate form. Then she spun around and sprinted across the snow for the far side of the keep. She dashed through the mob falling on the site of the fire, all of them so focused on the destruction that not one of them paid her any mind.

The gate was not directly in view from the armory, but a little ways further around the enceinte. Elsabeth took advantage of the chaos to slip into the shadows beneath the wall, and out of sight of the guards converging on the wreckage. She caught the muted flash of lamplight in the gatehouse, but everything else was deserted. The cacophony of many voices shouting over one another echoed throughout the grounds, and the sky was lit brilliant crimson as smoke billowed up overhead. Nothing else moved in the bailey.

A large stable complex was built up against the inside of the wall just ahead, and by fortune on her side of the gate. Lamps cast golden light onto a carpet of churned-up snow in front of the three sets of doors opening out onto the bailey, and the whole two-level structure was of stone on the lower level, giving way to half-timbering above, with a steeply-peaked tiled roof reaching up above the walkway topping the defensive works.

Elsabeth darted for one of the open doors and found herself alone; even the stable hands had rushed to tend to the blaze. The scent of fresh hay mingled with the stink of horse, and nervous whinnies and stamping broke the silence within. A lamp hung on a post near the door provided a dim light to see by. She quickly made her way among the stalls. There were a several palfreys and two strong coursers, though all were put up for the night and all their gear was removed and stowed away. With better light she might, perhaps, saddle one of the coursers, but it was too dark now for her to work, and it would not be long before her moment of surprise passed. However, at the far end in a stall nearest the gatehouse itself, she found three horses kept saddled for errand-riders.

Elsabeth threw open the gate to the stall, took one by the bridle, and led it out again. The horse obliged, though danced nervously over the noise of the explosion and the chaos of the guard rushing to investigate. Once free of the stall she swung herself up into the saddle, turned the horse towards the doors, and dug her heels into its flanks. It snorted and sprung forward, and the wind whipped against Elsabeth's face as the horse sped out into the bailey. She hauled on the bridle to steer for the gate, and then she was through, out through the gatehouse, and flying like a gale down the street and into the City with the gate guard yelling from their posts at her back.

20

OBIN THREW OPEN THE DOORS OF THE HALL AND stormed inside, with d'Alle close on his heels. Aimery and Baulduin filed in as well, along with a third, Thevot, who had assisted in the capture of the intruder, and intercepted Robin on his way out of the keep. The man had been returned to the great hall, where another bit of alarming news awaited them: Jacquemart and Agnez had disappeared, and Rapine and the guard left to watch over them had been found trussed and gagged in a cabinet.

The first thing Robin noted upon entering was Rapine slouched in a chair and nursing a wicked bruise marring her face. Laurens stood behind her with a comforting hand on her shoulder, and she had been given a drink of wine. The guard was not so fortunate, and lay on the floor with his head resting on a pillow, while the company surgeon looked him over. Last, slumped in a chair and surrounded by armed men, was the intruder, and Robin's heart clawed its way up into his throat at the sight of him.

The guard had not been gentle with him, and the tale of the struggle told on his features. One eye was blackened and swollen, and a wicked cut split his lip. A gash in his temple bled profusely and had been left unbandaged. His hands were tightly bound, so that the cord cut into his wrists. But beneath the battered, bruised, and bloody countenance, Robin immediately recognized the formerly handsome features of Jacquemart, the woodworker. Robin's blood boiled as the full weight of the implications settled over him, and he clenched his teeth so tightly he thought they might shatter from the pressure.

"What in God's name is happening, here!" he demanded, more out of a need to unleash his wrath than any desire for answers. Robin first looked to Laurens and Rapine. "Speak! Where is Agnez, the maid?"

"Gone, Monsieur de Sens!" Laurens stammered, and flinched behind Rapine. For her part, she cringed away from the fury in his voice, and her hands holding the cup of wine trembled. "I am afraid 'tis all a quite chaotic affair! I was coming to check on the progress when the guard stormed in with Jacquemart in their custody. I knew right away something was amiss when they arrived without his wife, so I came right here! That is when I found her gone, and I heard a knocking in the cabinet. Imagine my horror when I found the guard and poor Rapine locked inside!"

"'Twas that horrible girl!" Rapine bawled, finding her courage now that Laurens had spoken. Robin turned his attention now on her, and though the distress of her captivity still told on her features, her former air of superiority returned once more. "She struck me, if you can believe it! She struck me right in the face, and said such horrible things to me. I swear I have never been spoken to in such a manner before!"

Before anyone else could say a word, the sound of laughter broke the tension filling the hall. Robin wheeled around and, to his astonishment at such cheek, found it coming from their captive.

"Perhaps never to your face," Jacquemart said, "but I imagine there are quite a few who have said such things under their breath or behind your back, Mademoiselle."

Someone else snickered, but when Robin looked about he could not determine whence it came, though several of the guard stood red-faced, as if stifling the urge to laugh. Even Laurens hung his head and smirked.

Robin squared his shoulders and scowled at the man as he stepped round the chair to face him. The guard gave way for him, though remained close by so he would not try anything foolish. "I fail to see how you find this so amusing. Do you realize you face the hangman's noose, or worse?" He lowered his face until it hovered just in front of the prisoner's. "I want to know who you really are, and what you are doing here!"

"'Tis plain what he is really doing here," d'Alle snapped. "He is here for my *gonnes*!"

Robin turned and glared at the clockmaker, who stood at his side with his hands planted on his hips and trying his best to stand over their prisoner. Yet despite being bound and seated, Jacquemart merely smirked up at the fellow, not the least bit cowed or intimidated.

"Quiet!" Robin snarled, and d'Alle flinched at the fire in his voice. He reached out and seized the woodworker by the chin, and forcibly turned him back to face him. "Answer me: Who are you, what are you doing here, and where is your wife?"

The smirk never left Jacquemart's face. He said nothing, and just stared back. His patience already worn thin by de Carcassonne's foolishness and d'Alle's constant complaining, Robin's hand flew and struck the man hard across the jaw. Jacquemart's head wrenched around, blood sprayed from his busted lip, and though Robin's blow succeeded in knocking the smirk from his features, his countenance remained defiant.

"Where is she?!"

"I beg your pardon, Monsieur," Laurens interjected, "but are you sure she is part of this? She seemed such a timid, uncertain thing whenever I have seen her—"

Robin speared him on his glare. "Not one more word. I have been a goddamned fool! Every one of you I am sure would know her by sight. Monsieur le Comte has not been back a day and even he knows her! And because she is so recognizable 'tis obvious I would not even consider her a threat when Pierre is attacked by a woman yet cannot remember what she looked like. Of *course* she is a spy. And a perfect one, at that!"

He turned to Therot. "Take some men and secure the armory. Now! Then have this entire place searched for her. I want her found, and I want her al—"

Robin did not have a chance to finish. The great hall was rattled by a sudden roar like thunder, and everyone froze in shock. Then it passed, and he heard a commotion outside the hall and the rushing of many feet as people scrambled into motion. Sudden realization dawned on him, and icy fingers seized him by the heart.

"The armory," he muttered, under his breath. "The armory!" he shouted, and turned to the guards. "Aimery! Baulduin! Stay here and keep watch on the prisoner. Laurens, take Rapine and clear the hall. Master d'Alle, remain here with Aimery and Baulduin, and the rest of you come with me!"

Everyone snapped into motion. Laurens gathered Rapine and led her from the great hall, while the company surgeon helped the injured guardsman back to his feet and followed after. The rest of the guard formed ranks around him, but d'Alle danced about and wrung his hands on his apron.

"My *gonnes*! My *gonnes*!" he cried, and jabbed an accusing finger at Robin. "You said you had everything in order, and now look at what has happened! All of that work will be for nothing if she gets away!"

Robin rounded on him, seized him by the front of his doublet, and dragged him closer. "Do not test me now, Master Clockmaker.

I have had enough of it for a lifetime! Stay here and out of my way."

He released him with a shove, then spun on his heel and rushed for the doors. The rest of the guard fell into step behind him.

Robin rushed through the halls, shouldering his way past serving staff and guests who milled about in fright and confusion. By now everyone in the keep had emerged from whatever rooms they were in to see what the commotion was about, and it took a great deal of yelling, cajoling, and the guard making use of their halberds to push the crowds aside for him to reach the nearest exit to the bailey.

He burst out, heedless of the cold, and found the scene outside no less chaotic. Guards and workers rushed madly around the side of the keep, and Robin spied the telltale orange glow of a raging fire just around to the left along the side of the keep's outer wall. Cries of alarm echoed across the bailey, along with a deeper, crackling rumble. Robin slipped in the mush and mud churned up by the passage of so many people through the snow-swept grounds, and so staggered more than ran round the corner, and into a nightmare.

The armory had all but ceased to exist, with only a few timbers and shattered walls left to mark its former location. Great, towering pillars of flame leapt up from the wreckage, and poured thick black smoke into the sky. Debris continued to rain down, some of it falling dangerously close to the keep itself, as men scrambled to douse the flames with snow or water drawn from one of the wells on the grounds. No one could approach the wreckage of the armory itself. Guardsmen formed an orderly line of men bearing buckets in a desperate effort to extinguish the inferno, but the oil and pitch that had once been stowed within stubbornly resisted their firefighting. Others organized the men and women of the staff, and even a few of de Carcassonne's guests who had responded to the blast. Of de Carcassonne himself Robin saw no sign; not even his personal guard.

"Monsieur! Monsieur!" a voice called, and Robin craned his neck. One of the guard waved frantically for his attention from the far side of the crowd. He seized Theron by the arm and motioned to the blaze.

"I want every man in the guard not currently on duty summoned," he snapped. "Get these flames under control for God's sake before it sets the whole damn castle on fire!"

"Yes, Monsieur!" Theron replied, and directed the men who followed, while Robin dove into the crowd of onlookers.

He pushed through them, most distracted by the scene unfolding before them, but others recognized the sight of his arms and gave way so he could pass. After a few moments Robin emerged into an empty space where several men lay on the ground. Some coughed and hacked, others groaned. Frederick met him as he broke free of the mob and directed him to one of the wounded.

"How are they, Frederick?"

"Most of them just got too much smoke, Monsieur," the guardsman replied. "But, Monsieur, 'tis Pierre who is the worst off!"

"Pierre?"

Robin frowned as he was led to where Pierre lay. He moaned pitiably beneath several blankets, with more laid out beneath him on top of the snow, while several of the household staff tended to him. Robin stopped and knelt beside him. Pierre's face was drawn and pale, and he grimaced in pain.

"Pierre," Robin said, and reached out to take him by the shoulder. "Pierre, 'tis me, what happened?"

Pierre groaned. "The...whole thing. She blew it up!" he said.

"What?"

"'Twas the laundry maid, Monsieur. She was dressed up as a guardsman. She was with that other fellow; he struck her and ran off, and 'twas not until I came to help that I realized 'twas a ruse. But it was *her*. The one from Isabeau's."

Robin balled his fists. "Are you sure?"

Pierre nodded weakly. "Now that I saw her face again, I am sure of it. I don't... I don't know how I missed it before."

"Where is she now?"

"I don't know," Pierre moaned. "She asked me about passwords — I did not tell her, Monsieur, not a word! — and then she set the whole armory on fire. I think... I think she might have taken something, but there was nothing I could do. The whole thing blew up, and I got speared in my leg. When I woke up again 'twas to find myself lying here, and chaos all around."

"Damn it! How could I be such a fool?!" Robin spat. "'Twas all one misdirection after another! Jacquemart was just a distraction. She was the mastermind all this time!"

"I tried, Monsieur, I tried ..."

But Robin was no longer listening. He stood and stormed back to the ring of people surrounding them, and with a cry of "Guards!" plunged back through again, forcing past people until he reached the other side once more. "Guards! With me! With me!"

Those of the guard not occupied battling against the conflagration in the remains of the armory reacted promptly and gathered round. "Have my horse saddled and get as many others together as you can and quickly. We have a spy in our midst, and they may be attempting to flee the city. Sound the alert, and have the gates sealed at once!"

"Yes, Monsieur!" one shouted, and rushed ahead to carry out his instructions. Robin ordered his party then turned for the gate.

More people by now had joined the crowd around the burning armory, gawking at the inferno, or pitching in in the desperate effort to combat the blaze. But they had made no further headway. By now, de Carcassonne had also appeared outside the doorway, and watched the scene, dumbstruck. Robin turned his head aside to avoid a summons, but he need not have bothered; de Carcassonne's attention was held so rapt by the scene before him he never noticed him pass by on their way around the wall of the keep. Within a few moments Robin and his party were out of sight, with only the telltale orange glow of the fire, and the acrid stench of burning pitch and oil hanging in the air, to remind him of its presence.

As they neared the main gate, Robin observed a knot of bodies clustered together near the stable, all speaking animatedly. When they noted his approach, one detached himself from the group, and hurried to intercept him. It was the runner he had dispatched.

"Monsieur!" the man said, out of breath from the debate with the guard, and the effort of rushing across the frozen bailey. "Beg your pardon, Monsieur, but we have another problem."

Robin let a frustrated growl escape his throat. "What is it? And quickly!"

The guardsman blanched and stammered his response. "'Tis the horses, Monsieur, the ones Germain keeps saddled for the dispatch riders. One is... missing."

The icy fingers wrapped round Robin's heart since discovering the woodworker's wife gone and the armory aflame squeezed even tighter.

"Missing?" he repeated, having already guessed the implication.

The man swallowed. "Yes, Monsieur. When the folk at the gate heard the explosion everyone but the watchmen took off to help, including Germain and his stable hands, and the extra guard that was posted. One of the hands passed by another of the guard coming from that direction." He waved back the way Robin had come, where the orange glow of the fire illuminated much of that part of the bailey. "He did not think anything of it. I suppose he guessed he was sent to raise the alarm."

"Which guardsman? Did he get a name, or have a look at his face?"

"I don't know, Monsieur. I have not seen the lad, 'tis what Marin tells me; he mentioned seeing the fellow as well, and he seemed in an awful hurry. Marin is over with the gate guard, now. He was about to send for help from down in the City to put that fire out when I arrived with your instructions, and that is when the gate watch said someone took a horse and rode off, not much more than a few moments past, thinking that was what the fellow was doing. But he cannot recall anyone having given an order to send a runner into the city."

"Because no one did!" Robin snarled. He fumed and tore at his hair. "Damn it all! She is ahead of us, and already out of the castle. How quickly can the City be sealed?"

"That is the other matter, Monsieur," the guardsman said, and braced himself. "If the spy is already loose, we shan't get word to the gates before they can get out, especially if they are on horse and riding hard."

Robin stomped and buried his face in his hands as every waking nightmare he had experienced since Pierre was found unconscious at Isabeau's now played out before him. Presently, the dull thud of many hooves on snow forestalled any further command, and his horse was brought round, along with several others. Without preamble, he selected the fastest riders among the company present, and vaulted into the saddle.

"Seal the castle behind us, no one else comes or goes," he ordered. "Send word to Monsieur le Comte that we have one prisoner in custody and I am in pursuit of another. Sound a general alarm, and by God, I shall have every man and woman in the castle searched. If I should find any others either complicit or simply negligent in their duties, heads will roll!"

And with that he dug his heels into his horse's flanks and gave a cry, and his column flew from the gate and down into the City, kicking up a great cloud of powdered snow behind them as the icy winter wind whipped against his face.

His only hope now was in speed, and that his enemies had no further surprises in store.

D'ALLE PACED IMPATIENTLY AS THE GREAT HALL WAS cleared, leaving only the prisoner, Aimery, Baulduin, and himself behind. Laurens, Rapine, the surgeon, and the hapless guardsman watching over the woodworker and his wife departed first, and silently. Then came a great commotion and deafening rattle of gear as de Sens and the rest of the guard filed from the hall and hurried for the bailey. His stomach knotted itself as events spiraled quickly out of control, and he despaired at the thought that so much of his efforts over the past months had been forfeit.

He sighed, and paced, and fought to settle his nerves and the bile churning in his belly. Rapine left her cup of wine behind on the table, so rather than let it go to waste he finished it in a single draught, but, though it was a potent one, it did little to settle his nerves.

The prisoner sat calmly and silently with his hands bound behind him. He dared not move with Aimery and Baulduin to watch him, and their attention was focused on him. The slightest shift in his chair to ease his shoulders, bound as he was with his hands behind his back, provoked a twitch from their halberds.

D'Alle chewed the inside of his lower lip and wrung his hands. After several more minutes passed, he approached the guards from behind. Aimery turned slightly to consider him at the sound of him drawing nearer.

"I would stay back from this one," Aimery said. "I hear he put up quite a fight when they caught him. They practically had to beat him unconscious to take him."

"How much longer is this going to be?" d'Alle asked, slipping his hand into a pocket of his apron, and scrutinizing the battered man carefully. Despite his unfortunate condition, the prisoner's good eye was nonetheless bright and alert, and appeared keenly aware of everything happening around him.

"I could not say, Master d'Alle. If the whole armory went up... well, I can't imagine 'twill be contained quickly. The oil and pitch alone can burn for a long while. I suggest you have a seat before you wear a hole in the—"

D'Alle did not give him a chance to finish. His hand in his apron pocket seized hold of the carven handle he had been looking for, and before Aimery could react, he whipped his weapon out and struck Baulduin across the back of the neck. Aimery turned and snatched up his halberd, but froze at the ominous click as D'Alle lowered the dog and flint of his *gonne* into place on the wheel, and pointed it at Aimery's face.

"I would not! Drop it!" D'Alle said, and only through great effort did he manage to keep his voice even. Nonetheless, Aimery's courage failed him upon gazing into the gaping muzzle of the *gonne*, and he laid his halberd aside. "I have not had the opportunity to test this out myself, but it seemed only natural to me that my mechanism could work in a *hand gonne*, as well."

D'Alle smirked at the prisoner. "Quite ingenious, eh? I was working on it for myself while I was assembling the others. I suppose it shan't shoot as far, but 'tis much more readily concealable."

"I am sure the Baron will be quite impressed."

D'Alle turned his attention back to Aimery. "Now then, my apologies to poor Baulduin, but would you kindly take him to the cabinet and put him inside? Oh, and then follow him yourself, thank you!"

Aimery gawked, as if d'Alle had sprouted an extra head. "In the... are you out of your mind?"

"I was out of my mind when I agreed to de Carcassonne's wholly unsatisfactory terms!" He made a show of pointing his *gonne*. "Now go on!"

Aimery took hold of Baulduin beneath the arms, and his stricken comrade moaned as he was hefted up and dragged to the cabinet the conspirators had used on poor Rapine. Aimery folded Balduin's limp body in as best as he was able, then stepped inside himself. Never taking his eyes or *gonne* from the pair, D'Alle warily approached and kicked the cabinet closed. The latch clicked into place, locking the two men inside. He grunted in satisfaction, then carefully returned the dog to its safe position, and stuffed the *gonne* back into his apron pocket.

"Now then," d'Alle said, and returned to the prisoner. "Is all in order?"

He nodded. "The Baron's offer is ready to be delivered, we must but meet with him at Tuebingen," the prisoner said, and twisted his neck to indicate his bound hands. "If you would be so kind, Master Clockmaker."

D'Alle quickly undid the knots and helped the man to his feet. Despite his battered countenance, he stood with little real trouble and rolled his shoulders to loosen them again. "And what about my *gonnes*? Blowing up the armory was not part of the arrangement!"

"I do apologize for that, but circumstances required a degree of improvisation, and a need for a distraction. This should keep them busy. And rest assured, the Baron shall compensate you for your loss. And if fortune should remain with us, my companion will have salvaged one of them before blowing up the rest."

D'Alle grunted. "Do you really expect her to make it through? De Sens will be on her quickly, I fear."

The prisoner quirked a grin. "The Baron has the utmost confidence in her, 'tis why he hired her to keep de Sens's attention in the first place. Come on then, Master d'Alle, we must be on our way to make the most of her distraction."

D'Alle fell into step with the man as they hurried from the hall. Sure enough, the passage was deserted as everyone had rushed to the bailey, leaving them free to make their escape. "I don't think I ever caught your name. Your right name, at least."

"Kilianus. Michael Kilianus, at your service."

21

LSABETH RACED THROUGH THE STREETS OF Carcassonne as straight and swiftly as she was able. A few more minutes passed with no sign of pursuit, and for a moment Elsabeth held out hope she might even make it clear of the gates before an alarm was sounded.

The cry of a horn from the castle splintered any such hope into fragments. Another call went up, and another. Though it was late, doors opened, and residents poked their heads out into the night air to investigate the commotion. Most watched her rush past in a clatter of hooves and, catching the livery of the castle guard flashing in the light of the lamps illuminating the street, dismissed her for an errand rider. She urged her horse forward as hard as she dared on the icy cobblestones, and the clatter of hooves echoed in the night.

If the alarm is only just now going out they may not know to seal the gates. Perhaps the city watch will take me for a messenger and let me pass.

However, this time fortune was not on her side. As she reached the square not far from her apartment with Kilianus, her horse struck a patch of black ice on the cobblestones, and the poor beast squealed as its hooves slipped out from beneath it. She and horse both tumbled to the ground together. Elsabeth only just managed an awkward roll with the burdens of her appropriated armor and stolen *gonne* to control her fall, and she landed roughly on her backside. Her kettle helm clattered across the paving stones, allowing her hair to fly free. The horse was not so fortunate, and she heard the snap of its legs as it came down and rolled over onto its back and side, narrowly missing her head in the process.

Elsabeth got to her feet and gave herself a quick looking over, happily finding herself intact and uninjured. The horse, however, screamed in agony, and scrabbled trying to right itself again.

"Easy, love, easy!" Elsabeth murmured, and reached out to the animal, more from a need to quiet it lest it draw undue attention, than any real ability to tend to it. As she approached her throat tightened, and her belly churned; the breaks were bad, and wet bone speared from both hind limbs.

"Bugger," she muttered, and looked about. There was no one in sight yet, but if the horse continued on in such a manner, someone would surely respond.

No sooner did that thought pass through her head, when a new sound brought her up short; voices near at hand, and the rumble of hooves on stone coming from the castle.

"Fuck!" she snarled, and dodged for the shadow of the buildings and alleyways surrounding the square.

None too soon. Just as she vanished under cover, a small knot of men in the livery of the city watch appeared. One of them cried out, and as Elsabeth peered around the edge of the building sheltering her from view, she watched them rush to the side of the fallen horse. They were followed shortly after by a column of riders from the castle, which pulled up warily at the sight. The leader of the column separated from the others and dismounted. She strained her ears, but could hear little of what was said. However, the word "livery" managed to carry to her hiding place.

Elsabeth frowned and looked down at the tabard over her appropriated armor.

Bugger. They must know I am disguised as one of the guard. This will not do me any further good, for I shan't be fighting my way out of here.

She retreated deeper into the shadow of the maze of alleys, while edging further towards the gates in search of a quiet place to discard her gear. Elsabeth caught a glimpse of the column of horsemen dismounting and scattering in ones and twos into the back streets, accompanied by parts of the watch.

THE SIGHT OF THE SCREAMING HORSE LYING IN THE MIDDLE of the square brought Robin up short. He stopped before reaching the grisly scene and dropped out of the saddle as some of the city watch rushed up to investigate the commotion. The cause of the horse's fall soon became apparent: Robin nearly slipped on the same patch of black ice as he approached, and noted both of the poor beast's rear legs had suffered a bad break in the fall.

One of the watch snapped smartly to attention when he recognized him.

"Monsieur de Sens!" he blurted. "What is going on here? We heard the horn, and then a horse crying. By the time we got here ..." The man trailed off, and even in the dim moonlight Robin could see his face go white as he motioned to the horse lying in the street, nickering pitiably in its agony.

"There was an intruder at the castle," Robin said over the horse's cries. "'Twas a woman, quite tall, red-haired, with green eyes. She is impersonating one of the guard, and escaped by horse. This one, by the looks of it, though it seems she did not get as far as she hoped. Have you seen anyone come this way in the livery of Monsieur le Comte's service?"

The watchman shrugged. "Forgive me, Monsieur, but there was no one in the square by the time we arrived. Whoever was riding that horse must have slipped into one of the alleys when they heard us coming."

Robin bounced his hand off his sword-hilt in frustration. "Damn it!" He turned to his column and snapped his fingers. "The intruder is in the City, but unhorsed. I want three of you to follow me, and bring the horses! The rest, break up by pairs and find her. I want her alive if possible for questioning. Be sure to search the house she and her accomplice were using to be certain she does not seek refuge there." He then turned back to the watch. "Send your men to help them, and you come with me, I want the gates closed as soon as we can reach them. And someone deal with that poor beast, I'll not have it suffer any longer!"

He waited while the men moved to carry out his commands, then took his horse by the bridle and made his way up the road with the watchman at his side.

ELSABETH TOOK SHELTER IN THE DOORWAY OF ONE OF THE apartment buildings, and shed her cloak, sword, and baggage. The chill wind of deep winter penetrated all the way down to her bones, and her fingers clumsily refused to cooperate as she struggled with the points and straps of her armor. However, finally she had it undone and cast it aside, leaving her clad only in the remains of her dress and chemise. Elsabeth hastily wrapped her cloak about her again, though it could do nothing for her bare legs, clad only in stockings below her knees. She stuffed the discarded tabard and brigandine out of sight in the doorway and picked up the sword and her baggage once more, before slipping back into the shadow of the alleyways.

By now, the men pursuing from the castle had disappeared into the city streets, and moved from house to house and building to building, methodically knocking on doors and checking each and every yard, shed, and entryway. Elsabeth dodged between buildings, keeping to the shadows as she crept for the gates. She ignored the biting cold on her feet as the wet snow soaked through her shoes, and the chill wind blasting her legs (and swirling up her skirt and towards her nethers, against which her braies offered little protection). She clutched her cloak around her as best she could, and lowered her head to shield her face. Her breath misted in the air, the chill made her eyes water, and her cheeks stung from the tears freezing on her skin.

The outer wall of the City loomed ahead of her in the darkness, a black mass against the night sky. It was illuminated by winking lamps casting golden circles of light onto the ground in its shadow, with the odd fire burning in the many watchtowers. More lanterns lit the squares and markets as Carcassonne slept, and Elsabeth avoided these, sticking to the back streets and alleys, which were left dark and were largely empty of patrols by the watch. As she drew nearer to the wall, her mind turned to the practical matters of how she was to escape.

Even if the gate has not been sealed before I can get there — damn the delay with my horse! — I'll never outrun riders in open country by foot. As I recall there was a stable in the square inside the gate, but if they are alert now 'twill be a tall order liberating another ride without being spotted.

Finally, Elsabeth reached a point across from the gate itself. There was no further sign of the men pursuing her. Even the leader of the column could not be seen in the square, or on the main roads nearby. She did spy the flicker of lamplight on the helms of the watch posted at the gate, but as Elsabeth studied their disposition, she quickly determined from the way they leaned on their halberds that the men were not yet on alert.

She chewed her lower lip and considered the gate carefully, peering into the shadow of the fortified gatehouse for any sign of an ambush. However, nothing moved there that she could see. Next, she considered the walls themselves; the battlements were accessible by means of stairs built alongside the inner surface of the wall between the towers regularly spaced along the enceinte. Perhaps if she kept low as she ascended, she could keep the stairs themselves between her and any watch from the gate or towers, and use the shadow of the wall as cover from anyone who might be watching from the street.

Unfortunately, that still left her alone and on foot, in the dead of winter, and without supplies. By a cruel twist of fate, the stables were on the opposite side of the gate square, and she could not reach it from her current hiding place without being spotted. Worse; she now spied the leader of the horsemen pursuing her, walking in company of four other men. Three led the rest of the horses, offering her hope she might yet be able to get hold of a ride. The fourth, however, broke away from the group and rushed to the gate, and his voice echoed across the square.

"Hoy there! Close the gate, by order of le Marechal de Carcassonne!" he cried, waving his hands over his head to signal the men on guard.

Damn it! So bloody close only to be trapped now. I suppose my best hope is up and over the wall, and then find some sort of hiding place.

Elsabeth was just about to make a move towards the wall, when a voice from behind brought her up short.

"I have her!" someone cried, and Elsabeth felt hands seize her round the middle, nearly pulling her off her feet in the process. "I have her!"

She did not have time to chide herself for losing track of her surroundings, as two more men rushed in from the side. The racket quickly drew the attention of the men in the square, and they, too, turned in her direction.

Elsabeth stomped her foot down on her assailant with all her strength, and blindly struck at him with the back of her head, but her shoes made no tale against him through his sabatons, and he easily ducked her blow. She beat at him furiously in an effort to escape before his comrades could help subdue her, but her hands connected with his armor, and she could not find an exposed point to strike with him behind her. The others closed around her as she kicked and scratched at anyone who came close, but soon one had her leg, and the other caught hold of her fist.

The click of a latch nearby caught her attention, and from the corner of her eye she spied a face peering out from a nearby door, shielding a lantern against the wind to investigate the commotion.

"Hey there!" someone called, "What is this all about?"

With other more dignified options exhausted, Elsabeth screamed.

ROBIN WATCHED THE WALLS OF CARCASSONNE LOOM UP black and forbidding against the night sky, lit only by the lamps fixed to the inner surface, and the fires warming the watch towers. His breath misted, and as he wound down from the rush of the pursuit, the cold began to creep in on him once more. He hunched down into his armor, but it offered him little protection from the chill. The other men with him weathered the cold without a word, though the horses snorted irritably. The only other sound was the clatter of their hooves as they were led into the gate square.

Upon passing into earshot, the watchman broke from their side, and called out to the gate guard leaning on their halberds and shrinking into their cloaks against the chill.

"Hoy there! Close the gate, by order of le Marechal de Carcassonne!" the watchman cried, waving his hands over his head to signal the men on guard. They snapped to alertness upon noticing his approach, then hurried to do as commanded once they recognized him.

However, before they could manage it, the sound of voices on the opposite side of the square drew their attention. Robin and his men stopped and turned, as the watchmen hurried in that direction.

"Stay here!" Robin snapped to the guardsmen with the horses, and started across the square after them.

Moments later a woman's scream shattered the stillness of the night.

Robin instinctively released his horse at the sound and broke into a run. *'Tis her! I am sure of it, but from the sound of it I best get there quickly before this gets out of hand!* As he drew nearer, he spied two men engaged in a furious brawl with three of the castle guard that the watchmen scrambled to break up. His hand found his sword, and the drawing of steel hung in the air as he completed his charge. However, none of the combatants paid heed to the sound; one of the guardsmen lay crumpled on the ground, his helm knocked aside, and shielding himself from the blows of a lantern swung by a rather large fellow standing barefoot in the snow. Two more of the guard wrestled with another man nearly as big, who had a broom in one hand. The watch seized the first by his arms and hauled him off the fallen guard, and he kicked and thrashed against them, nearly hurling them both off their feet in the process.

"Enough!" he cried "Enough!" However, no one responded, and the two big men continued fighting against the guardsmen and the watch, who restrained themselves from striking in the confusion. "For God's sake, stop this at once!"

Finally, the flash of the big man's lantern on his naked sword caught their attention, and Robin interposed himself between him and the fallen guardsman. The watch finally succeeded in separating everyone and restrained both assailants.

"What in God's name is happening here?" Robin demanded hotly, looking from the denizens of the City, to the watch, to the guard. All of them hung their heads in chagrin; the guard at having been so handily battered by the two men, and the men having finally recognized the livery of de Carcassonne on their tabards. "Speak up! I want an answer, now!"

"We had her, Monsieur," the fallen guardsman muttered, as he unsteadily returned to his feet. "She was right here, and I had her. Adrian and Bridoul were coming to help restrain her. Gods, but she was strong, and put up a terrible fight! If I did not have my armor she might have done some real damage even with her bare hands. All of a sudden she screams, and next I know these two come rushing in. Before I could even think of what was happening, I am struck across the face and down in the snow, and the woman is gone!"

Robin turned his glare on the two men, both dressed in simple homespun, and now shivering in the cold and wet. They both ducked their heads sheepishly, but the bigger of the two (now relieved of his lantern) stood forward to address him with bowed head.

"Forgive me, Monsieur!" he said, and his voice trembled, both in fright and the cold. "I heard a commotion out in the yard, and when I looked out my door I saw three men accosting a woman! Her dress was torn, and she was screaming, and in the dark I did not see that they were in Monsieur le Comte's service! What was I to do?"

Robin eyed him closely, and the big man averted his gaze after a few moments of searching in the light of the lantern held aloft now by the watchman. "That woman is a fugitive from Monsieur le Comte," he said, and both men paled. "You swear to God that you are not accomplice to her crimes?"

"I swear, Monsieur!" the other man stammered. "'Tis as he said. My brother said, that is! We heard a commotion out back, and he went to have a look. That woman screamed and all we saw were three men with their hands all over her!"

Robin studied them both, pinched his nose, and let out a sigh of frustration. "God damn it! Just who *is* this woman? Some manner of devil in disguise? And where has she gone now?"

"I don't know, Monsieur," one of the watch said. "We were so focused on breaking up this fight before someone was hurt, I never even saw her!"

Robin turned to his guards. "Adrian? Bridoul?"

Both shrugged.

"She must have slipped away during the confusion."

"Damn!" he said again, and angrily jammed his sword back into its scabbard. He eyed the two men and jerked his head towards their open door. "Go on, back inside and out of this damn cold. I will trust your word that this was all a misunderstanding, but you shall answer for your assault upon Monsieur le Comte's men, nonetheless." He turned to the watch. "See to it they stay inside. This will have to wait until—"

Robin was interrupted by a sudden cry from his horse, forgotten for the moment in the confusion. He spun round, just in time to catch a flash of the woman's bare legs as she swung up into the saddle and jammed her heels into its flanks. She gave a cry, and then she was gone, her cloak and fall of burnished copper hair floating behind her like a horseman's banner.

For a moment Robin could only stand dumbstruck, before he cried out in a mix of anger and exasperation, and sprinted toward his men waiting with the horses.

ELSABETH LANDED HARD ON HER BACKSIDE AS TWO BURLY men rushed from one of the houses adjacent to the gate and fell upon her assailants. The first, carrying the lantern, struck the man behind her, knocking his helmet aside, then seized hold of him and flung him away. The other interposed himself between her and the other two, swinging a broom to ward them off. In the few precious moments of confusion created by her cries, her rescuers failed to notice the armor or livery of the guardsmen; instead, all they saw was the dark shadow of three men seizing a woman in the dead of night.

She scrambled on her hands and knees out of the middle of the brawl, ignoring the stinging bite of the snow, and keeping to the cover of the shadows as the gate guards responded and joined the fray in a desperate effort to separate her pursuers and the men attacking them. The sound of steel rasping on wood hung ominously in the air as the leader of her pursuers, streaking across the square, released his horse, charged into the fight, and cried out an order to stop which at first went unheeded.

A smile came to Elsabeth's lips; in the confusion and haste his horse was left unattended. The rest of his column remained behind, bewildered by the unexpected turn of events, and watching uncertainly.

Elsabeth kept to the shadows of the wall as she crawled clear of the fight. *'Twill not keep them occupied long, but perhaps long enough to secure a way out of here!* She crouched and waited. The horse, stamping irritably as its breath misted in the cold air, was a good few paces away, still far enough that she would not reach it without being spotted. It was a fine courser, swift and sure-footed, and left to its own devices now wandered aimlessly, nosing through the slush and awaiting its master's return.

She gathered her legs beneath her and edged closer, watching both the waiting guardsmen observing from the opposite side of the square, and the fight itself, which soon ended once the leader of her pursuit entered the fray. The horse was now within reach of her hiding place. The attention of the men nearby was focused on their debate, while the guardsmen conversed quietly with each other.

So she braced herself, took a steadying breath, and broke from cover. Her long legs covered the distance in a single spring, and she seized hold of the bridle. The horse whinnied and reared in alarm at the unexpected movement, but Elsabeth kept a firm grip, spun the horse to face the gate, and swung up into the saddle. She jammed her heels into the horse's flanks with a cry, and hooves scrabbled against the cobblestones as it lurched forward. Her hair and cloak rippled behind her and the icy bite of the wind stung her eyes, but in moments she was out of the gate, and speeding along the road away from Carcassonne.

HE ROAD OUT OF CARCASSONNE BRANCHED about two miles from the gate. The fork on the right led westward and deeper into Navarre. On the left, if Elsabeth recalled her geography, the road ran relatively straight towards the Ain River, before turning aside to follow its course southwards, and eventually joining with another road that crossed the river and led to Teubingen. This made it the swiftest passage into Boehm.

They daren't pursue me across the river. If I can reach Boehman soil I ought to be in the clear. I can shelter in Teubingen for the night and can then make for Pruck in my own time.

So Elsabeth took the left fork without checking her pace. The horse, whose blankets and gear were decorated with the arms of de Sens, surged onward. The dark countryside of eastern Navarre flew past her as she thundered down the road, but even the swiftest and strongest of coursers could not run the thirty miles between the two cities without a rest, and soon the horse snorted and labored, and its pace began to falter.

Trusting she had enough of a start on her pursuers, Elsabeth drew the animal up and slowed to a trot. By now, the overcast obscuring moon and stars had passed, and silver moonlight glittered on the smooth, windswept snows blanketing the fields of east of Carcassonne, and the whole world seemed to glow.

Complete and utter silence, interrupted only by the rattle of the horse's gear, smothered the countryside, and stars glittered cold and silver overhead. Elsabeth shivered and huddled into her cloak, but it was too thin on its own to offer her much protection from the frigid winds rolling across the snowy plains. Her legs were still exposed, and now her dress was cold and wet from falling during the scuffle at the gate. She shivered fiercely and clutched her cloak tighter against her chest.

She frequently looked behind her to check for pursuit on the road. She did not have an opportunity to give the other horses in the column a looking over, but she risked a guess that the common soldiery would not be riding a horse the like of de Sens's courser, so she ought to gain ground on them. *If I cannot gallop all the way to Teubingen, nor can they.*

At times Elsabeth spurred her horse forward for a short run, ever with an eye behind her for signs of her pursuers. But so far, the road remained empty, and she pressed on against the cold and her own growing weariness. In the excitement of her escape she had lost track of the time, and the night now was growing old. But she maintained a good pace, and by the end of her second hour out of Carcassonne the ground began to gently sink down a long, smooth slope towards the Ain. There it turned south to follow the banks of the river, flowing swiftly and steadily north where it would eventually empty into the sea.

However, as she continued south her heart sank somewhere into her bowels; for as she approached the point where the road crossed the river, she saw the black shape of a fortified tower spanning the near side of the bridge deck. Lamps glowed on the walls and in the watchtowers, and at times she spied the flicker of light on the helmets of the guard watching over the cold waters.

"Fuck," she murmured as she drew her horse up, and surveyed the scene below. The gate was closed, barring further passage, and a second tower guarded the far side, though whether the towers were manned by Boehm or the Navarrese she could not tell in the darkness.

Her horse steamed and stamped, and it snorted irritably after having been driven so swiftly in the cold only to be stopped short. "Hold your bloody... self," Elsabeth grumbled. "Perhaps you have figured for yourself that I am in a damn hurry, and that gate yonder will only slow me down!"

I can't imagine I have all that much of a lead, now, and if they delay me long, I could be caught before I can get across!

Elsabeth considered the road and noted that perhaps two or so miles from the bridge it joined with another coming up out of the southwest. *The road up from Pruck forks somewhere south of Carcassonne to circle round the farmland. My ride in took the westward branch, but I suspect this one connects back. If I am very lucky, I might be able to ride all the way around and they will lose some time figuring which way I have gone.*

She dug in her heels and started off once more; none too soon, for as she debated with herself, the distant rumble of hooves behind her broke the stillness, still some way off, but too close for comfort. The horse broke out into a run, and Elsabeth lowered herself in the saddle to make herself as small as possible and shield herself from the wind behind the horse's great neck. She reached the turning with no sign the watch in the bridge towers had spotted her, and spun the horse around the bend, racing back to the west.

OBIN'S COMPANY RODE AS HARD AS THEY DARED FOR A short distance along the road east to Boehm — though their quarry had already passed out of sight by the time he was able to get his men into the saddle once again, the watch atop the wall had seen her strike off hard along that fork. However, soon they had to slow their pace lest they ride the animals to exhaustion. Even if she had to do the same, the woman had *his* horse, which could easily outpace the palfreys of de Carcassonne's stables.

I am beginning to take this entire matter very personally! God help me I have no desire to slaughter a woman, but I may very well make an exception once I have her.

The rest of the company followed him. No one spoke, and only the steady thudding of hooves in the muddy road and rattle of the gear broke the silence.

After perhaps two hours of riding, they drew nigh the crossing of the Ain, fortified on both banks by bridge towers held by de Carcassonne. All seemed quiet down below as he led his men down the slope and approached the western tower. The gate stood closed fast, and Robin frowned. The woman was not so far ahead of him that she could have already cleared the watch at this time of night. Woodland stretched south away from the road, separating the Ain's floodplain from the farmland further west. It was too dense and tangled to accommodate a rider, and with no shelter for someone on foot and without provisions.

Robin stopped his column as they approached the meeting with the road leading up from the southwest. "Wait here for me! I will be back shortly," he commanded, then turned his horse towards the bridge and spurred it to a gallop. He covered the distance swiftly, and only checked his pace once he was within hailing distance of the watch upon the river.

The tower rose some four stories over the surrounding plains, though in the dark even the sharpest of lookouts would not see far. Sure enough, the gate stood closed, though there was a sally port that could be opened quickly to accommodate a single rider. Lamps illuminated the landward and river-side facings of the tower, and fires burning within lit the windows a welcoming, warm red. His arrival had also not gone unnoticed, and as Robin drew nearer a voice rang out in challenge.

"Who goes there at this time of night?"

"'Tis le Chevalier Robin de Sens, Marechal de Carcassonne!" Robin called back, while his horse stamped and shook itself from the hard ride. "I am in pursuit of a fugitive who has fled the City, and was last seen heading this direction! Has anyone passed the bridge tonight?"

"Not since before sundown," the watchman replied. "Only a fool would be abroad in the dark in this weather. Beg your pardon, Monsieur!"

"Damn her again!" he murmured to himself. "Have you seen anyone on the road, perhaps?" Robin replied, loud enough for the watchman to hear.

"I am afraid not. 'Twas a quiet night before you rode up, Monsieur. Shall I open the gate for you?"

"Nay! Keep the gate closed until further notice! I shan't have our quarry double back and slip across!"

Without waiting for a response, Robin wheeled his horse around and rode hard back to rejoin his company. He found them waiting as he had commanded at the fork.

"She has not been this way," he said upon his arrival, and slowed to gather his company with him. "Leave two men here to keep watch, the rest of you with me. If we have not passed her, she must have taken the southern road."

Without waiting for a word of response, he turned his horse onto the southwestern road and raced off.

LSABETH FOLLOWED THE ROAD AS IT SKIRTED THE northern eaves of a deep woodland stretching southward. Her fingers were frozen and numb, and ached at the effort of holding tight to the reins of her horse. She slumped in the saddle, and a deep weariness was steadily falling over her. *Stay awake, girl! 'Tis the cold and you know it. Fall asleep now and you shan't wake again!*

Her decision to bypass the bridge and take the southwest turning paid dividends; it cut behind a small fruit orchard that screened it from the road out of Carcassonne to the north, and as she rode back west, she was hidden from view as she heard the hooves of her pursuers thundering past. That, at least, bought her more time.

As the night grew old, Elsabeth knew she could not make Pruck without finding a moment's rest out of the cold, certainly not unless she could find clothing better suited to the temperature. But other than a few groves and orchards, or the forest near at hand, the country was too open. She might find shelter from the wind in the forest, but the undergrowth was thick and tangled, and her horse would never be able to navigate it. She had no food or provisions, and a fire might still be seen from the countryside and draw too much attention.

That left one of the farms dotting the snow-swept fields around her, but most crowded too close to the main road and would be easily searched. However, as she neared the end of the woodland on her left, she spied a faint track branching off and running south, skirting the western edge of the forest. Though narrow, it was rutted and wide enough for a cart or wagon, and seemed to get regular use. *'Tis no game trail, I am sure of that. But not heavily traveled, either. If I had been riding any faster than a trot I might have missed it. Let us see where it leads! At the very least I shall cut a bit off my ride, rather than going all the way round this farmland.*

So Elsabeth turned her horse off the road, and onto the path following the edge of the woodlands at as brisk a trot as she dared. Though clear of snow, (the better to mask her passage, rather than cutting across the undisturbed snow blanketing the fields) it was nonetheless muddy, and she proceeded with caution lest her horse slip on a patch of ice from the water pooling on its surface.

She followed the path for some three hours. By then, a rosy blush smudged the horizon to the east. Ahead in the dark she came upon a sight that greatly lifted her spirits: A low fence with a gate, and thin wisps of wood smoke rising into the air. She rounded a corner, and there before her she spotted a small, half-timbered house tucked into a corner abutting the woods, with an attached barn. Elsabeth allowed a smile to cross her lips and patted the horse's neck.

"Looks like the Lord of All is with us, love," she muttered to the horse. "Three or four hours of rest in a warm barn, and we ought to be good for the last race!"

The horse merely nickered softly and twitched its ears in response.

Elsabeth spurred forward, and soon she passed the fence and cautiously approached the barn. Other than smoke rising from the house's chimney there was no other sign of life or activity. The windows were still dark, and the only sound was the wind hissing through the naked branches of the woods behind the homestead. Elsabeth dismounted and, ignoring the cold bite of snow leeching through her shoes, led her horse the rest of the way to the barn as quietly as she was able. There was a latch, but no lock, and it was simple enough to have it open. Needing no urging from her, the horse gladly stepped inside and out of the cold. She followed, quietly closing the door behind her.

Though lacking the comfort of a good fire, the barn was nonetheless a welcome relief from the frigid air outside, and

Elsabeth's fingers and toes were soon stinging and tingling as warmth coursed through them once more. The whole place smelled of livestock crowded too close together. Hogs occupied a pen fenced off from the rest of the area, and cows, sheep, and two big draft horses occupied stalls within, warming the space with their bodies. There was also an old Hackney, which snorted at the disturbance of her entry, but otherwise remained silent.

Elsabeth shed her bag, sword, and stolen *gonne*. She led her horse deeper into the barn, next to the Hackney, which received its guest without complaint as the courser huddled up to it for warmth. She quietly removed its gear, particularly those bits that identified it as belonging to de Sens, and stashed them out of sight in one of the stalls. Then she found as warm a place as she could on a pile of straw and threw herself down. As she wrapped herself in her cloak, one last conscious thought passed through her mind as she drifted off to sleep.

The things I am doing for a thousand pfunde.

23

OBIN STORMED AWAY AS THE HOUSE'S DOOR SHUT behind him and returned to his party. For the past hours they had been knocking at every farmhouse along the road and searching every barn and outbuilding, yet there was not so much as a rumor of the woman's passing.

They had now reached the end of the southwest fork, where it met with another road coming north encircling the fields occupying the stretch of land west of the river and woods. More woodland rose up in front of them on the other side of the northward road. The first light of dawn stretched searching fingers westward cross the snowy fields, tinting them pink as the limb of the sun crested the horizon in the east. The horses shivered and lowered their heads wearily, and the men slumped in their saddles. Man and beast might be able to push far beyond their limits, but the cold, the exhaustion, and the frustration told on all their features.

Robin swung himself up into the saddle again, and the men gathered round him. He swept his eyes north and south across the road, seeking some sign of their quarry. But it was empty in both directions, and though he spied the occasional trail left in the snow by the passing of a hare, fox, or deer, there was nothing to mark where a horse and rider might have darted across the empty fields.

"What are your orders now, Monsieur?" Bridoul asked. His voice trembled from the cold, and he breathed onto his hands in a desperate effort to warm them. Frost had formed on his beard and mustache throughout the night, as his hot breath condensed in his hairs, then cooled and froze.

"She must be here," Robin replied, but spoke in a low voice as if to himself. "Even on my horse she cannot have gotten that far ahead of us in this weather, and she certainly could not have simply sprouted wings and flown away!"

"Beg your pardon, Monsieur, but we checked every house along the road already."

Robin glowered at him. "I am quite aware of that, but this is still the waking world and not some work of minstrel's fancy! She is flesh and blood like any other man or woman, though she may have the Dark One's gift for trickery, and more than her share of sheer good fortune."

He sighed and mopped his face wearily. The cold was telling on him, as well, and never before, though he had certainly endured many a grueling march and hours of battle on end, had he felt such weariness as now threatened to settle over him. *'Tis but the cold. We have been out here for hours with hardly more than our meanest cloaks for warmth.* When he looked up again, he turned eastward to face the sun, and though it was still no more than a bright sliver peeking over the woodland to the east, he let its light wash over him, and it seemed then that some warmth found its way across the drifts piling alongside the narrow cart tracks scoring the fields.

Robin frowned as realization dawned on him with the sun.

"Fuck!" he snarled, and all the men were taken aback by the vulgarity. "Fuck! Fuck! Fuck! 'Twas right there in front of me all along!"

"Monsieur?" Bridoul asked, his features screwed in confusion.

Robin angrily waved towards the fields. "'Twas not just the main roads! There are riding trails, footpaths, and byways all throughout this area so the laborers can reach their fields or move goods about! She need not leave a trail through the snow to cut across them, she might have left the main road at any time while we have been stumbling about in the dark. God damn it, I am a fool!" He smote the pommel of his saddle in frustration. "She might even have already slipped across into Boehm."

He turned his horse onto the southern road. "Form up and prepare to move! We ride for the southern crossing."

"But Monsieur, the men and horses are both exhausted," Bridoul said. "We have been at it all night and need a rest!"

"There will be rest to be had when the job is done, I'll not lose her now!"

And with that, Robin jammed his heels into his horse's flanks, and sped off like a shot without waiting to see if the men followed.

SOMETHING RATHER HARD AND BLUNT JABBED ELSABETH in the side, and she moaned softly as she was roused to wakefulness. She cracked one eye, enough to see that the gray light of early morning was streaming through the slats of the shutters sealing the windows of the barn. Her neck and back ached from the floor, and straw stuck in her hair as she slowly and painfully lifted herself up on her elbow. A shadow fell over her, and Elsabeth scrambled back from the figure standing over her. Her hand took hold of the handle of her rondel stuffed into her belt.

"Who are you, and what are you doing in my barn!" a stern voice demanded.

Elsabeth blinked the sleep from her eyes. She mused she had managed no more than four hours of rest. Her belly also rumbled in protest of its empty state; she had not even had an opportunity for supper before she and Kilianus set their plan in motion.

"Go on! Answer me, or I'll have the guard called from Carcassonne!" the voice repeated insistently, followed by another nudge with the handle of a pitchfork, gripped tightly in the hands of a man perhaps a few years her elder, and dressed in simple woolen hose and doublet beneath a ragged cloak. His features were rough, but not unkind, though his countenance was perturbed at finding her sleeping in his barn uninvited.

"Forgive me! Please! Don't hurt me!" Elsabeth shrieked, and made a show of shrinking away from him. "I... I was lost, and cold, and so very tired. I saw your barn and... I just needed somewhere to put my head down for a moment!"

"What in God's name are you doing here?"

"Please, Monsieur, I need your help! I was riding and there was a gang of men on the road. They grabbed me, and I only just got away from them, but they nearly tore my dress off before I could, and I was left with only my cloak and last night was so very cold."

Elsabeth forced tears into her eyes and lifted her thin cloak away to show the ragged end of her dress, along with a flash of her legs beneath. She hugged herself and clutched her cloak to her chest. "I daren't try to ride on much further, lest I freeze to death!"

The man's expression shifted now, and his annoyance at her intrusion faded as the implications of her story sunk in. He sighed and set aside his pitchfork.

"You poor thing!" he said. "I am sorry if I gave you a fright just now, but I would think there were better places to find shelter for the night." He knelt beside her, and whatever sympathy was in his features, the brief glimpse of her bare legs put a gleam in his eye, and Elsabeth smiled inwardly.

This will be entirely too easy.

"As I said, I was lost. I got so turned around when I tried to get away. If not for my horse I don't think I would have made it at all." She waved vaguely at de Sens's courser, and the farmer frowned.

"Where is it you are from? 'Tis no common beast of burden or riding horse."

She sniffed. "We have a little estate near the City. I was so bored and lonely from being cooped up while the weather has been so foul and my father was away in town, and thought I would just take a little ride. Please, could you help me? I assure you, I can be very appreciative!"

Elsabeth made a pout and fluttered her lashes in unspoken promise, and knew she had the poor man in her pocket without another word needing to be said.

IN THE END, SHE NEEDED NOT BE AS APPRECIATIVE AS SHE had with the watch captain the morning before. *A welcome respite, for this business has been excessive, even for me!*

She fastened the farmer's cloak round her shoulders, belted the sword at her waist, stuffed her rondel into her belt, and adjusted the fit of his doublet and hose. Both were too large for her frame, but were much warmer than her tattered dress, and her old cloak was still somewhat damp and not fit for travel. Her shoes she could do little about, but were less of a concern since she need not walk.

The farmer glared up at her from the floor of the barn, clad only in his braies and shirt, with his hands knotted behind his back (he had stripped off his doublet and put his hands in the bindings himself, even before she drew her rondel). A part of her dress served as a suitable gag to keep him quiet while she worked, and he dared not get to his feet with her standing over him with a weapon close at hand, so she did not bind his legs.

"I won't tie you up completely; 'tis much too cold in here for my liking," she said, "And as I shall not be coming back this way again and it seems you are alone if you were so desperate for company you would let a strange woman get you out of your clothes so readily, I would hate to leave you here to freeze. So long as you wait 'til I am gone, you can go back inside your house and free yourself."

Elsabeth hurried to saddle the old Hackney. One look at de Sens's horse told her the poor thing would be unsuitable to ride any distance that morning. Though she would lose quite a bit of speed, she decided having a fresh mount would serve her better on the final race to the Ain. With the saddle in place, she secured her bundles on the horse's back (fortunately, the *gonne* and spare parts, and the powder with it, had remained dry during the previous night's adventure) and then led it out of the stall. She paused at the door and returned to the farmer.

"I am also afraid I must take that old fellow with me; my horse is exhausted and is no good for riding today, and I am afraid I am in need of haste. But I will leave him here with you, so at the very least you are trading up. I, ah, would be careful who you let see him. His gear is tucked away in one of the stalls. Best you not let anyone see that, either, unless you know of a good fence. If not, if you know of an inn nearby I have it on good authority the keeper ought to be able to point you in the right direction. It ought to be worth a pretty *pfennig*.

"Now then, I really do thank you for your hospitality, after the fact. I am afraid I can't do much to repay you, but..."

Elsabeth dropped into his lap, straddling his hips, and pulled the gag from his mouth. Before he could make a sound, she kissed him fully on the lips. He let out a muffled grunt of surprise, and then she parted from him again before he could take advantage of the situation, stuffing the gag back in place.

"...at least a little something to keep you warm until I am away, and you can go."

With that, she rose and hurried for the barn door. She threw it open, leading the Hackney out with her, then closed it again.

Thin gray light spread across the rolling, snowy fields as the sun climbed higher in the east. It was still cold, but seemed not as bitter in the first light of morning. The land to the west was empty and serene, nor did she see signs of anyone approaching from the north or south. *Fortune, it seems, is with me; my hunters must have missed that track in the night.* She swung up into the saddle, turned the Hackney towards the south, and urged him forward into a trot.

It took some two hours to reach the main road again, with the track rejoining it some ten miles west of the crossing of the Ain near Pruck. South of the road was a wide expanse of woodland, and it was as she drew nearer than she finally caught sight of what she had been dreading the whole flight from Carcassonne: horses on the road. They were still a few miles behind her to the west, little more than an indistinct black shadow moving against the white of the snow, but the distant rumble of hooves confirmed it was no mere trick of the light, and they were heading east for the river.

"Bugger!" Elsabeth growled. "Come on, love! We best get a move on."

And with that she urged the horse into a gallop as she turned onto the main road. The old Hackney snorted irritably at her pace, but complied as best as it was able. However, between its age and the treacherous footing in the muck and mud, Elsabeth knew she could never outpace her pursuers. She heard a cry in the distance behind her, and when Elsabeth glanced back, she watched her pursuers surge forward.

The wind whipped her hair and cloak, and stung her cheeks. She kicked the horse again and again, desperately urging it on, however within only a mile or so its pace faltered, and she had to slow once more to a trot while her pursuers gained ground against her. Now she could make out the individual horses and their riders, though eventually they, too, had to check their pace. If she held any advantage now, it was that old as it was her horse was fresh, while they had been in the saddle since the night before, with no means of securing fresh mounts.

And so, the pursuit continued; Elsabeth spurred her horse into a run for short bursts before reining him in once more for a rest, as her pursuers did the same. But slowly the distance between them closed, and now the rumble of their hooves was not so distant, but rolled like thunder, as if a storm were sweeping up out of the west behind her.

Soon the ground began to descend towards the crossings of the Ain, and as she crested the slope and started down, she could see the river not more than two or three miles ahead. Once more, Elsabeth kicked the old Hackney into a gallop, and pushed him as hard as she could for the bridge. The floodplain flew past her, and the sun glittered coldly on the rolling black waters of the Ain. The Hackney's hooves struck the stone deck of the bridge, and it skidded and scrabbled from the thin layer of frost building up on the damp stones. Still, she did not check her pace. The horse snorted and gasped, its mouth frothed, and its hooves clattered against the stone as it charged across the bridge. Boehm loomed up ahead of her, and Elsabeth still did not check the horse's pace. Behind her, her pursuers were no less determined to close the gap and catch her up before she could reach the safety of the far shore. Her horse faltered, and though she urged him on, his pace slowed. She could now see de Sens in the lead, swatting his horse's flanks with his naked sword to drive it on harder.

And then, just halfway across the bridge, her horse let out an agonized bellow. It gasped in vain for breath for several paces, and blood frothed in its mouth and nostrils. Then its front legs collapsed beneath it. Elsabeth cried out as she was pitched forward out of the saddle and shielded her face and head as the stonework of the bridge deck rushed up to meet her. She struck the ground on her forearm and twisted her body to throw her weight into a roll. She tumbled a few dozen feet across the hard stone, while the horse crashed to the deck, where it lay twisted and unmoving.

Elsabeth scrambled unsteadily to her feet. She was still on the bridge, perhaps a hundred feet or more from the far end. Her head spun and her arm and shoulder ached from the impact of her fall. Her baggage was thrown clear of the horse as well, but de Sens bore down on her with his sword raised. She set her feet and lay a hand to her sword, but just as it cleared its scabbard a crack like thunder split the air. Blood spurted from the neck of de Sens's horse, and it squealed and reared, batting at the air with its front hooves and breaking the charge. De Sens cried out and hauled on the reins to master the animal, but blood continued to pour from its neck, and it, too, collapsed, throwing de Sens to the stones of the bridge. The rest of the party brought their horses up in a sudden stop, and they all looked about wildly in confusion.

As the echo of the shot died away, Elsabeth looked back towards the near side of the bridge and gawked.

Sitting astride his horse on the road as it climbed away from the river was Cuncz with a small *gonne* in his hand, flanked on either side by Kilianus and an older, wiry figure she did not recognize, and with a host of men at his back.

N

O ONE MOVED, OR EVEN DARED BREATHE AS
deathly silence fell across the bridge. The only
sound was the panting of horses, and the quiet
burbling as the Ain swirled past the columns
supporting the bridge spanning its waters. Elsabeth blinked in
astonishment at the sight of Cuncz and Kilianus, but dumbstruck
as she was, she could not even call out.

Nearer at hand, de Sens extracted himself from the tangled
body of his fallen horse and retrieved his sword from where it lay
nearby.

"Marvelous!" Cuncz crowed in delight. "Simply marvelous!
My dear Master d'Alle, I must congratulate you on your
craftsmanship! I would say that shot was placed from nearly fifty
yards, do you agree?"

"So it would seem, Monsieur," the mousy little man agreed.

Cuncz casually poured a measure of powder down the barrel
of the *gonne*, placed a ball in the end, and then tamped it all down
with a wooden rod held in a channel carved into the underside of
the tiller. He then turned a wrench on the wheel until it clicked into
place, poured a measure of powder into the pan, and lowered the
flint against the wheel.

De Sens strode forward a pace, but froze when Cuncz leveled the *gonne* at him.

"In the name of Monsieur Ethor Odson, Comte de Carcassonne," de Sens shouted, "I demand you turn over that weapon, along with Master d'Alle and those two!" He motioned between Elsabeth and Kilianus with his sword. "Master d'Alle, it seems, is a traitor to Monsieur le Comte, and these two are charged as spies."

"I offer you a counter proposal, my good Monsieur de Sens," Cuncz said lightly. "I suppose you have not noticed, but you now stand on Boehm's side of this bridge. And should you seek to argue the point, I have you quite outmanned."

He casually motioned to the side, and the men backing him all leveled crossbows at de Sens and his party.

"I consider your presence here so-armed an act of hostility on the part of Navarre, one which His Imperial Majesty shan't tolerate."

De Sens's face went red. "Hostility? You dare speak to me of hostility, when His Imperial Majesty sends spies into our midst?"

"I really don't know what you are talking about."

Elsabeth looked between Cuncz and de Sens, the former sitting smug and confident on his horse, the other impotently fuming and knotting his fist round the hilt of his sword.

"If Monsieur le Comte wishes to issue formal charges, by all means he may send a message to his Excellency the Prince-Bishop in Bremen, and he shall address it with His Imperial Majesty. But, in the meantime, if you don't wish to die here, I suggest you and yours retreat across the Ain, and make your way home."

De Sens studied Cuncz for a long moment, then looked to his own men. They were clumped together on the bridge, and with the two dead horses sprawling over the deck, they were in no position to force the issue. Finally, he sheathed his sword, and spit Elsabeth with a glare.

"You have caused me considerable trouble and humiliation," he spat. "I best never see your face in Navarre again, or by God I will have your head to decorate my wall!"

"Tch. Best you get in line, love," she said at his back as he turned and retreated to join his men. "There is only one of me to go around, and a considerable number with desires on it ahead of you."

De Sens did not favor her with a response. Instead, one of his men reached down and helped him up behind him in the saddle, then together his column turned and retreated, and it was only once they had cleared the far side of the bridge that Elsabeth relaxed and gathered up her scattered baggage. The *gonne*, fortunately, was still intact, and the rest of her pilfered goods had not been dumped out across the bridge.

She slung the bag over her shoulder, took the *gonne* in hand, and limped the rest of the way across the bridge. Cuncz, Kilianus, and d'Alle had by now dismounted, and awaited her on the road. Clement, Jacobus, and Thaddeus stood with them, leaning on their halberds. The guardsmen kept their features neutral, but Kilianus looked away from her sheepishly, while d'Alle watched with a sour expression. Cuncz simply smirked that same, superior smirk as he welcomed her back onto Boehman soil.

"Ah! My dear, I knew you would come through for me!"

Elsabeth glared at him, and dropped the *gonne*, still wrapped in tarpaulin, at his feet. D'Alle shrieked and darted forward to snatch it up off the ground. He protectively cradled it against himself.

"Be careful with that, you foolish girl!" he snapped in passable Boehman. "This is worth more than your hide! Especially after you blew up all the others!"

"Oh shut up!" Elsabeth snapped irritably. She then turned her eyes on Kilianus. Her temper faltered at the sight of his bruised and battered face, but she screwed herself up and jabbed a finger at him. "And what in the name of the Dark One are you doing here?"

Elsabeth rounded now on Cuncz, and her face heated at the amusement dancing in his eyes. "This was another of your fucking games?"

Cuncz chuckled and stepped forward. "My dear, as I told you before this venture began, the games never stop! But as I know that is not the answer you are looking for, I do have a confession to make:

"You see, I was not entirely forthcoming with your role in all of this. 'Twas not enough to have a working *gonne*. Oh, I am sure His Imperial Majesty's artificers could have worked out how to replicate the device once they had a working example, but you see, that takes time. We needed the maker, who could teach us the secrets that only a Master of his craft knows."

He threaded an arm around her shoulders. Elsabeth shrunk away reflexively and put her bag between them. "And well, Master d'Alle was quite dissatisfied with his financial treatment by the Graf de Carcassonne, much less the other demands placed on him. So, once he made this known to me, I resolved to liberate him. That was my good Kilianus' actual mission. But I needed a distraction to give him an opportunity to rescue Master d'Alle. And my dear, you are quite a distraction."

Elsabeth fumed. "You used me. Again!"

"Oh, believe me, I greatly appreciate you managing to recover an intact *gonne* in the end. But 'twas merely one part of a much more elaborate piece."

She turned her wrath now on Kilianus, who idly scratched behind his head to avoid meeting her eyes. "And you!" she snapped. "After all your disapproval about how I go about my work, all this time you knew about this and lied to me!"

Cuncz put his hands on her shoulders, and forcibly turned her to face him. The playful sparkle in his eyes was gone, and he looked upon her solemnly. His change in mood was not quite enough to soothe her wounded pride, but the seriousness in his countenance cooled her temper. "My dear, I told you before that this is a very deadly game we play. I came to you because I knew I could trust you to see your part through, and that the chaos you inevitably leave in your wake would be the perfect cover. You have my, and His Imperial Majesty's, sincerest thanks."

Elsabeth held his eyes for a long moment, then let her shoulders slump wearily. "I will be holding on to this, then," she said, and lifted the bag. "'Tis a few extra bits and pieces I salvaged from the armory before it exploded. You have your intact *gonne*, and your clockmaker on top of it, so I suspect you shan't need it."

Cuncz shrugged, and Elsabeth ground her teeth at his cavalierness. "'Tis a perfectly reasonable request. Now, as for our agreement, I shall hold up my end. One *gonne*, for one thousand *pfunde*."

She nodded. "Thank you."

"Should I have the certificate of account given to you directly, or shall I have it sent on to Father Ottin in Pruck?"

As those words left his mouth something in Elsabeth snapped. Almost before she realized it her rondel was in her hand, and she had its point at Cuncz's throat. Everyone around her snapped into motion. Kilianus sprung forward to seize her, the horsemen raised their crossbows, and Clement, Jacobus, and Thaddeus readied their halberds. However, all froze at a single raised finger from Cuncz, and to Elsabeth's consternation his expression never changed from that same infuriating sense of control despite his circumstances.

"Let us make one thing clear, you and I," she snarled, and her voice trembled in rage. "Stay away from me, and stay away from Pruck. I am not your courtesan. I am not your woman. I am not your *anything*. I want you out of my affairs."

Elsabeth stepped back from him, her rondel still raised to his throat, but shifted it to her other hand so she might remove his ring from her finger. She dropped it into the mud at his feet. For a moment something flickered behind Cuncz's eyes that might have been *hurt*, but it passed with a literal blink.

"Just leave me — and my life and everything in it — alone! Do we have an understanding?"

"Quite."

She lowered her hand and returned her rondel to its sheath, then looked at Kilianus standing beside Cuncz, still tense and ready to spring to his Lord's aid at the slightest gesture. Without word or preamble, Elsabeth seized his face in her hands, and kissed him full and deeply on the mouth. Kilianus' body went rigid in surprise, and an embarrassed silence fell across the riverbank.

Elsabeth quirked a playful grin, but her eyes flicked to Cuncz to leave him with little doubt the show was for his benefit. "If I shall remember anything fondly of this whole bloody misadventure, 'twill be our night together. All things considered, I really did enjoy the tilling."

Kilianus's face flushed, and his eyes went big as saucers. "Herr Baron, I swear, I never meant... I mean she just has this way—"

Cuncz waved him off casually, and Elsabeth gritted her teeth at his flippancy. "You hardly need to explain yourself, my good man. Were our positions reversed I suspect I would not have been able to resist, either.

"Now then, *Frau Soesten*, I will have the papers of account drawn up for you, and will have Thaddeus see you safely back to

Pruck. I do believe Michael retrieved the rest of your belongings when he made his escape ..."

25

ELSABETH ANXIOUSLY PACED FATHER OTTIN'S office while she awaited his arrival, wringing her hands while the bile churned anxiously in her belly. She had worked through what it was she would say over and over in her mind throughout the ride back to Pruck after receiving her note of account, nonetheless it did not prepare her for the jumble of thoughts and feelings that struck her once the walls of the monastery came into view. Such was her urgency to see the matter done she only stopped at the inn long enough to deposit her baggage, then rushed up the hill before the monastery closed its doors for the night.

A vision of chestnut eyes beneath a fringe of strawberry-blonde hair, peering at her from a rounded heart-shaped face sprung unbidden to mind, and Elsabeth steeled herself for what was to come.

What do I say to him? How do I tell him the truth? How do I even explain why I did what I did, and 'twas what I thought best? Is he even old enough to understand?

She vainly fought to banish such musings from her thoughts, but they clung tenaciously, burying their claws deeply into her mind and refusing to be cast aside. A thousand hopes and fears warred for prominence at the prospect of her secret anguish of the past years finally coming to an end, and that just made her stomach knot itself even tighter, and her heart hammer so hard against her breastbone she thought it might shatter and the offending organ burst from her chest so that all might see the weight settled over it lift.

The minutes stretched on to nearly an hour of waiting, and Elsabeth wandered aimlessly about the cramped space, unable to sit for more than a few moments at a time before her legs began to bounce restlessly and she was up and pacing again. There was no decanter of wine at hand; she had been left without so much as a drink of small beer to steady herself, or any other means of distraction or entertainment but her own thoughts running wild of what was to come.

Finally, the door to the office creaked open, and Father Ottin glided inside.

Elsabeth returned to her chair and perched anxiously at the edge of the seat as the Prior rounded his desk and solemnly lowered himself behind it.

"Elsabeth," he said gravely, and folded his hands in front of him. Something niggled at the back of her mind over his demeanor and tone, but Elsabeth forced it down; after so many years she could finally lay aside her greatest regret.

"Good evening, Father," she said, and her voice tremored nervously. "Thank you for seeing me so late, but this really could not wait."

She reached into her doublet and withdrew the paper containing the certificate of account.

"I have had something of an unexpected windfall, and our last conversation gave me a great deal to think about, so once I had it in my hands I came straight here. 'Tis no meager sum, and this alone is enough to live comfortably on for a good length of time, perhaps I might even use it as something to grow on. Regardless, 'twill finally allow me to put things right."

A bit of excitement worked its way into her voice, and she stood and extended the certificate with shaking hands.

Father Ottin heaved a sigh and lowered his head. Alarm bells blared in the back of her mind, and Elsabeth drew in and held a breath as icy fingers seized her heart.

"I had not expected you back so soon," he said, and she could not mistake the regret in his voice. "Had I known you would be returning ..."

"You would what," Elsabeth prompted, when he trailed off and did not continue. "If you had known I would be returning you would have what?"

Father Ottin gestured to the chair. "Please, Elsabeth, sit down."

Elsabeth slowly did as he instructed. A hollow feeling spread through her at his tone of voice, and a thousand dreadful thoughts rushed through her mind at once. "Has something happened?" she asked, and she could not keep her fear from her voice. "Is Paulus all right?"

"Perhaps a week after you departed Pruck," Father Ottin said, slowly, solemnly, and deliberately, and Elsabeth's bile burned the back of her throat as she waited for him to come to his point. "Herr von Aigel and Frau Aigelen returned for my answer. As you instructed on our last meeting, I let them know that Paulus was free to be taken if they still wished to proceed with their plan. He left with them several days after."

The icy fingers round Elsabeth's heart began to squeeze, and it seized in her chest. Her limbs went cold and felt as heavy as lead. She swallowed, but she could not draw another breath as Father Ottin's words struck her in the belly as if it were a fist of iron. "I see," was all she could manage to say, as tears welled up in her eyes. With a great effort she held them at bay, but she clenched her hand tightly round Cuncz's note and slumped in the chair.

"I did relay to them your requests for Paulus' education, and they were agreeable to honoring them, especially as the accounting has already been arranged. He will also continue his studies of the sword with Brother Simon, for now, and the sword you brought him was among the possessions he took with him. Once he is ready, Herr von Aigel, I believe, is amenable to seeking more advanced instruction. I will, of course, continue to maintain his finances per our agreement, until he comes of age, which Herr von Aigel agreed to."

Elsabeth nodded dumbly as Father Ottin's words echoed in her ears. She felt suddenly ill and desired nothing more than to throw up, but she fought back the rising lump in her throat rather than make a mess of his office.

"He very much hoped to see you again, though arranging a visit at the estate may prove rather awkward, under the circumstances," he continued.

"Of course," she said hoarsely. Elsabeth unbunched the note in her hand, smoothed it out, and tossed it onto his desk. "Do see to it that this is added to his accounts," she said. "It seems I don't have use for it myself, after all."

Father Ottin picked up the note and glanced over it, and his face paled and his eyes widened in astonishment at the sum scrawled across it, alongside Cuncz's signature, with His Imperial Majesty's very own seal stamped upon it. "Elsabeth this is... are you certain? As you said, this is no small sum, and you could live in considerable comfort."

She nodded and stood.

"Everything I have done these past years has been for him. Why should that be any different, even if he no longer has any need of me?"

He sighed, set the note aside, and the sound of the feet of his chair skidding against the floor as he rose drove anguished spikes through her reeling head. "Elsabeth ..." He rounded his desk and put a comforting hand on her shoulder, but she angrily shook him off.

"Don't! Just don't!" she snapped, and Father Ottin raised his hands defensively lest she lash out in her grief. "I don't need condolences or comforting. As you said, I agreed to this. 'Twas my decision to make, and for his good I made it! 'Tis done! 'Tis over! And that is the end of it!"

Father Ottin solemnly folded his hands in front of him and lowered his head. "You and I both know that you shall never convince yourself of that."

Her lower lip trembled, and her face heated. "What I can convince myself of makes no difference. He will be cared for, and I have provided as well as I could, so he will have no small fortune when he comes of age to perhaps make something of himself. What more is there for me to do? He is lost to me, now, and that is that."

"Elsabeth—"

"Thank you, Father, for all your efforts on my behalf. I will trust you to continue maintaining his accounts per our agreement, and I shall continue to add to them as I may."

He opened his mouth to speak, but his solemn eyes met hers, and he merely sighed and nodded at whatever he saw within them. Father Ottin lowered his head and made the sign of the Wheel to her. "Very well, I will see to it. Go with God, my child. Know that you will be in my prayers tonight."

Elsabeth nodded curtly, then turned and threw open the door. Father Ottin followed her to the doorway as she stormed from his office and flung the door shut behind her, but he caught it before it could slam to, and gently pulled it closed to leave her to her misery.

She stumped down the hallway in a desperate effort to escape the inhabited areas before she lost all control. Other brothers of the monastery scattered at her approach — accustomed as they were to her visits no one questioned her presence, nor offered her an escort from the premises, or more than a passing greeting which she did not hear.

The icy fingers round her heart now clenched it so tightly she thought it would burst. Hot tears, held back until now, broke free from the dam she had built up to hold them back over the past years, and now streamed freely down her cheeks. Her breath came in ragged gasps and her whole body shook, her hands clenched so tightly her nails began to cut into her palms. Her legs began to wobble, and she collapsed her shoulder against the wall beside her for support as if she no longer had bone nor muscle nor sinew to support her. She buried her face in her hands as choking sobs wracked her body.

Then she fell, sinking to her knees as a wail of anguish burst forth and echoed along the hall of the monastery, and all she could do was weep.

APPENDIX: READING BLAZONS

The coats of arms herein are presented in the form of the blazon. This is a particular heraldic language used to describe a coat of arms in a succinct manner that will automatically be understood.

The arms are always described in a specific order:

1. Any divisions of the shield which exist.

2. The field is described:

   a. In the case of a solid color, the tincture of the field (capitalized, even if the color is not the first word of the blazon) is given, followed by a comma.

   b. In a complex field, such as *chequy* (that is, checkered of two colors) the pattern is described, followed by a comma.

3. The principle ordinary or charge is given, followed by in order:

   a. Its attitude (IE the pose of a bird or beast)

   b. Its tincture

   c. Parts that might be colored differently

   d. A charge may have another charge placed on it.

4. Any additional charges placed around the primary charge described as above with their positions.

5. Any additional charges *on* the principle charge, again described as in the principle charge.

A blazon is always given from the *bearer's* perspective, not the viewer's. Thus dexter refers to the part of the shield on the bearer's right (viewer's left).

On a divided shield, the divisions are described beginning at the chief, (top) from dexter to sinister, then the base (bottom) in the same fashion, much like reading a book. Thus in a quartered shield, the top row would be quarters I and II, while the bottom row is III and IV.

For example, the blazon — *Quarterly 1ˢᵗ and 4ᵗʰ Azure, on a bend Or three bears statant erect Sable Quarterly 2ⁿᵈ and 3ʳᵈ Gules, two longswords in saltire proper in chief a gauntlet Or* — would describe the following shield:

The bearer's upper right and lower left quarters are blue, each with a gold diagonal band from (bearer's) upper right to lower left. On this band are three black bears standing on their hind legs. The bearer's upper left and lower right quarters are red with two crossed swords with points angled upwards. The swords are colored naturally (silver blades and gold hilts). Above the swords is a gold gauntlet.

There are other elements of a coat of arms, including achievements, mantling, and supporters, but these do not appear on the shield itself.

GLOSSARY

ARCHITECTURE

Crenel The gap between merlons on a battlement.

Enceinte The main enclosure of a fortification, including the main defensive wall and towers.

ARMS AND ARMOR

Bombard A large cannon of the 14th and 15th Centuries, of indeterminate size or material.

Brigandine A form of lightweight armor consisting of many small oblong metal scales riveted to the inside of a garment, typically a doublet. This outer shell can be linen, canvas, wool, leather, or even richer materials such as velvet.

Couter A component of plate armor that fits over the elbow. It is often articulated with other components of armor for the arm, such as the vambraces.

Cuisse A component of plate armor worn on the thigh.

D . E . WYATT

Longsword   A two-handed, double-edged sword with a blade ranging from three to three and a half feet in length. Longswords are generally well-balanced between cutting and thrusting, and are quite fast and agile swords.

Pavise   A tall, oblong, square shield with a prominent central ridge and faced with coarse canvas, primarily used by archers and crossbowmen as cover against opposing archers while reloading. The shield would either be held in place by a *pavisier*, or in some cases planted into the ground by a spike at the bottom. *Pavises* were often painted with the coat of arms of the town which produced them. Religious icons were also common subjects.

Pavisier   A specialist page or soldier who carried a *pavise*, and held it in front of a knight, archer, or crossbowman for protection against opposing archers.

Poleyn   A component of plate armor that fits over the knee. They could be strapped directly to the leg, or attached to a cuisse.

Rondel   A dagger with a long, slender blade of lenticular, diamond, or triangular cross-section ending in a fine, needle-like point designed for punching through mail or penetrating the gaps in plate armor. The grip is cylindrical, with a disk or similarly-shaped guard and round pommel. One or both edges could be sharpened. It was particularly favored by knights, and often served as a sidearm or personal defense weapon.

Sabaton   Armor for the foot consisting of articulated steel plates.

Tabard	A broad and short garment with open sides and short sleeves, typically no longer than the hips or mid-thigh. A tabard is often decorated with the wearer's coat-of-arms, and is frequently worn over armor.
Tiller	The stock of a crossbow, to which all the other components are attached. Some early guns used a similar handle.

ARTS OF DEFENSE

Vom Tag	"From the Day." A principal guard of the longsword in German fencing traditions, held either with the sword above the head, or with the hilts just below the left or right shoulder. The blade is held point-upward and angled back slightly. It is typically assumed with the sword on the fighter's strongest side, with the opposite foot leading (thus a right-handed fencer leads with his left foot, and the sword is held at his right shoulder).
Hengen	One of two defensive actions in the German longsword tradition. The upper *hengen* is similar to *ochs*, but with the hilts further out from the head, and the point angled downward and across the body to cover against attacks from above. The lower *hengen* is similar to *pflug*. As with the upper *hengen*, the hilts are extended more away from the body. It can cover against attacks from below, and is also the natural endpoint of the *Zornhau*.
Ochs	"Ox." A principal guard of the longsword in German fencing traditions. The hilts are held above the left or right shoulder, with the blade pointed forward towards the opponent and angled

VII

slightly inward. The lead foot is the opposite side from the sword (thus if the sword is on the right, the left foot is leading).

Pflug   "Plough." A principal guard of the longsword in German fencing traditions. The hilts are held at either the left or right hip, with the point angled up at the opponent's face. The lead foot is the opposite side from the sword (thus if the sword is on the right, the left foot is leading).

Zornhau   "Strike of Wrath." One of the five Master Strikes of the German longsword tradition. It is a powerful falling diagonal strike most commonly used to counter an opponent's cut from above. Executed properly, the *Zornhau* should both defend against the strike, and either strike the attacker in turn or allow the defender to threaten his opponent with his point. It therefore most commonly ends in the lower *hengen* rather than cutting all the way through, as this both binds down the opponent's blade, and aims the point at his face for a follow-up thrust.

HERALDRY

Argent   One of the two recognized metals, either silver or white.

Chequy   A pattern of the field, indicating that rather than a solid color the field is instead in a checkerboard pattern of two colors.

Chevron   An ordinary in the form of an inverted V across the shield. A chevron can also be inverted, so that it forms a V. In addition to an ordinary, multiple objects can be placed "in chevron," in which case they are positioned in an inverted V. A chevron can also describe a division of the shield, "per chevron."

Ordinary — A simple charge or device, generally in the form of a line, bar, cross, or other simple geometric pattern. An ordinary is considered a primary charge, and can have another charge placed on it, for example "on a fess."

Overall — A charge described as overall means that the charge covers the entire shield, rather than being confined to a particular division.

Purpure — In some heraldic traditions, one of the five recognize tinctures, referring to purple. However, in French heraldry purpure is considered uncommon and "ambiguous," thus treated as both a tincture and a metal.

Quarterly — A shield divided into quarters. Each quarter is numbered 1st through 4th from dexter to sinister, and then chief to base. Each quarter of the shield can have its own blazon.

Recursant — Similar to regardant, but reserved for birds.

Regardant — An animal charge with the head turned backwards. Typically, the body faces to dexter and the head to sinister.

Sable — One of the five recognized tinctures, referring to black. Although English and French heraldry follows "Rule of Tincture" and does not allow tincture on tincture or metal on metal, in Central Europe (including Germany and Poland) sable is not restricted in this manner. Thus, the frequency of a sable charge on a gules field (or vice-versa).

| Vert | One of the five recognized tinctures, referring to green. |

HORSES

Courser	A light, strong, and swift warhorse. Though not as heavy, powerful, or expensive as the destrier, the courser was faster, and thus favored for the rigors of hard battle.
Hackney	A powerful, but attractive, general purpose riding horse. Their trot made them better suited as war-horses than amblers.
Jennet	A small, compact, and well-muscled riding horse of good disposition, noted for its ambling gait. It is smaller and frequently less expensive than the palfrey. The modern Spanish Jennet is very similar in appearance and gait, though the historical jennet was not a specific breed.
Palfrey	A highly-valued riding horse with an ambling gait, that is larger than the jennet. It was popular both for general riding, as well as hunting and ceremonial use, and was particularly popular among the nobility. A well-bred palfrey could be just as expensive as a knight's destrier.

TITLES AND RANKS

| Chevalier | One of two positions in the system of French peerage. As a rank, a Chevalier was a member of the most noble families or possessors of particularly high dignities in court. As a title, |

chevalier is the French term for a member of an order of chivalry; a knight.

Comte   The French term for a count.

Courtesan   A courtier, or one who attends the court of a monarch or other person of wealth and rank for financial or political benefit. The relationship between courtesan and benefactor was a mutual exchange: The courtesan provided companionship and other services to their benefactor, who rewarded them with financial compensation and elevated status. Courtesans could come from both common and noble birth, and use their position either as a primary form of employment or for the social or political benefit of themselves or their spouse. Most commonly associated with women and prostitution, men could also be courtesans, and the courtesan's services were not necessarily or exclusively sexual. Courtesans were often trusted with sensitive tasks that a servant could not be.

Freiherr   The German rank equivalent to a French or English Baron.

Gnädige Frau   A German honorific, meaning "Gracious Lady." Archaic and seldom used in modern German, but formerly used to address a woman when her name was not known, or not used.

Graf   German nobility roughly analogous to a count.

Marechal   The French term for Marshall, the officer in charge of war and defense.

Prior   One of three ecclesiastical positions. A Claustral prior is a superior of an abbey, and is the most senior officer below the abbot or abbess, and assists them with administration of the abbey. A

Conventual prior is the head of an independent monastery that is not a full abbey. An Obedientiary prior is the superior of a satellite monastery of an abbey.

Ritter
The second-lowest rank in German nobility, below *Freiherr* (Baron) but above *Edler*. A hereditary knighthood roughly analogous to the English baronet.

WEIGHTS AND MEASURES

Livre
Short for *livre tournois*. The largest coin in Medieval and Renaissance France, roughly equivalent to the English pound sterling. Never minted, and typically used as a unit of account.

Pfennig
A silver German coin roughly equivalent in value to a penny (about 1/240 of a pound).

Pfund
The largest coin in Medieval and Renaissance Germany, roughly equivalent to the English pound sterling. Very seldom minted, and typically used as a unit of account.

Span
A unit of measure defined as the distance between the tips of the outstretched thumb and little finger. It equates roughly to nine inches.

Skilling
A silver German coin roughly equivalent in value to a shilling (1/20 of a pound).

OTHER

Braies
Any of a variety of breeches worn as undergarments by the late-Middle ages and Renaissance, and typically made of undyed linen.

They could be anywhere from briefs to knee-length.

Nunnery   Ironic slang for a brothel.

Pattens   Raised wooden soles attached to shoes, often by lacing or straps, to lift the wearer out of the mud and protect the softer, thinner soles of the shoe itself while traveling.

Rollmops   Pickled herring filets rolled into a cylindrical shape, often around a savory filling. Traditionally used as a hangover cure.

ABOUT THE AUTHOR

D. E. Wyatt was born and lives in St. Louis, Missouri. When not writing he is an occasional gamer, a student of German swordsmanship, a saxophonist, and works in IT.